The Franklin

Avenue

Rookery for

Wayward Babies

Also by Laura Newman

Parallel to Paradise

The Franklin Avenue

Rookery

for Wayward

Babies

and other stories

Laura Newman

Delphinium Books

THE FRANKLIN AVENUE ROOKERY FOR
WAYWARD BABIES
and other stories

For information, address
DELPHINIUM BOOKS, INC.,
16350 Ventura Boulevard, Suite D
PO Box 803
Encino, CA 91436

Library of Congress Cataloging-in-Publication Data is
available on request.
ISBN 978-1-953002-08-2
22 23 LSC 10 9 8 7 6 5 4 3 2 1

First Paperback Edition

Jacket Artwork and Design by Colin Dockrill, AIGA

Guppyman,

What a wonderful world.

Travel makes you speechless,
then it turns you into a storyteller.

—Ibn Battuta,
fourteenth-century Moroccan traveler

CONTENTS

Tourette's of the Heart

*Can a starving girl ride her bicycle 400 miles to Kathmandu, fortified with a stolen wheel of
yak cheese and a side of ham?*

Berkeley, California, 1996

Dorje almost always carries fat in her pockets. Usually in the form of yak cheese which she makes herself and flattens into little squares of wax paper. If not for city ordinances, Dorje would keep a yak in the backyard of her rent-controlled bungalow in Berkeley. When the food co-op is out of yak milk (often), she settles for a wedge of French Neufchatel. Dorje is making up her packets while she waits for her ride.

Dorje's daughter-in-law comes in the front door like a blockbuster movie, all noise and graphics on her T-shirt. Amplified hair. "Ama La, I have your *chuba*; I finished it last night!"

She pulls a full-length wraparound dress out of a reusable Whole Foods bag. The dress is in shades of gray and white, like fog on mountains. Beautiful. Not flashy. Well, it isn't a real *chuba* or it would be sheepskin, but it's May and they aren't in Tibet. They aren't at 12,000 feet. "Here's the apron!" The apron is made out of thin stripes of turquoise and ruby fabric. Her daughter-in-law can tell by Dorje's face that she's pleased. That little crease of a smile that shifts the abundant wrinkles on Dorje's fifty-six-year-old face. A face that looks more like eighty,

atop a body that stands about four-foot-eight. Dorje goes into her room to change, securing the *chuba* with the apron, pulling loose the front of the dress, making a pocket on her chest. She waits until her daughter-in-law isn't looking and then puts the wax-covered pats of yak fat into the pouch. In the past, her food bowl would have gone there too.

"Okay, let's go," her daughter-in-law shouts, because for some reason she is convinced Dorje is hard of hearing. "We don't want to be late!" Dorje's husband is already waiting by the car, patient as a monk. They are going to see the Beastie Boys.

Let's leave the three of them here, climbing into the Subaru, concert-bound.

Tibet Mid-Twentieth Century
Dorje was just a flea. A mayfly. Born in Tibet in the winter of 1940, too early in the pregnancy and sure to die within a day or three. Her mother gave her the strongest name she could think of—Dorje, meaning diamond or thunderbolt. She chanted *om mani padme hum* over her tiny body almost nonstop, both to keep herself composed so her daughter would not know her sadness, and so that when Dorje died she would pass with the kindest mantra in her baby ears. But small things can live, and Dorje did just that. Not in a thriving way, but like a patchwork doll made out of old fabric scraps, sure to be someone's favorite. Dorje would ever be small, with barely covered bones. But her hair was black and lovely and her fingers quick. Invisibility came to suit her. It seemed people looked straight through the child like a bowl of broth, or a winter wind. Dorje grew up at her

mother's feet listening to the machine-gun sound of her mother's sewing machine. Keeping time to the up-down-up-down foot pedal. In fact, in 1959, when Dorje first heard the real guns in front of the Potala Palace some blocks away, she thought she was hearing a sewing machine, but it was bullets.

How could Dorje know that she lived on the Roof of the World? For Dorje the mountains are just there. Like barley, or wood in a fire. Common. The click-clack of the prayer wheels releasing good intentions into the world, the maroon monks. Potala Palace with its one thousand rooms and copper foundations, a red-and-white layer cake rising above Lhasa. She knows the Dalai Lama, just five years her elder, lives in the palace. Is he allowed to play Sun and Moon? Certainly not Horse Thief.

Dorje could not know that the air she breathes is so pure it almost isn't air. Air with holes in it. Holy air. December is the clear, cold month when the sun becomes an inquisition. People avoid this month. Eyes are lowered, hearts race for oxygen. It is hard to tell a lie in December. But Dorje loves this month of bright light because she can stay indoors and learn to wield the tin needle. She mends socks with a flower stitch by the fire. Her mother, Ama La, runs the sewing machine, whose sound is the mantra of Dorje's young life, and her old Mola sits with Dorje by the fire, nodding along, teaching Dorje her stitches. Pala, her father, runs a six-seat Smoke and Tea Bar in the old town, where the money is thin and smoke thick.

When winter finally breaks its back on the mountains, it is Dorje's job to take the straw basket that forever smells of summer and walk the alleys of Lhasa looking for

cloth. Any kind. A lost kerchief, a blanket on the verge of despair. Balding sheepskin. She is in competition with moths. Ama La repurposes these threadbare threads and the resulting garments could be in a museum. If they survived. If anyone still has them.

It is also Dorje's daily job to deliver the *sha phaley* to the Smoke and Tea Bar, a bar staple like pickled eggs in England. Even now she can conjure the smell—she would wear it as a perfume if someone would just bottle it, dab dab dab wrists and just behind the ears. Spicy beef and cabbage, folded into barley bread and deep fried for an afternoon snack. Always she would eat one herself before heading out to the bar. Except on the day she burned a batch. She took the *sha phaley* outside and buried it all to avoid being scorched by Ama La. The *sha phaley* ghost haunts Dorje still. Clear to California it stalks her.

Dorje's little brother Tashi came late in the spring of 1950. Like a lucky duck egg in the chicken coop. For the first four months of her pregnancy Ama La assumed it was menopause. Surprise, surprise, a baby boy! But none would call it a fortuitous year. On October 7 Mao Zedong liberated Tibet. *From whom, Mousy Tongue? Shhh. Say that again and I'll wash your mouth out with lye soap.*

Tashi became Dorje's best friend. First he was her little doll. She sang him sleepsongs and poured water through his fingers for a game of Catch the Impossible. His giggle was like bubbles. Eventually the two were inseparable, running through the streets of Lhasa. There were always prayer wheels to spin. Monks to chitchat with (except in the month of July when the monks sequester so they don't accidentally step on just-born insects). Insects to step on. The mountains were always talking, the sky told a story a day. The Yogurt Festival

in Norbulinka Gardens and the Dalai Lama's birthday. School days. There was always food to make and food to eat.

As Dorje headed into her teen years, life seemed a reasonable venture. Her first deep sadness came on the morning that Dorje's old Mola died. She died of old age with a clay cup of butter tea, hot, just past her lips and then spilled on thighs that did not flinch. A good death. If it hadn't had been for the spilled tea, Dorje wouldn't even have known she died. They left her sitting in her chair for twenty-four hours.

Well, that's normal. It takes forty-nine days for a person to be truly dead in Tibet.

That evening in a house of sadness, Ama La told her children how first Mola will lose the earth. The earth will dissolve into water. The water will then dissolve into air, and Mola will be surrounded by smoke. (Dorje pictures the Smoke and Tea Bar.) Then her soul will separate and she can disappear into the light. (Dorje envisions a white December light.) "Then," Ama La said, "Mola will come back in her next body in forty-nine days." If Ama La believed the words, you couldn't tell it by her face, the saddest little face in Tibet. She had lost her mother. Pala holds her enduringly tight.

Here's what really happened: The lama came and read the prayers. Then he took the body up to the monastery, where it was cut into pieces and put out on the Sky Burial site. Then the vultures ate the old grandma and, if there is any justice in this world, carried her soul up over the Roof of the World into the yonder.

In the years to come Ama La was greatly comforted that her mother had died an easy death with a stomach full of breakfast rice.

And that there was one less to care for.

The Great Leap Forward 1959
Mousy Tongue, were you thinking this was a game? Like hopscotch or the long jump? Follow the Leader?

Everyone knows a journey of ten thousand miles begins with a single step. There is always the first drop of the monsoon, although none could say which one, exactly. So it was with the Chinese liberation of Tibet. *(From whom?)* For the first nine years there was the 17-Point Agreement and the Dalai Lama stayed in his layer-cake castle, and if he was there then they were still Tibet, weren't they? But slowly Dorje noticed that businesses in Old Town had Chinese signs over the doors and there was a lot of moo shu pork stinking up, let's admit it, the already stinky place. The adults were wrinkling faster than usual. There was talk of monasteries being shut down. Who would shut down a monastery? *Mousy Tongue. Shhh, say that again and I'll wash your mouth out with lye soap.*

Her father closed the Smoke and Tea Bar and re-opened behind the shutters of their own little house. Ama La still ran her sewing machine in the back room, but Dorje could tell she was angry by the speed of the needle. Or afraid. If she sewed enough clothes, could she save them? Could she sew a safety net?

There are things that cannot be arrested: the moon, the tides (although almost no one in Lhasa had ever seen one), and the Dalai Lama. So pick up your kitchen knife, your shovel, your spade. Potala Palace has foundations of copper and you can't come in. On March 10, 1959, Dorje's father and thousands more stood in front of Potala Palace and would not let the Dalai Lama out.

Or the Chinese in. Three days later the Dalai Lama escaped to India and lives there still. That night the prayer wheels did not spin, although an ungodly wind did blow and blow.

Dorje deeply felt she had lost a friend, though they had never met. It was an avalanche of the heart.

But that was not the worst of it. All of China and Tibet were headed for Three Bitter Years. The Terra-Cotta Warriors turned over in their grave, but that was of no help. All the Emperor's horses and all the Emperor's men couldn't put China together again. Because there was no Emperor. Only fat *Mousy Tongue*. Sesame-oil-soaked dumplings in an oxblood broth for breakfast. Peking Duck for dinner.

Mousy Tongue, if you issue a decree to kill all the sparrows, it is true they won't be able to eat the grain seeds. But who, Grasshopper, will eat the locusts when the sparrows are gone? It might be true that if the farmers plant the seeds deeper the roots will be stronger. But it is certainly true that if the farmers churn up rocks in order to plant deeper, it's going to ruin the topsoil. And why would you, *Mousy Tongue*, force the farmers to switch to wheat when barley has been your tenant for centuries and has paid the rent so well? While these deforming reforms were being enforced, China increased its grain exports to Russia by fifty percent and sent grain for free to comrades North Korea and Vietnam. By 1962 the death count soared to some thirty million. But only Buddha can count how many sparrows.

First there is just a fear of hunger. A rumor running through the streets like a poor sewer system, a scent of hunger. Word of failing crops. No one is yet truly hungry, in Lhasa. There are wheels of yak cheese behind the

counter of the corner store, plucked chickens hanging in the window. The alley cats are in no danger. This was never a country to waste food, so nothing changes at the kitchen table; there never were table scraps. But somehow the women know. It is time to gather what you can, hide it, don't talk about it, and hope you are wrong. But here is the problem for Ama La and really all her friends: money. They don't have it. So while there are still stores available, they don't have the money to finance a stockpile. It was ever a buy-what-you-need-today life. A pinch of spice, a bone of beef. And so the first pounds that Ama La lost were from nervousness. Anticipation of a bony winter.

Then there it is: a famine. Come over the mountains like a snow beast to settle its weight on your breastbone and eviscerate your guts. Dorje dug up the burnt *sha phaley* but found only dusty ghosts. Food came in bits and bugs. Cats taste like chicken. Rat soup, only you call it something else. Stone soup with minced onion. Dorje ate a candle in the dark. She was invisible.

It is said some people ate some people.

In the spring of 1960, the second Bitter Year, Dorje knew that death was more possible than life. They all knew it, except Tashi who was too young to conceive of a world without him in it. Tashi's parents gave him the lion's share of the cat, but his eyes bugged out of his sweet, skinny face and his stomach was starting to distend. Dorje and Tashi slept together at night and barely looked like one person under the quilt.

So much was suspended. It seemed even the prayer wheels made a hungry sound. Every prayer was for food. Her father, with his shop closed down, could not find a job. Many men couldn't. Her mother earned an extra

food ration by mending for the Chinese Army. Tashi, who was quite good with a slingshot, became a hunter of small things. Dorje volunteered nights at the new tent hospital, which was mostly just watching people die. When they did, she looked for small valuables to pilfer, even buttons to make her mother smile. The night shift came with a meal, half of which she ate and half she brought home. Never enough. Rations were cut almost weekly. When her mother fell sick Dorje brought home the full meal and forced Ama La to eat. But Ama La would give the food to Tashi when Dorje was out of the room, or to Pala, who had begun to look like a whooping crane, such skinny legs and feathery hair. The cough.

One very early morning after her shift, Dorje walked home on the quiet streets of Lhasa. The morning birds, who used to be so cheerful, had all left the city by wing or in a pot. People were too hungry to get up early. Even at age twenty Dorje remained the invisible girl, her gray wool *chuba* turning her into a shadow, her dark hair the color of shutter paint. Her step was quiet. The young Chinese woman pushing a baby carriage came around the corner and walked just feet in front of Dorje, and did not see her. The metal wheels of the old carriage scraped the cobblestones. Walking a baby. A common thing in an unusual hour. Dorje stopped and watched her. She saw a wink of blue silk under her dirty coat and akimbo hair; a go-go girl for the Army. Suddenly Dorje hated the Chinese woman. Because she had a blue silk dress, because you could tell just by her ankles that she wasn't hungry, because she was a go-go girl, because she was Chinese. Surprising both of them, Dorje ran full speed up to the girl, pushed her aside and took off with the carriage. There was so much rage in Dorje that the

blue-silk girl didn't even have time to protest, and Dor-je was gone. As suspected, there was no baby. But there was a wheel of yak cheese the size of a dinner platter and a side of smoked ham. *Om mani padme hum.* Holy shit.

Dorje found a safe corner and ate three big bites of ham. It was smoky and greasy and it reminded her teeth of their job. She pictured her family. Today they would eat a meal that required knives! But even in her small euphoria she knew it wouldn't be enough food. To send Tashi's eyes back into their sockets. To turn Ama La's hair from white back to black. To save them.

Dorje was a Buddhist, of course she was, born in Lhasa. But she never really practiced the religion be-yond clacking a few prayer wheels. Without ever really thinking about it she assumed that because she lived in the same city as the Dalai Lama, his prayers, his efforts, spread an aura over her. Divinity by proximity. But he was gone to India, and she was still here. She always con-sidered herself a good girl; she was a good girl. But hun-ger is a taskmaster with a whip. She looked at the cheese, cool and waxy, the color of butter. The ham smelled of autumn and chestnuts. Slowly she allowed the unthink-able thought. Slowly she whispered to herself the one thing she needed to convince herself of, but that she knew was not true: *They will be better off without me. I'm just another mouth to feed.* And then she stopped think-ing at all. For what is love to a starving person? Salt in the wound of an empty stomach.

Dorje waited and entered her home like the thief she had become. She knew her parents would be in ra-tion lines; each person had to collect their own food or else it would be suspected that you had the ration cards of dead people. She cut and packaged the glorious food

so she could carry it on her body. Not one bite did she leave because then, what would they think of her? *Or the truth, Dorje, you already thought of that ham, that cheese as yours, didn't you?* She bottled water. She took her winter coat, which would not be odd because the hungry are always cold. She climbed up on her old bike, red faded barely pink, with a frayed wicker basket on the handlebars. If there had been any dogs left in town, they would have chased her, she smelled so good. Hours down the road she realized she had not even left a note. *Or the truth, Dorje, you did not want to leave a note. Did not want them to know that you had left them purposely and in layers of food, pounds of fat.*

For Kathmandu.

It felt so good to leave the responsibility of her family behind, and that good feeling made her feel sick.

Can a person pedal four hundred miles to Kathmandu on ham and cheese? Even if she is the invisible girl? Probably not. But Dorje knew that the Newari trading caste from Nepal still followed the thousand-year-old trade route and she might run into that pack of yaks. She wasn't the only one on the road. Some seven thousand people traveled over the Himalayas in the diaspora of the Bitter Years before China closed the borders. And there are monasteries and villages and the snow on the mountains glows at night like cold silk. She would lick the famine, or become a Hungry Ghost. When thoughts of her family came to her, she destroyed them. She concentrated on the sound of her bike; the chain became her prayer wheel. Each day a Sky Burial of the heart.

So it came to be that Dorje was indeed taken in by the Newari. They were not in a habit of this, especially in these times, but one of the cooks was quite taken

by the idea of a girl riding her bike to Kathmandu and championed her passage. What she would remember most about the trip is drinking warm milk. She would remember Chomolungma, the highest mountain in the world. The thin razor's edge of the exact summit is the boundary line between Tibet and Nepal. Wind will decide the nationality of the single falling snowflake, and if it lands in Tibet, the Chinese will try to claim it. Dorje slept out on a borrowed sheepskin blanket, looking at the night sky. Chomolungma, Holy Mother, stars catching on her shoulders. Hillary and Tenzing walked to the top in 1953 and an irritating line of people sleeping on her back would soon follow, but there's no conquering Everest.

Some might say it would be easier to walk to the top of the highest mountain in the world than to walk away from your family.

At last, Kathmandu. The traders dispersed at ancient Maru Square, a caravanserai built by the Newari in the twelfth century at the crossroads of the Indian and Tibetan trading routes. In the bustle, Dorje was ignored. At any rate, the Newari had no responsibility to her. She wandered on into the maze of shrines, temples, royal lodges with pagoda roofs, markets. She was stunned and hungry. There were some who were looking for people like her. A man came up to her and asked, "Are you lost, child?" His words fluttered around her but did not quite dovetail. He asked again in Tibetan and she understood. He touched her arm. She did not flinch. He pressed a little harder. "Come with me. I have food." He gripped her wrist. It excited him. He would take the wench home and break her in and then trade her to the brothel in the Thamal district for more go-rounds with

slightly less angular girls who had bathed. He *would* feed her first; he wasn't an animal. He had done this several times before. He placed his arm around her waist like a grandpa to urge her forward. But their passage was stopped by a monk, suddenly in front of them. He had been watching, too. "Come with me," he said, putting out his hand. "I am the safer choice." Dorje thought he was the Dalai Lama so she took his hand.

Let's leave Dorje and the monk there for now, holding hands . . .

. . . and go to Miami, Florida, 1966, the year Magnolia Augusta Van Zandt was born.

Magnolia came out howling, and her anthem would ever be John Mellencamp's, "Authority Song," *I fight authority and authority always wins.* Her mother, Avery, intended to call her Lia, but that was too soft a sound and it was Maggie from day one. Maggie weighed in at nine pounds three ounces and she threw that weight around. Maggie's daddy, Jack, who wasn't going to have to stay home with the little howler, thought her perfect. His first child.

The new family went home and Jack went back to his medical residency at the hospital. It's what men did. Jack grew up in Miami and there was something about the clear sunlight, the way it glinted off the glass buildings and turned the Atlantic to steel, that made him want to be a surgeon. It was such a blue-sky-and-silver town, everything looked like it was cut with a knife. Plus, there are a lot of old people in Miami. No shortage there.

Jack met Avery while he was in med school. She was a waitress at the Cuba Mama Café, where the Cuban

sandwiches could not be beat. She looked so out of place. Most of the waitresses seemed almost to dance salsa steps while they slung the hash, and they had trashy mouths and hair held back by bandanas. Beautiful. But then there was Avery, this sort of misplaced southern belle, awkward and blond and like she didn't hear the same music as the other girls. Jack didn't know how she got the job. She would have fit better at Howard Johnson's, where the old men overtip a girl like her. But she was so *sincere* about the job. So sincerely awkward. One day he was sitting in her section and as he opened his book-style, large plastic menu she tipped the coffee pot to fill his cup. The two actions intersected and she poured the coffee right down the crease of the menu and onto the crease of his pants. Before Jack could even react to the heat she grabbed his glass of ice water and threw it on him. Half of it splashed up on his shirt. Then for an instant they just looked at each other. Avery spoke first, saying, "Would you like some eggs with your coffee, sir?" and Jack just had to marry her.

Maggie announced herself two years later. Avery never wanted to be anything more than a wife and mother, and maybe write a few folk songs on her guitar. She was happy to bake a cake. When Jack came home, she always had on heels. Until Maggie. Then things got a little raggedy but Jack didn't mind. He never needed perfection, Avery was never that to him.

Maggie caterwauled for the first six months of her life. It must be said that Avery loved her daughter best when she was sleeping, her little fingers in tight fists. Maggie spent quite a lot of time in her plastic baby seat perched atop the clothes dryer, lights low, dryer on. The hum of the dryer, the escaping heat, the small pitch side

to side like a faerie boat. It lulled the baby to sleep and sometimes Avery, not really intending to, would sleep too. Until the timer went off like a fucker.

But Maggie did like the folk songs. So they had that.

Around the time Jack became Ginsu Knife Certified (as Avery teased him), the Vietnam conflict escalated into war. Two years earlier, when North Vietnam did or did not fire on the USS *Maddox* floating serenely in the Golf of Tonkin, America had the moral initiative it needed for Congress to write President Johnson a blank check. Operation Rolling Thunder, or at least the media event, got underway. Jack's brother was already over there. Now that Jack was a doctor, some combustible combination of patriotism and history made him want to volunteer. To somehow protect his brother, his country, the grainy footage of Vietnam on the CBS Evening News, it all distilled into his decision. He would carry knives instead of a gun and stitch the wounded world back together. Walter Cronkite was like a grandfather practically admonishing him to enlist, you coward.

Avery was not amused. But it happened, and Jack went to Nam as an officer and M.A.S.H. surgeon. What Jack found out was that war is badass. Soldiers and civilians came to his surgery looking like they had been attacked by tigers—one of them had. In less than a year Jack contracted Tourette's of the heart. He took to cussing like a son of a bitch, but so did everyone else. He developed facial tics, but so did everyone else. He sometimes used his own ether, not so common. When he woke up he shook like a dog come out of the river. None of this was a problem for the U.S. Army, but the tics in his hands were. Accidentally slicing the femoral artery of a patient on the operating table and earning

the nickname *Jack the Ripper* among the nurses got him reassigned to Da Nang on the South China Sea.

Jack spent the rest of his war as chief medical officer of the free clinic for the Da Nang prostitutes. This was a fairly successful attempt by the Army to keep U.S. servicemen from catching the clap.

While Jack was sifting for his sanity in the hourglass of China Beach, Avery and Maggie continued their own little war. Maggie would-not-could-not eat those peas. Maggie hated pink. Maggie would only sleep if she could sleep next to Mama and when she did she ended up sideways and kicked her mother all night long. Maggie put her pudgy hand around the stem of one of Avery's prize parrot tulips in their pocket garden. "Maggie, don't even think about it!" her mother warned. Her daughter stared back her, hand still around the stem. "I'm thinking about it," the two-and-a-half-year-old said, serious as lead. The mother/daughter war waged and both of them wanted Jack back.

When Jack came home he would not find the wife he left. Somewhere along the line Avery changed out her full skirts for bellbottoms she hand-embroidered, thought about burning her bra, and wrote some damn straight war-protest songs on her guitar. Jack would be proud of this new wife, a sort of hippie debutante. She grew out her flip and her ears stuck out, just a little bit, of her now straight blond hair. While Avery never marched on Washington she did seep Maggie in a tie-dyed attitude, which frankly increased Maggie's rage against the machine stance, especially against her mother. So Avery's protest phase was not to her personal benefit.

When Jack was discharged he was certain that the only thing he wanted to slice was the Thanksgiving tur-

key. Avery was tired of the the rumba of Miami and Jack was just tired. They moved to Panama City, Florida, near Avery's sister, and bought a bungalow on the Gulf Coast. Nothing much to speak of, but the house had a nice view and siding faded to the perfect shade of sea-glass blue. Jack became a family physician with a small practice for small injuries and things that can be fixed with pills. He played golf on Fridays. Two more babies followed, Violet Camille, seven years Maggie's junior, and then a son, Ashley Grant, just eleven months later. Maggie was not amused. But Avery was, because these new babies ate their peas.

Then came Eloise, September 23, 1975.

The Van Zandts had experienced hurricane evacuations before so they had very little anxiety. They packed up the station wagon with the essentials, which mostly meant diapers. No doubt they would be back in the morning. As a running joke, they hoped the high winds would knock down the old oak in the backyard that was too expensive to remove. They headed inland to a Motel 6. They stayed one day too long.

A school of silver ballyhoo got caught up in the excitement of Eloise. The little fish were sucked into the swirl of the hurricane and had a somewhere-over-the-rainbow experience. An E-Ticket ride. After Eloise completely destroyed the Van Zandts' house (but left the tree), the ballyhoo were deposited among the exposed foundations in a displaced ocean puddle. A kindergarten class of seasick ballyhoo survived, at least for a few days. Maggie saw them when the family returned, although she was looking for her bedroom.

Well, that was that. The house was splinters. Avery took the kids back to the Motel 6 and Jack volunteered

long hours for the Red Cross. Two nights later Jack called to say he was on his way home, would pick up pizza. "Hurry," said Avery, "Maggie's in fine form tonight." While her parents were processing the loss like adults, not without grief but with logic, Maggie was just a kid. She was ping-ponging around the motel room, out of control over the loss of "EVERYTHING, MOM I LOST EVERYTHING!"

Jack and Avery did not know it, but they were in the eye of the storm; it wasn't over yet, it hadn't even hit full velocity. Maggie couldn't contain herself. Her little red pony, her canopy bed, the glow-in-the-dark stars pasted to her ceiling. Her Snow White silverware and plate! It was a never-ending list. She felt like puking. Her mother kept telling her to *sit* down. Violet was singsonging, "Maggie's in trouble, Maggie's in trouble," like it made her happy, which it did. Ash was eating his peas, but suddenly decided to fling them around the room. Her mother's voice was escalating. Maggie let out a rebel yell, opened the front door of the motel room; they were on the second floor. She ran down the steps, around the swimming pool and out onto the twilight street. Avery freaked. She put Violet and Ash into the empty bathtub, which had just presented itself as the playpen, and ran after Maggie yelling her name like a magpie.

Here's where the hurricane really hit. Avery ran down Maggie. It didn't take that long, as Maggie was only nine. But back in the playpen, little Violet, just two years old, stood up, pulling on the faucet for leverage. The water came on. Ouch, hot. Violet, no fool, pulled herself up and fell out of the tub. She hit her head and started to cry. Ash, just barely a year old, had no such skills. He was at the back end of the tub. If the drain

worked properly, the hurricane would have flowed right down the pipes. But the drain was a little rusty and not open all the way. The water started to reach Ash. He tried to pull away, but of course he only slipped and slid further into hot water. Then he cried too, but with an urgency that was so intense Violet shut up.

Avery picked Maggie up and beat her bottom to almost child abuse levels, she was just so frustrated. She hurried back to the motel. Halfway up the steps she heard Ash and literally dropped Maggie and her heart at the same time. When she saw her son she knew nothing would ever be the same again. It would always be before this day, and after this day. Maggie knew it too. She was certain her mother would never love her again. She might have been right.

Avery lifted her son into her arms and three days later laid him to earth. Ash to ashes. Avery stayed in the hurricane for a very long time.

In the aftermath Jack made the unilateral decision to move his family to Sedona, Arizona. A place of cultivated peace. If the evening news so much as reported on tropical storms, the channel was changed. In the dry reds and golds, the cactus, they never spoke of the past. They were no longer Southerners. They wore cowboy boots. Violet's boots were pink and she stomped over the bridge of sighs without difficulty. She had no memory whatsoever of the Eloise Event. Guiltless. Maggie hated her and her pink foam curlers. Her turquoise-colored barrettes. *You're the one who turned on the water*, she thought, but never said.

The fights between Maggie and Avery ended. Because really there was only one fight left. The guilt between them a cactus of the heart. Who was more at fault—Maggie for

running out the door or Avery for putting the babies in the bathtub? It was a ball they bounced between them, a hot potato. Avery, at her core, knew she shouldn't blame a nine-year-old. Jack tried his best to intervene—"You shouldn't blame *anyone*." Maggie remained the apple of his eye, but even with her father's sustained affection, in her self-punishment she downgraded herself. Pink Lady to Macintosh. As a teenager she sneaked tattoos onto her body in hidden, painful places. And once a year Maggie, without anyone knowing it was on purpose, seared her palm on the kitchen burner or burned her thigh with the iron. Small flagellations.

Years gathered. Maggie graduated from high school and moved out. She attended the Sedona Center for Arts and Technology to study textiles and design. She thought moving away from her mother would make her feel better, or feel less, but pencils fell out of hands and all her designs were violent. Her concerned drawing teacher said she knew a good therapist who had helped her overcome great grief. (She didn't mention that her great grief was menopause.)

Maggie went. But because it was Sedona her therapist was really just a New Age acolyte with crystals in the window and a sideline of essential oils. He talked of guilt and self-loathing. Forgiveness, or at least transference. She could blame the whole thing on her mother like every other American kid. And then forgive her mother! Massage. She should do something artistic, or take a trip . . . (LSD?) No! Somewhere far away and out of her comfort zone (comfort what?) like Kathmandu.

Kathmandu. Maggie left her therapist and rolled the name around like a talisman in her pocket. Nearly every college student, and certainly those living in Sedo-

na, had heard of, dreamed of the Hippie Trail. Istanbul, Goa, Bangkok, Kathmandu. Lyrical, mythical places. Really, just a backpack away.

Maggie continued her classes and worked night shifts at The Vortex. The club was an underground Ecstasy rave, and Maggie's job was to sell lollypops and water to dancing idiots while they fell in love with each other and said really really really important things that they couldn't remember the next day. But the tips were good.

In late August of 1990 she bought a ticket to Kathmandu. *Leaving on a jet plane, don't know when I'll be back again.* Like her mother, Maggie loved a good folk song.

Maggie's body and psyche have grown used to the American Southwest. She wears her cowboy boots without irony. What she values is space, the lone saguaro cactus in the Sonoran Desert. She believes her weekend hikes up the difficult Cathedral Rock and Bear Mountain trails have conditioned her for Nepal. Kathmandu just laughs at that concept.

Walking out of the small airport Maggie is sure she will see the Himalayas. What on earth would the earth's highest mountain range hide behind? But the Himalayas are not so very easy to find. Nor is a taxi. A sudden rush of male humanity offers to carry Maggie's luggage. Although she only has one bag, she feels forced to choose a porter, which immediately becomes three men ushering her into the dilapidated taxi of their choice. As she reaches into her bag to get a few dollars for the porters, hands come in the window. Voices, dirty nails, car engine revving, the driver looking at her, cigarette smoke.

She gives them too much money. The hands depart, the cab departs. Maggie sinks back into the small sojourn of the cab, exhausted by thirty-six hours of travel and ten minutes of interaction. She checks into the Kantapur Temple House, an oasis of teak and quiet, showers, and goes to bed. She falls asleep thinking she should have gone to Hawaii.

In the morning Maggie stands at the gate of the Temple House. Inside, she hears the little bells of the hotel's Buddhist garden. Outside is the dark carnival of Thamel, Kathmandu's tourist zone, and she has to go through a puddle of mud to get there. She jumps the puddle and goes.

Kathmandu comes at Maggie like a landslide: Goats, rats both dead and alive, unattended cows and unattended cow shit. Long-haired sheep from Tibet painted pink on their backs marking them for dead sheep walking. Vendors, vendors, vendors. Meat without refrigeration. Dark clouds of flies on the meat. Narrow streets. Women in saris, pops of color. Power lines in great clots of tangled wires balled up and dangerously hanging. Piles of garbage, strata of garbage; fresh orange peels could almost be pretty. Cars, bikes, rickshaws, all carrying items that are sticking out. Goats on motorbikes, pink sheep on top of busses. Walkers, walkers, walkers, hawkers, hawkers, hawkers. Food smells. Nuts with spices, fruit on bicycles. *Tiger Balm, buy my Tiger Balm.* Children. Buddha Eyes painted on stupas, imploring everyone to tolerant chaos.

Maggie is overwhelmed.

But slowly Kathmandu stops vibrating. She comes to realize that no one is shouting, pushing, no evil eye. *Make way, make way,* everyone makes way. Within the

week, Maggie makes way too. And she has a friend; she has begun to speak to Ash. She speaks out loud, because what's one more crazy? She pictures Ash as an adult, but hazy and a bit see-through, walking by her side. Maggie feels less alone with her brother. He helps her make decisions.

Maggie's favorite place comes to be Maru Square. She doesn't know that it's a caravanserai built by the Newari or that Dorje took the hand of a monk in this very crossroads. Of course she doesn't.

Ash gets impatient with Kathmandu. He tells Maggie he wants to see the Himalayas, for God's sake. A long line of buses leaves every morning for Pokhara, six or seven hours west from Kathmandu. Pokhara is the jumping off point for the Annapurna trekking trails. Maggie buys her ticket. The Prithvi Highway is a course of switchbacks whacked out of jungle traversing a river gorge. Goats, sheep, chicken in cages, and passengers ride on top of the buses. Ash rides on top for free. Maggie rides inside, looking out the window, a voyeur peering through a dusty lens. She sees a solitary villager on a suspension bridge carrying a black-feathered chicken. Clothes, dishes, children being washed in public fountains. A woman with tumors on her abdomen showing in the open space between the skirt and bodice of her sari. When the bus stops, vendors run chips, fruit, cucumbers out to the bus windows to sell. A sign that says, *Thank you for visiting the first defecation-free zone in Nepal.*

Maggie takes a cheap room in the tourist district of Pokhara and finds an outdoor restaurant for lunch. She is the only late afternoon diner. While she is having her curry, two cows wander into the garden and start eating the plants and flowers. Instead of shooing them, Maggie

just watches like a child because cows don't generally go to restaurants in Sedona in a still-living state. But she feels ashamed when the waiter comes out and picks up a broken hibiscus branch, a single yellow flower hanging by a woody thread. The flower floats to the ground and he just shakes his head. He knows what happened. Ash giggles. Sometimes he acts like such a one-year-old.

For the next few days, Maggie watches the many-colored rental canoes ply the quiet water of Phewa Lake. Above, the many-colored sails of the hang gliders look just like upside-down canoes. It looks as if the lake is mirrored in the sky. On clear mornings the Annapurna Range appears and three out of the ten highest mountains in the world stand out like show girls. By afternoon a curtain of clouds will end the show. "Maggie," says Ash, "I'm tired of the peep-show. Those mountains aren't going to walk to us."

The most common commodity on the main tourist street is trekking supplies. And if North Face is really North Façade, it's good enough to last a month or two. Maggie bought what she needed and looked to hire a guide—her own personal sherpa. Like the porters at the airport, there is no shortage of men willing to carry your backpack and guide trekkers through the high passes. Eenie, meenie, miney, mo, how else to choose? If there's a fork in the road, follow the sherpa. Tenzin Sherpa filled out her permit paperwork and misread her name on her passport. He calls her Mongolia.

The next day Tenzin hires a cab to drive them to Naya Pul and they start the walk to Ulleri. They are in the low hills on a constant upgrade through rice paddies and all things green. Tenzin walks as if life is a picnic in a basket. Ash sits on top of the basket. Maggie wonders

what happened to all the air. Midafternoon, Maggie hears a sound, far off as if she is only catching the wind that carries the sound. They enter a wide meadow hosting a herd of grazing donkeys. The donkeys are wearing bells. "A donkey concert!" whispers Ash. Some are in costume too, with tasseled, embroidered harnesses and color-striped saddle blankets. Maggie thinks the donkeys look as pious as monks and the bells are like the wind chimes that line the monastery roofs.

Reaching Ulleri, Tenzin finds them rooms at the teahouse Luxmi Lodge. Maggie learns that all teahouse lodgings on the trip will be similar: thin mattress beds in plywood-walled rooms, shared bathrooms, and a large dining room. Cold showers. The food items and the cheap prices on the menus will be exactly the same at each stop. The guides eat by themselves, but Maggie insists Tenzin eat with her. She doesn't want to talk to Ash in front of all the other trekkers. Ash sulks off in a corner but then turns his gaze out the window to the kitchen gardens and on into the yonder.

Tenzin speaks English, Hindi, Korean, and several local dialects. He shrugs his shoulders; how else can one be a guide? And he is born to it. Sherpa is the name of the occupation of mountain guide. So all guides can be called sherpas, but not all guides belong to the highly regarded ethnic group with the surname of Sherpa. Tenzin Sherpa does.

In the morning Tenzin leads Maggie up the countless staircases cleaved out of the mountains to Ghorepani. The steps are carved out of granite and tree roots and are always, always, always uneven. They climb through a dim forest skirting a stream so clear it lights their passage. Ash plays with the wood faeries because they can

see each other. Maggie thinks she is going to die, her heart fast as a hummingbird wing, she starts counting steps fifty at a time. Forty-seven, forty-eight, forty-nine, rest. Tenzin is fine.

Other trekkers and guides pass them, fall behind. Porters (Tenzin is *not* a porter) with large cone-shaped baskets secured by cloth around their foreheads pass them, fall behind. The porters carry everything up the mountains, from banana gum to refrigerators. Every one says *Namaste*. Hello, goodbye.

They reach Ghorepani, 8,792 feet, and stay a few days at the Nice View Front teahouse because it has a nice view, a large broiler in the dining room which acts as a fireplace, and the apple pie is tarted up with a dollop of peanut butter on top. Tenzin normally wouldn't sit by the broiler, wouldn't talk much to his clients. He has usually been part of a bigger group; never alone with just one girl. Just a girl like this one. Mongolia. He knows she's traveling with a ghost and it doesn't bother him; his mother does the same.

They drink ginger tea and ginger beer and he tells Maggie that he is at university in Kathmandu for a degree in engineering, but it's slow progress. He goes to school half a year and then guides half a year to raise tuition and to give money to his parents. After he says this he is embarrassed because he thinks she will think he is angling for a larger tip. He shouldn't be here, sitting with her. But she one-ups him and says, "I'm here because I killed my brother." It's a confession, she has never said the words aloud before. She looks at Ash and his burn scars flare up, or is it just the broiler behind his shadowy self? Tenzin is hesitant to reply. Americans! He is unsure if she is telling a truth or exaggerating. He

wants to ask questions. But Tenzin is from a quieter culture, he has a Buddhist understanding of the nature of suffering. Sometimes words should be swallowed. They drink their tea and eat their pie.

Before the dawn Maggie and Tenzin (and Ash) climb from 8,792 feet to 10,531 feet without resting. There is a line of people on the ascent. Seeing the sun come up at Poon Hill is like watching it go down at Key West—it's a party. Tenzin tells Maggie that Poon is a Mongol tribe name. At the top is a wide knoll with an unobstructed view of the entire Dhaulagiri and Annapurna Range— fifteen massifs. Maggie wanders. She would like it to be quiet. She wants to sear the sight of the mountains into her soul and hear the wind through the prayer flags, the sound of the dry thistle breaking beneath her feet, the small poof of feathers from the passing bird. She would like to hear the sun pull itself over the top of Dhaulagiri and be just quiet enough to hear the snow melt at first light. She wants to hear the ancient memory of the hoofprints of the Golden Horde.

Eventually the trekkers trek back to Ghorepani and the numbers dwindle. But Maggie lingers, even though it is very cold. A plane on its way to Jomson flies by. She is not disappointed. She never expected quiet. But she didn't expect to hear James Taylor either.

There is always that backpacker with the soul of a minstrel who carries his guitar and knows that when the maddening crowd has thinned, his time is at hand. A young national sits on a bench, fifteen mountains behind him, and plays that guitar. He sings a local folk song in Nepalese, and Tenzin finds himself quietly translating the song to Maggie: *My heart flutters like silk in the wind. I cannot decide whether to fly or sit on the hilltop. The*

folk song is followed up with "Fire & Rain" and "You've Got a Friend" in English. Ash is smiling like he set this up. Maybe he did. When the minstrel finishes, Maggie knows it's time to go. They walk back to Ghorepani.

Midmorning the little group heads out for Tadapani farther up the mountains at 8,891 feet. It is a quiet day of walking through the *lali gurans*—rhododendron trees. The trees have lost their leaves to fall but Maggie imagines the trail of petals in spring. Dhaulagiri comes into view like the giant it is. Tenzin tells her there are only fourteen mountains on earth over an elevation of 26,000 feet. Dhaulagiri is the seventh highest rising out of and creating the Kali Gandaki Gorge, the deepest in the world. Maggie is silenced, to see something so deep.

That evening as the sun falls out of the sky, the clouds gather and they see just the tip of Machapuchare—Fish Tail Mountain—in the distance, rising higher than the clouds, struck end-of-day gold. Tenzin tells Maggie that is the direction they are heading.

The road to Chomrong is downhill, only to climb right back up, almost all of it through a tangle of jungle, thicker than what they have been in before. The light is green and comes in shafts like art lighting in museums. A ray highlights a single tree covered in moss and canopied with ferns, many falling into each other, rotting slowly, others thrusting up. Maggie sees white-faced monkeys. The path leads down staircases of roots. When the sun breaks through, it follows Maggie's blond hair and puts a halo-light around her.

Eventually they leave the jungle and walk through rice paddy terraces and fields of buckwheat, the trail cutting through front yards. Playing children stop to look, or don't stop. Trekkers are a common sight. One

of the children sees Ash, and she sees him as a toddler. He stops and plays with her, *rice pattycake*, everyone knows that game, and then catches up.

At last they reach Chomrong, 7,200 feet. Directly across the valley looms Annapurna South, over 26,000 feet; to the east is Machapuchare, over 22,000. Maggie sits out on the stone patio of the Kalpana Lodge drinking ginger tea and watching the late afternoon fan dance of the clouds. From the angle of Chomrong the two-pronged tail of Machapuchare is visible, splashing out of the tide of clouds. Maggie thinks the mountain looks like a Japanese koi. She could draw it on white rice paper with a few black strokes of ink.

Chomrong is a bigger village with terraced farms, a school, and a sports field. It has shops with items from Tibet and there is a German bakery and an Italian pizza parlor, but really they are a Nepal bakery and a Nepal pizza parlor. On the patio of the teahouse, an old woman has set up a small store with knit hats and gloves and intricately sewn scarfs. The merchant says she is from Tibet (she calls it Tea-bet) and Maggie wonders if her life in Chomrong is better than it was in Tibet, and what the term *better* might actually mean to her. Maggie buys three scarfs—for her mother, Violet, and herself. While she is paying, Tenzin is pleased to find them together, comes over and introduces Maggie to his mother. Dorje. Dorje puts her hands together. *Namaste.*

Let's leave them there for a moment . . .

. . . And go back some years ago when Dorje stood in the caravansari in Muru Square and took the hand of the Dalai Lama (who wasn't the Dalai Lama at all).

Now here is a strange thing, and Dorje and the monk

both knew it: women don't touch monks. It is forbidden. But they did it. And for Pradeep it was the first time he had been touched by a woman since his mother hugged him goodbye on the monastery steps when he was six years old. He was the youngest of four boys, his parents could not afford him and so gave him to Buddha, a common thing. Pradeep was never discontent with his life until he held Dorje's hand. Which is of course exactly why women aren't allowed to touch monks.

Pradeep took her back to his monastery and she was left with the nuns to regain her health. It took over a year while they fed her little bits of fatty meat and yak cheese and doses of oil and butter tea. The monastery was away from the city, up in the low hills, a very quiet place of bells and the sounds of water and prayer wheels. Dorje found the silence elegant. For in this year of outward silence she screamed on the inside. Each piece of food she ate, could not resist eating, was a slice of guilt.

Dorje believed the only thing she could do to redeem herself was to become a nun. But once a person has been weak in this world, has abandoned what is known to be right, it's not so hard to do it again, now is it? Pradeep sought out Dorje in the quiet places she liked to go, inside the hay barn where the cats sleep, in the copse of aspens, to the donkey meadow. They never touched again. But a year later, when Pradeep asked Dorje to leave the monastery and marry him, she said yes, yes, yes. Because she did not want to be a hungry ghost, because she wanted to forget, because she wanted to be touched and full. Because he had Dalai Lama eyes.

Pradeep and Dorje were ever poor but they had their son, Tenzin Gyatso Sherpa, and Dorje buried her past

somewhere high up in the Himalayas where mostly it stayed under snow.

Dorje invites Maggie to their home for dinner and serves platters and platters of food. They all get a little drunk. The cat jumps up on the table. Maggie kind of falls in love with Dorje. Dorje recognizes that Maggie has some sort of wound and she tries to salve it with a good soup.

Chomrong is the last year-round village stretching out in terraces a thousand feet down to the Modi Khola River. Beyond are only seasonal teahouses to service the trekkers. Maggie and Tenzin (and Ash) cross the river on a suspension bridge that feels like its true job is not to transport travelers to the other side but to weed out the weary and the knock-kneed with a quick, plunging death. Tenzin holds Maggie's arm for the slow crossing. On the other side they climb right back up into a creaking bamboo thicket. There is only one way into the Annapurna Sanctuary. As they climb higher the jungle recedes and the gorge opens up wide, deep, and vast. The gorge is gorgeous. If Vincent had been allowed to paint there, he would have cut off both his ears, or neither of them. They climb higher and seem at last to meet October. The jungle is gone, the plants more hardscrabble, the vertical cliffs of the canyon split by a hundred nameless falls. Last flowers grow close to the ground and lose a petal even as they pass by. A mist falls from the north and makes the trekkers quiet. Machapuchare is hiding, but they know exactly where.

A lone Nepalese with a light load in his wicker basket and a cheerful Dhaka topi hat emerges from the mist. He carries a fistful of wildflowers. Maggie wonders

where has he come from, where is he going? She'll never know but imagines him with his wife at their dinner table that night, flowers in a jar. It marks the soul of a man who will stop to pick the late last blooms of autumn and carry them the long way home.

The next day they continue the trek through the valley to Machapuchare Base Camp at 12,139 feet, the last stop before Annapurna Base Camp at 13,549. They are high in the mountains now. Tall dried stalks of a summer plant lining the path make a scarecrow sound as they pass. The teahouses emerge in the mist. They have the same blue tin roofs of all the teahouses but appear more solidly built, like barracks. Maggie's room is small and narrow, lined with windows that the 2:00 a.m. cold will completely ignore.

Maggie and Tenzin (and Ash) bundle up and head out behind the teahouse to climb a steep rise. Tenzin takes her to a place he usually keeps to himself. The mist slips away with the sun and the sky turns that final shade of blue just before black. They head for a line of prayer flags on the far crest. To Maggie they look like forgotten laundry, but if you know how to read them, they tell a story as clearly as a stained-glass window in a church. *Lung Ta*—Wind Horse, surrounded by four hundred mantras, rides the middle of each flag, a symbol of speed and transformation of bad fortune to good. Tenzin tells Maggie that Tibetans believe the mantras will be blown by the slightest wind to spread compassion. They are not individual prayers but for the benefit of all. "Including me," thinks Maggie, standing downwind. The moon comes out from behind one of Machapuchare's lower peaks, large and oddly shaped as if the thin air can't quite support the October moon.

That night is ice-on-the-windows cold. Tenzin wakes Maggie at 4:30 a.m. with a knock at her door. Ash wants to sleep in but Maggie makes him come. They climb into the bowl of the Annapurna Sanctuary in a complete sur-round of very close mountains, not one of them under 20,000 feet high. It's a clear day and they can see forever.

On the longest day of summer there are only seven hours of daylight in the Sanctuary. Desolate and stark, the mountains command the environment. Maggie thinks they are speaking, if she only had the ear to hear them. Annapurna 1, the tenth-highest mountain on earth, shrugs its shoulder and snow drops like a white velvet cape. The glaciers in the crevices below them creak and creak and then break with a muffled boom. The wind goes where the mountains tell it to go.

The grass at their feet is at year's end and damp with morning. When they walk, the smell of hay and ice ris-es. It is a place of Wind Horses, cairns, and avalanche. Tenzin tells Maggie that the Gurang people believed the Sanctuary was the repository for gold left by the Indian serpent-gods, the Nagas. When the sun breaks over the crest of the peaks, the snow is gold, and Maggie believes it. She believes the mountains could get up and walk around if they wanted.

Tenzin is a good guide and he knows when Maggie wants to be alone. She wanders off with Ash, and at last gets her nerve. "Ash," says Maggie, "can you forgive me for killing you?" She starts to cry. It's taken her fifteen years and a desperately high walk to ask this question.

Ash looks at his sister and says what he came to say from the beginning. "You don't really remember me." It's a true but blunt opening salvo. She has to look at photos to recall his face. "My death is more alive for you

than the memory of my life. You have forgotten about me. It's the loss of me that lives." From the mouths of babes. "That's broken, Maggie."

Maggie pauses. "Did it hurt?" she asks.

"Yes. And then it didn't." They stand together in thin air.

Maggie takes a thin breath and asks what she came for. What she just realized she came to do. "Can I leave you here, Ash?"

"Yes," says the hazy ghost. Maggie can see the mountains right through him. "But I have two requests." Maggie listens. "Forgive me for causing you pain."

"Ash, you never meant to . . . !"

"Did you mean to?!" interrupts Ash. And some of the broken things are fixed.

"What's the second request?" Maggie asks a few moments later.

"Go ahead and shtup the Sherpa, Mongolia. You know you want to!" With that the smiling ghost of Ash Van Zandt turned into air and blew right through the prayer flags and out into the yonder.

Maggie walks by herself. Tenzin walks well ahead, out of her sight, then waits. When he sees her, he walks ahead again. A true Sherpa. As Maggie drops out of the bowl of the Sanctuary she passes wild lupine just giving up the ghost of purple. Tibetan sheep are grazing on the hillside. Porters rest in the narrow sun and take their time. There is no time here. Time can't make it over the mountains. Maggie takes slow steps and stays as long as she can in a very high place.

She starts to weave a plan out of thin air . . .

San Francisco 1996

Maggie and Dorje hurry out the door, join Pradeep in the Subaru, and drive to Polo Fields in Golden Gate Park. Maggie will call her parents tonight to tell them all about the day. As they make their way through the crowd, Maggie waves to Tenzin, who is already there, saving them places up front, holding their son, Ashley Tashi Sherpa. Ashley has little headphones on to protect his ears. The baby sees his grandma and reaches out. It's only been a year now since Maggie managed to secure legal status for her in-laws to come live in the United States. They are getting ready to open their store in Berkeley, where there are a good number of expats from Nepal and Tibet. Everything will be handmade, quite a bit of it by Dorje and Maggie.

The family is settled in their seats well in time to see the Beastie Boys take the stage for the first ever Tibetan Freedom Concert. Dorje sways with joy even before the music starts. *Free Tibet!* She passes out wax-paper-wrapped pats of yak cheese so none go hungry. Ever again.

Swisher Sweets

As a mother navigates her children's grief, she is surprised to find her own is decades deep.

Lake Tahoe, Nevada Late Summer

I pulled open the top of my one-piece bathing suit and poured a good amount of my ex-husband's ashes down the front. It felt like gritty talcum. When I let go of the elastic front some ash dust puffed up into my face. I managed to resist licking my lips but I could feel it in my eyes. The best thing to do was to just hurry up and jump in the lake. So I did.

The lake was heartlessly cold—it'd just as soon kill ya' as anything; freeze a body into a sunken, blue-veined alabaster statue. But I'd been in this lake many times, water so clean a child could drink it through a straw. I knew what to do. Big breath, start kicking. My goal was an outcropping of granite rocks not too far away. The idea was that as I swam the ashes would dissipate from my suit and follow the drift in some spiritual, afterlife way. Peaceful. But I kind of felt the way I would feel peeing in someone's pool. I was pretty certain it was illegal to dump human remains in the environmentally protected Lake Tahoe. But this was *our* lake. Ben's lake.

Dead at fifty-eight, heart attack. Imagine being attacked by your own heart.

I could see some of the ash coming out and floating on top of the water. Little pieces of Ben, floating away,

sinking, glinting like mica in the late afternoon sun. He was literally next to my heart. I remembered the way Ben looked behind the oil-glossed wooden steering wheel of his Boston Whaler, a place that did not require a college degree. The big mackinaw trout and the smaller rainbow, color ghosted out of their scales as they drowned in the air. The smell of pine needles and fish scales, the thwack of the waves on the side of the Whaler and the thwack of the fish on the deck. Ben cleaned the fish with efficiency, but I felt the little deaths and smelled them on his fingers.

Did I love him then, in those early years when we went fishing and after we jumped off the side of the boat together and cooked the fish in a cast-iron pan over a rose-gold fire? On those nights, when it was cold even in deep summer, I know I loved his shoulders and the way he filled up the space of the plaid flannel sleeping bags, side by side, zipped together.

I climbed out on the rocks, expecting my suit to be empty. But as the water shed off my body, I realized the bulk of the ashes remained in my suit and had turned into a sort of mud, clumping to my skin. The weight of it pulled my suit down a bit and collected at the low point of my one-piece. I sighed. He was in parts of me I had not intended. I had no choice but pull open the leg of my suit and start pulling out globs of ash. It was wet cement. I had to shake it from my hands and hunks of it splashed into the water or splat onto the rocks. This was not what I had in mind. Most of it ended up on the granite. The thought came to me that when the ashes dried in the sun it would look like those rocks that are covered in bird shit and harvested for fertilizer. I wondered how long it would take for Ben to erode.

Oh well, I had tried. To do something nice. When I got home I had to shower the rest of the ashes off and watch my ex-husband go down the drain in a swirl of gray. Some of it clumped around the drain and I used my toes to squish him down. I threw away the suit. Who wants that memory? Then I realized that part of Ben was in the garbage too. What a mess. No wonder people bury people.

I still had his prosthetic arm though. With the hook-hand and the tattoos.

Two Months Earlier, Five Days Before the Wedding

My darling friend Debbi was with me when the phone rang in the car. Later it occurred to me that the Internet of Things people should teach the ringtone to be intuitive and give a little warning. I was expecting a wedding-bells type call, but what I got was Tubular Bells. I put Piper on speaker phone.

"Mom, where are you?"

"I'm with Debbi driving back from the nursery. I got a gardenia plant." Piper probably doesn't even know what a gardenia is, doesn't know that if a wedding could be contained in a single flower it would be the elegant gardenia. "Coming down the mountain if I lose you."

"Dad died."

All the gardenias ghosted away.

Could I have planned for that? Along with the taco bar and the twinkle lights in the stream that would be fallen stars in the night. Somewhere in the lists we made and checked off, could there have been a line for "Dad died"?

The road was more clairvoyant than the phone. A pull-out presented itself just around the bend, a little

safety sanctuary. I wanted to accelerate, vibrate, teleport myself to my daughter. So Debbi was going to have to do the driving.

Debbi said I was—what's the word for the way to feel when the man whom I was married to for fifteen years and I divorced twenty years ago dies? I don't know if there is a single word. There was a time I wanted him dead. I would get the insurance money. Back when I tried to escalate our fights from the fuck-you-bitch level to the breaking-my-arm level so that, like America, I could take the moral high ground, wounded soldier, purple heart. Sort of a Pearl Harbor approach to entering the war of separation. But we had reached an armistice years ago, my arm intact. (His long gone.)

I could feel relief. In old age Ben would have been a burden on the kids. He was a house built of sticks. Or I could feel a sort of laurel-wreathed victory that the living has over the dead. Or I could have felt numb, the way I feel when I smell pine branches encased in icicles in a December forest.

Plus, we had all lost our handyman.

"I don't even know where to bury him," was the last thing Piper said before we hung up the phone, Debbi now at the wheel.

"I know where, I know exactly where," I said, and all the things I could be feeling, could be thinking, dissolved into melancholy and I felt like a sad guppy in a cloudy fishbowl.

Debbi hurried me home and I cried the whole way. A surprise of tears. Not for myself. For the phone calls we had to make, the packages of grief, like dog shit, we were going to deliver. For my son, Jude, who lives four hundred miles away and no one was going to be there

with him to ride out the wild. And sadness for Ben. For what he never had and and what he would never get. For Steven, because Piper was going to dance right off the edge and Steven would have to be the one to two-step Piper back. For Steven and Piper's wedding. How do you have a wedding five days after the father of the bride dies?

A Memory
In the first summer after the divorce we didn't really know how to end the marriage. Ben and I talked on the phone in the dark hours. Went for walks in the birch trees by White's Creek, old carvings in the bark. A bleeding heart, maybe 1917, maybe not. The little round birch leaves made that quiet leafy sound when the wind moved through. We had walked this path many times. "Ben," I said "if neither one of us remarries, let's be buried side by side." Ben knew I was serious. I like graveyards.

"That seems a long time to wait to lie down next to you," Ben softly replied in the birdsong grove.

The Phone Call to Ben's Sister Angie, Who Lives on the Oregon Coast Where the Ocean Polishes Agates into Sea-Jewels and Then Buries Them in the Sand for Children to Find on a Windy Day
The girl's neurotic, it's just a fact. It's like it's always Halloween night and there's candy wrappers all over the place. Her Indian name is *Runs at Mouth*. Piper got in a hello and then a word-cloud surrounded us. And I was lost in that cloud. Her voice, her excitement. Piper couldn't interrupt. Angie spoke as if commas were be-ings of a lesser world. It was almost like listening to a

poem. I caught Piper's eyes with mine. We both knew it. We were going to deliver that singular edge of time where life would always be counted as *before* or *after*.

I lost my concentration and started pulling sad haikus out of the word-cloud. Finger-counting syllables in my mind.

Dad's heart stopped like that.
He drank too much and smoked pot.
Death by KFC.
Or
He deserved to die
He deserted his children
He reaped what he sowed.
Or
Pretty boy, blue eyes
You never stood a true chance
Shame your mom and dad.

"Angie," Piper finally cut in, and I shook off the haikus. "Dad died, he had a heart attack." She had to get it out really fast and said it twice so she could put the brakes on Angie and make her hear. The circus tent collapsed and was never going up again. All the elephants went home.

Silence, but not golden. "My brother died," Angie said, tentatively trying on the ill-fitting words. We all felt sick.

We had more calls to make. His job, his best friend. A shorter list really, than it should be. His mother. Jude.

"Oh, my beautiful boy," said Ben's mother, Mariam, with a sigh like the last violin note played on the *Titanic*. Is it a true sign of my humanity that in that moment I felt nothing but sorrow for her? All the years of flicking

blame on her flicked away for the duration of that call, and I could share her pain. She had lost her son, after all. And I was worried about mine.

What this call was going to do to Jude. We saved him for last, for as long as we could.

The Phone Call to Las Vegas Where All That Glitters Is Fucking Plastic

God, what a town. No one really lives there. It's all dress-up and *Let's Pretend*. Jude told us he was at a stoplight by the Strip and a woman's wood-heeled shoe fell out of an open-sided high-rise parking garage and broke through the back window of his hatchback. Size 7.5, Topshop. He took off before the body followed.

My beautiful boy. He and his sister were all I cared about. The rest of my emotions I pushed to the back of the underwear drawer, right next to the gun. They can blow up later. I spent my life watching these little souls run na-ked into the world. I wanted to clothe them in petals.

When he was growing up I told Jude don't do that, do this. And he listened to me, he really did. But every broken bone, every snowboard accident was a bottle of doctor-prescribed Vicodin lining up with his father's genes. Bad genes in black jeans—that's what I married. Five years of sobriety, three of graduate school, and still I was worried that this phone call could send Jude straight to the Queen of Hearts, open twenty-four hours, two-for-one shots 6 a.m. to 12 noon. *Whiskey, if you please, four deep.*

"Hi Jude," said Piper and I said it too. "Whatta you doin'?"

"Just got back from the gym. Making breakfast." Ba-con and eggs. His house always smells of bacon, which I

think is a counter-girlfriend smell. I'm going to send him a diffuser. Orange oil. God, my brain is a sick chicken, I can't hold on to a straight thought. I took over.

"We have some really bad news, Jude." No need to stretch this out. "Dad died. He had a heart attack, it was quick."

His reaction was immediate. "I knew it," said Jude. I could have imagined a hundred responses and it wouldn't have been that. "I woke up this morning and I was sad. So I just went with it. I put on sad music and cried for two hours and went back to bed. I knew it."

"You knew it was Dad?"

"No, just something. I gotta go. I'll call you back, don't worry. I love you guys." He hung up.

Oh, I'm going to worry. I'm worrying so hard I'm going to break out in a sweat like it's hot yoga. Cow Face Pose. I told Jude a dozen times, a baker's dozen, "Call your dad, you'll be sorry if you don't." Piper had her dad over for dinner two weeks ago (brisket). She had him fix things at her house and yelled at him regularly. She was going to be sad, but she wasn't going to be guilty. Jude was due a double shot of guilt and remorse—bitters and absinthe. I wanted to get on an airplane and fly to him, but I wasn't going to be able to save him from that cloudy glass. Only he could do that.

Well, Cow Face, you didn't need to worry, oh ye of little faith.

Finding recovery is like finding God. Plenty of paths to the top of that mountain. An addict can sit around with a bunch of sick dicks at AA and talk about it. Rock climb until the wrists will hold no more. Slit a wrist. Jude did those. Why not? They work. Turns out, meditation is his jam. So when he tells Piper and me that he

woke up sad and didn't try to figure out why, just let it get tugged along by a song, we buy it.

Jude didn't turn to the Queen of Hearts. He turned to stone. He told us later that he stayed up all night in meditation to help his father pass from this world, to bear witness. He built a stairway with a big neon exit sign out of memory and kindness and he kept it flashing until it was dimmed by the dawn. Then he wrote a letter to his grandmother. He told Mariam what he had done for her son and that when she died he would do the same for her. Only he would do it with the pure and hot intention of making her transition hard, harder, hardest. When that time comes, Jude will grind those pearly gates to dust.

Piper, Later That Same Night
God, what a day. Evening now. Piper set up her ironing board and heated up the iron. She took the plastic wrapper off the shirt, pulled out the straight pins holding the square shape, unbuttoned the shirt, laid it on the board. Ironed it. The steam smelled of minerals and desert. She ironed her tears into the shirt. A secret message. She got out the gray wedding suit and into the inside pocket of the jacket she put two photos of her and Jude when they were kids. She put the suit, the shoes and socks, the tie, the pocket square into a bag. To take to the mortuary tomorrow. Ben's life had no use for a suit. He bought it for the wedding, at the JC Penney outlet store, but it was nice. Ben told Piper the only other time he would wear it was for his own funeral, *hahaha*, so that's just what she was going to do. She knew he would have preferred Carhartts. Or that jacket with the fur-lined hood he brought from Alaska, all those years ago.

Piper remembered when just the two of them went to Bryce Canyon and got caught in a windstorm. Red dust. Ben put a bandana over her face, bandit style, and they went out into the grit, just to feel it scour their skin, to taste the old earth. Face it down. Ben taught her things like that. How to throw the knife. Rip with your teeth. Sew up what needs sewing.

A Little Bit About the Arm
You've never made love until you make love to a man with a hook for a hand.

Well, we each had our own things to think about that night.

Four Days Before the Wedding
(For the record, the only reason Ben took Piper to Bryce Canyon was because I called him and told him if he didn't pay some attention to his daughter she was going to transfer all her love, one hundred percent, to me. Which I wanted. Which I deserved. Earned. But I loved Piper, so I made that call. Honestly, it cost me something. Sorry, Piper, that I didn't teach you how to eat grit and sleep in dirty sleeping bags. I'm just the one who bought the lice shampoo.)

Here's what I learned about calling people to tell them someone they cared about was dead: They keep the call short, they hang up quickly. The terrorist's bomb has just exploded and they need to count their fingers and toes, check for internal bleeding. Then they call back and the second call takes much longer. That's the *who, what, when, where, why* call. And with that second call they want me to become responsible for what they need, or their concepts of what should be done. Fuck

'em. Why are they even calling me? I only care about Piper and Jude. I had four days until a wedding. I decided to give Ben two.

Steven set us up at a mortuary. Piper and I were headed over when Mariam called. "I need to see Ben; I just need to do it." She lives in Portland, a nine-hour drive if she can hold her pee.

"You don't want to do that, Mariam," said Piper. "He had a heart attack and they did an autopsy." Piper's a badass emergency nurse and Steven does triage from a helicopter. When Steven wears his flight suit around town people thank him for his service and give him things like free oil changes.

"I have to see my boy," said Mariam. Sadness so sad, her heart a bug caught in amber.

And I could understand that. "Okay, Mariam, I'll ask them what it takes and call you back."

Piper and I sat with Morticia; I never did remember her name. Could there be a worse job? Well, I guess shoveling the body into the box was worse. I expected Morticia to be slack-handed and gratuitous but actually she was quite normal and nice. She probably had a name like Lisa. She addressed her questions to Piper— the true next of kin. I was just the checkbook. $1,300. I said no to all the extras. Piper didn't care.

We went out to the car to get the clothes Piper brought. "You're going to bury him in the wedding suit?" I asked, looking into the bag. I hadn't known until that moment.

"He told me to," she said. She told me about ironing her dad's last shirt. She looked like a mudslide about to happen. I would have followed her down.

I rescued the tie, pocket square, and socks from the

bag. All in bright colors. Things Ben had picked out. "Could we give these to Jude to wear at the wedding?" She nodded yes. Jude was taking Ben's place and walking her down the aisle. I found a pair of boxers in the bag.

"No one wants to be buried commando," said Piper, squaring up, stepping back from the edge.

Morticia looked in the bag and handed us back the shoes. They don't burn shoes. "We don't actually put the clothes on the body. We just lay them on top. It's $450 extra to dress the body and make it presentable for viewing." I looked at Piper.

This is something that I know. If Piper died, she wouldn't go in the box naked and have clothes put on top of her. And I wouldn't let anyone else dress her. I would do it myself. I found I understood how Mariam felt.

I thought of a night, so many nights ago, when Ben fell asleep on the couch and I came out to get him. He had beautiful skin. The moon was coming through the window, but his skin was the candle in the dark. The blanket had arranged itself in a twisted way exposing his body as if he were a model in repose for a classically trained painter. His missing arm, his flat stomach, breath rising, falling. I wished I had the nerve to ask Morticia how much extra for me to dress him. Then I snapped out of it.

I went outside and called Mariam. "Hi." I skipped the *How are you doing*s. "It's $1,300 to have Ben cremated and $450 to make him presentable to view. I'm paying the $1,300." This is where Mariam is supposed to remember that I am the ex-wife. That I have no obligation to pay for anything and she jumps in and offers to help. I pause. No? Okay, I go on. "But I'm not willing to pay more. Do you want to pay the $450 to have him dressed?"

Silence. The next person who talks loses.

"I'm feeling better now," said Mariam. The cow. I'd pay $4,500 to make sure Piper was dressed. But even as I thought it, I knew I was harsh; her response was tied to her income.

Piper didn't blink when I said we were fine with the standard deal. Then Morticia brought out Ben's arm and laid it on the table. They don't burn prosthetics either. Good Christ.

A Bit More About the Arm

The tattoos are hula girls. Pinks and greens. A tiki torch. I think Ben used Tommy Bahama shirts for his patterns.

On our first date I reached across the table and ran a finger up a florid hibiscus. "What's the story?"

"I was born without it." My fingers dropped back to the cold hook, pressed my fingerprint onto the metal.

"That's sad." But reasonable, certainly believable.

"You don't miss what you never had."

"I like the tattoos."

We kept dating. Eventually the family albums came out. Thanksgiving. Baby Ben at the beach, two arms reaching up as if the sun were his to keep. I flipped him the stink eye. He countered with the bad-liar shrug. Later that night he said, "Frostbite."

Just because I was sleeping with him didn't mean I owned his past. But everyone knows the past is never past. It isn't even over.

What Really Happened to the Arm

How to explain Sand Mountain? Imagine an ancient Gargantuan fills his hourglass with the sands of time

from the eternal Sahara. The sand is as fine as silk, almost the feeling of water in his hands. The Gargantuan goes to visit his auntie to take her this exquisite gift—an egg timer. His auntie meets up with him in what will later be named Nevada and she loves the gift! But the hourglass slips through her gnarled fingers and shatters on the harsh earth. Two miles of sand dunes rise six hundred feet in the air, completely incongruous with the low pinyon pine and the borax washes of the high desert that surround it. The dunes appear out of thin air, a mirage, a broken hourglass, all of Time poured out.

Seriously, Sand Mountain is so out of place it seems a faerie tale. And it is extraordinary, one of only thirty-five places in the world with documented singing sands. When the sand moves, it sings, it whistles and barks, booms and roars. It gives voice to the desert and to Lake Lahontan, which gave up the ghost of water nine thousand years ago, the prevailing winds prevailing upon the remaining sand of the exposed lake bed to *Rise up, Brothers!* and make the dunes.

If the prehistoric beasties are willing to talk, should we not sit still and listen? Just turn off the radio and shut up. But no. It's an off-road wonderland. No glass allowed, that's the only restriction. When the wind blows and the dunes whisper secrets, all that will be heard is the sound of two-stroke engines fucking it up.

Mariam and Pete took their children, Ben and Angie, out to Sand Mountain. Really Pete was drunk before they got there because he was always drunk, it was just a question of how much. Today, too much. Pete put seven-year-old Ben in the ATV with him and headed straight up the mountain.

"I remember being afraid," Ben finally told me.

"When we got toward the top we were so vertical I remember thinking the sand would pour over and bury us. We were digging in deep and there was a wake of sand behind us. Dad had on goggles, but I didn't and the sand was needling my eyes. My eyes were watering and I saw nothing but the color gold and I thought we were burrowing into the mountain, rather than going up. I had the strangest feeling. And then Dad flung the ATV over the crest of the dune, full speed, and we went out into the air, as if we could fly, and for a moment I thought we could. But as the ATV stopped flying and started to come back to earth Dad fell sideways into me and his body pushed me out. I don't know what happened. My arm landed under the ATV.

You would think the sand would be soft, no? But it's not. It's as hard as a chopping block. My forearm looked like steak tartare.

Did you know there's a butterfly out there—the Sand Mountain Blue? It's the only place in the world it lives. Right before I passed out one landed on my chest."

We never talked of it again. But about a year after he fessed up we drove out to Sand Mountain, arriving as the sun was on the wane. I saw three of the Blues flying in a little vortex pattern, wings like geisha fans. We waited until all the off-road vehicles had departed with their throaty, juvenile roars. We waited for the singing sands to come out with the stars, we listened to the creaking old song. We hiked the dunes by moonlight and went where the prevailing wind told us to go.

How the fuck can a mother stay with a father who's a drunk? Pete died relatively young, but it wasn't until after Angie and Ben were adults. She never left him. What was it about my destiny that kept this critical piece of

information from me until it was too late, until I was already in love with the beautiful one-armed boy? How could I have expected him to know how to be a good husband, a good father? He knew more about hiding in the closet than he did about one-two-buckle-my-shoe.

When Ben started drinking Tequila Sunrises with the sunrise, like they were in cahoots, I was out. He could live inside the lyrics of a George Thorogood song if he wanted, but I was out.

Morticia was looking at us. Business was done; it was time to go. I always liked that damn arm. I picked it up and tossed it in the trunk of the car. Piper and I went home.

Three Days Before the Wedding
Debbi called. "Why don't you let off some doves in Ben's name after the ceremony? Then he'll be part of the day."

"Nice. But then I'd have to give everyone guns to shoot the doves, because Ben never saw a dove that didn't look like dinner," I said. "And it's not his funeral. It's not about him."

Piper called. We were waiting for Jude; he was driving home. "I've been thinking about it and I don't want Dad talked about at the wedding. I can't be, 'Oh, you look so beautiful, congratulations. I'm sorry about your Dad.' I can't go back and forth like that."

"If you do that you'll crack your makeup from going up-smile, down-smile," I agreed.

"Well, yeah, but I was thinking more about my emotions," she said.

"Oops."

Angie called, "What are you doing with Ben's arm?"

"Why do you ask?"

"I think I'd like to keep it. I feel it belongs to me. He used to throw it at me when we were kids."

He used to throw it at me when we were fighting. Here it comes. People are going to start claiming things. "I burned it up with his body." Nothing belongs to anyone except Piper and Jude. And maybe me.

Mariam called. "I heard you and the kids are cleaning out Ben's apartment tomorrow."

"Yes."

"Why so soon?"

"Well, because Piper and Steven are going on their honeymoon for two weeks and I don't want them to come back to that. And because Jude is coming up now and goes home right after the wedding and I don't know when he'll be back. So this is the time that everyone is here to get it done," I said.

"I can be there in a few weeks. I'd like to go through some of his stuff."

"Mariam, that's not going to happen. The kids are going to take what they want and the rest is going to the dump. His rent is due in a week. If you want to pay it, I'll lock the door and you can go through what the kids don't take. I'm not paying his rent."

"It just feels like you're sending his life to Goodwill," Mariam said.

She did not offer to pay the rent. "I don't care. I don't care about anyone but Piper and Jude. This is what works for us and this is what we are going to do." Did she honestly think I should pay the rent to wait for her? Did this woman forget that I hate her?

"Will you keep his pillow and one of his shirts for me?"

She had just lost her son. "Yes."

Really it wasn't my best day.

Two Days Before the Wedding

Jude, Piper and I drove over to Ben's house with a truck and two cars. We didn't know what we would find; none of us had ever been there. It was in a sort of compound of 1940s bungalows built around a common driveway. Sears siding and asphalt shingle roofs, scruffy paint. Inside were arched doorways and built-in nooks. A small, rusty pull-down ironing board attached to the wall in the kitchen. Front room, kitchen, one bedroom, bathroom. It was relatively clean.

How invasive to go through someone's belongings when they didn't have a chance to curate, to leave out the proper things, set up the story. They say dead men tell no tales, but their stuff does. His weed and pipe were by the stove, a bottle of Jack on the shelf above, right next to the salt and pepper. A steak in the fridge, a little past its prime, but who isn't. His bed was made. We found letters and photos of the kids, cards and artwork they had sent him, Father's Day cards and bills and IRS notices. *This is your final notice!* Damn straight on that one.

We found the old coat from Alaska with the fur-trimmed hood and his Carhartts and fishing poles, Indian axes, scrimshaw knives, a turkey warbler. We found one thousand pieces of the puzzle but we couldn't assemble it. We only pulled it apart. When we were done packing up there wasn't enough left for anyone to pay the rent on.

I looked around the sad artifacts and suddenly I wanted to smudge his house. I wished for sage and twine and to open all the windows and set Ben's spirit

free. It seemed the holiest thing to do in the wreckage of this ransacked space. By his reading chair was an ashtray and a carton of little cigarillos, two-to-a-pack in red-and-white packaging. We went room to room, opening windows, except those held fast by layers of old paint. Smudging Ben's home with smoldering cigarillos.

Swisher Sweets.

Ben would have liked that; I know he would.

One Day Before the Wedding
One of Jude's reactions, or actions, to his father's death was to get a tattoo on his back. The Ouija Board. The sun, the moon, the alphabet, the numbers, *Good Bye* at the bottom. It took up half his back. What the hell was that about?

Day of the Wedding
Piper was as beautiful as a bright idea presented in lace and tulle. When Piper took Jude's arm the three of us believed Ben was with us; if it's true that he can be, he was. And then we mostly forgot about him. For the whole day every time I opened my mouth bubbles came out, I was spreading bubbles everywhere. Piper was marrying the right man and they married in my garden with the stream and the granite bridge, the Japanese lanterns, and Japanese maples, passionately red. Winks of gold and orange koi. Debbi said, "You gardened seventeen years for this day," and in that moment that felt true.

The band had asked us if we wanted them to play any special songs. Secretly I asked for Fleetwood Mac's "Landslide." It is Piper's and my song. When the band started "Landslide" I went and got Piper, and Jude came too and we danced together. Yes, I was drunk. The café

lights were just now coming on and the twinkle lights in the stream, just like I'd planned, looking like fallen stars. Color everywhere, and all the people we love and a soft current of goodwill that hinted of gardenias.

Partway through the dance Jude said, "We talked about it, Mom, and we're glad it was Dad who died and not you. It would be so much worse if it was you." Piper was agreeing. "We're giving it to you. We love you more."

I might like to think that the better part of me would have spoken up for their dad. But I didn't. It was the best dance of my life. There will be none better.

A Last Bit About the Arm

It's in the trunk of my car. I don't bring it in the house, but it goes with me wherever I go. Every once in a while I let a bag boy bring my groceries out just to watch his face when he sees the detached arm, the hook and hula girls, when I open the trunk. Freaks 'em every time.

Sweet Nothings

Gómez has a date with destiny in the syrup aisle. Chuy is carrying Jesus on his back through the traffic lanes at the San Ysidro border crossing. The gun is in the lake.

In the mornings Gómez liked to pour himself a good strong cup of coffee-flavored tequila and a small bowl of Grape-Nuts. No milk. Just a bit of crunchy fiber to aid his digestive system. He would finish it off with a fig. And then a nap. At ninety-four he was hoping that he would make a hundred and ten and that some American news crew like 20/20 would do a story on him asking to what he attributed his long life, and he could say, "Figs. Figs are the thing."

After his nap, Gómez would most often get on his bike and make his way through the streets of Tijuana to the house of his young, but really not-so-very-young, friend, Chuy. It is no easy thing to ride a bike in Tijuana; Gómez always felt that the drivers of the cars tried to hit him on purpose, rather than realizing that, between his age and the tequila, he had a tendency to stray into the road. About halfway between the few blocks that separated him from Chuy's house, Gómez would stop at the OXXO for a six-pack of Del Sol. By this time he was exhausted, what with the exertion and the exhaust from the Most Visited City in the World. He would pop a can, then continue his journey, five more Del Sols in the basket between his handlebars so he could keep an eye

on them. Most of the time he would lose some or all of the beers, either from swerving to avoid being hit by a car, or from throwing cans at the cars. His pitching arm was weak, so mostly the cans would just fall at his feet, burst open and spray up at him, usually making him look like he'd peed his old-man pants. Children would ask their mothers why the *abuelo* was throwing beers on the ground. Mothers would shake their heads and sometimes discreetly put pesos in his basket while they quickly walked by. Because Gómez's peripheral vision had long since departed this earth, he usually did not see these items being deposited in his basket (sometimes bread, fruit, or even eggs) and he had no choice but to consider them proof of the existence of our Lord, Jesus Christ.

Gómez never knew if Chuy would be home or not. If he was home, Chuy would most likely be in his garage, and this would be quite evident because the garage door would be up. If the garage door was down, Gómez would leave his bike just outside the garage, use the key that Chuy had given him to get into the house, and take a nap on the soft green velvet couch. It was like sleeping on the wings of a parrot. When the mariachi clock in the kitchen went off, Gómez would wake, be it in ten minutes or an hour.

But if the garage was open when Gómez arrived, he would slightly alter his routine by adding in a nod to Chuy before leaving his bike just outside the garage, and going inside to take a nap until the mariachi burst out of the kitchen like a band of knife-wielding banditos. Who the hell could be expected to sleep through the assault of a mariachi band? Then Gómez would join Chuy in the garage and start the conversation as if he had just

arrived. Which in a sense, he had.

They were the best of friends. "Chuy, would you like a beer?" Gómez would ask, offering up a now warm Del Sol.

"I do not drink, my friend, but thank you."

"No? I did not know that or I would have brought Coca-Cola." This is how they started the conversation most days, unless Gómez had lost all his beers on the journey over. Then Chuy would say, "Gómez, my friend, you look hot and thirsty. May I offer you a beer?"

"Why yes! Why did I not think to bring some with me?" And Chuy would go to the garage refrigerator and get Gómez a beer.

"Will you not join me?" would always be Gómez's response at this time, and Chuy would say, "I do not drink, but thank you." And the two men would smile small smiles, for they enjoyed this exchange. Anticipated greetings resolved, they would get on with the day.

Chuy's garage opened to a small alley. A high fence opposite clipped the harsh summer sun and a golden light filtered in. Rather the color of the Del Sol in Gómez's hand. Gómez took his regular seat, opened up the resident chessboard, and began to set up a solitary game. He had to push wood chips out of the way. Chuy was well into his project; the wood chips were everywhere. Chuy's short-haired Chihuahua, Queenie, sleeping in the corner on her red blanket, looked like a curly poodle. Queenie sneezed, and for a moment Gómez thought she'd exploded. Curls of wood floated up into the air and settled into drifts and eddies.

Gómez had a soft spot for Queenie because the dog was responsible for his friendship with Chuy. In Queenie's much younger days, she was a feisty beast. If she was in the

open garage with Chuy, the little dog would charge any-one who came down the back alley. It must be more than seven years past that Gómez chanced down the alley on his morning constitutional and was attacked by what he took to be an outsized Mexican jumping bean. He sus-tained quite a spill, mostly to the detriment of his beers. Two cans burst open, and when Gómez came to, he was surprised to see the jumping bean drinking the foamy puddles. Chuy was aghast that his dog had felled what looked like an apple doll on a girl's bike, and brought the old man into his garage to get him out of the sun and into a chair. Queenie immediately jumped into Gómez's lap and started licking his bristly face, which both men chose to interpret as an apology. Gómez looked around the cozy shop. It had the atmosphere of a barber shop or cigar store, someplace rather nice to be. Gómez noticed the chessboard and the first thing he said to Chuy was, "Do you play?" Thus began an unexpected, if not quite May-December, at least a July-December relationship.

Even with the door open the garage smelled like a Pacific Northwest forest, although there was always an undercurrent of beans. But Gómez had to admit that just might be him.

"How do you find Jesus in that block of wood, any-way," asked Gómez?

Chuy stopped his hammer from hitting his chis-el and looked to Gómez. "I say He is in there. I *say* it. Then I go looking for His big toe. If I can grab that, I can wrestle out the rest." On this day, Jesus had in fact fully emerged. Some three feet tall, with His knees bent but closed together (so as not to see up His loincloth), arms outstretched, head slumped. Oiled black walnut body. Chuy was just finishing the matching cross.

On the table lay the already completed crown of thorns, symbol of suffering. Gómez ran his fingers lightly over the carved thorns, points sharp as wit. Through the years Chuy had come to understand that it was really the crown that made the sale. A briar ouroboros, a prickly scrambling thing of beauty. Instinctively Chuy knew that people would want to put the crown on their own heads for penitence, prurience, or Halloween. But his Jesus was only three feet tall. So he created a way to hinge the crown with extra pieces that would slide and lock into place, expanding the circle to human size. Who would dare to wear Jesus's crown? Many, it would seem. He knew that he could sell the crowns alone and ease his back. Indeed, one woman donated her purchased Jesus on the cross to a church she didn't even belong to and put the crown on a marble pedestal in her library as a piece of art. And it was a piece of art. But for Chuy, carving just the crown would be a shortcut that would miss the point of the journey through the wood.

Chuy always carved the crown and the nails from purpleheart wood, a color a mother would wish for her daughter's eyes. Startling.

While Chuy nailed Jesus to the cross (figuratively, as he actually used glue), Gómez went into the kitchen and made lunch. The damned mariachi band clock was going off again, little ensemble coming out of tiny saloon doors, playing "La Cucaracha" and then popping back in. The clock drove Gómez cuckoo, but at least Chuy was over his Swiss clock stage. There was a time when several clocks in the garage would go off all at once and Gómez would have no choice but to drink more.

Gómez had earned his living as a cook at Caesar's; he knew his way around *la cocina*. He made bean bur-

ritos with cilantro, salsa, and avocado and carried them
out to the garage on paper plates, only dropping one of
the burritos. That was Queenie's. Well, it was now. Gó-
mez saw that the crown was placed on Jesus's head and
Chuy was polishing the purple nails in Jesus's hands and
feet. The buttons of wood glowed from the inside like a
good glass of Spanish sangria.

"You'll be heading out with this one soon, then,"
said Gómez with a nod toward the cross.

"Day after tomorrow."

"I'll watch after Queenie." The dog had just finished
a burrito half her own size and now looked like a Bean-
ie Baby. Plus, an almost translucent, curling wood chip
had landed just above her right eye, transforming her
into a long-lashed drag queen.

"She'll watch after you."

"Okay, but just so you know, I'm slaughtering the
mariachi band while you're away and I'm going to blame
it on an earthquake." Gómez was fond of charcoal pills
to aid in his digestion and this statement ended with a
burp and a puff of black ash.

"Gómez! You're like an ancient Xiuhtecuhtli. Fire in
your soul." Chuy really loved the charcoal burps.

"On his deathbed," agreed Gómez.

"Someday I'm going to paint you draped in tur-
quoise with ash clouds coming out of your mouth."

Gómez liked the idea of being depicted as the Az-
tec fire god, and nodded his approval. "But paint me
young." The two gentlemen finished their lunch; Gó-
mez returned to the velvet parrot couch for a siesta
before he pedaled the long way home. Chuy set about
cleaning the garage, as his Jesus was complete.

Today, when Gómez got home, he was surprised to

find a roll of toilet paper and a rubber spatula in his bas-
ket. They both looked new. God is good.

When Chuy first saw Silvia, of course he did not know
her name. She was several rows over and he thought he
was looking at a Pablo Picasso painting, one of those de-
constructed, cubist portraits. Which in itself would be an
odd sale item for the Tijuana-San Ysidro border crossing
line. But there was no frame around Silvia, beyond the
shimmering halo of the pale sun. She was a face of trian-
gles. Chuy would not be surprised if she had one brown
eye and one blue. He had to get closer. He cut across sev-
eral rows, no easy feat carrying Jesus. He smacked the end
of the cross into a windshield and kept on going. While
it is hard to be discreet while carrying Jesus, he stayed a
few rows away from Silvia and watched her. As her face
dipped in and out of windows, he came to realize that
one of her eyes was set closer to her nose than the other.
Her symmetry was askew. Neither side of her face was
particularly remarkable, but if you looked at her straight
on, it was disconcerting. She obviously knew this and al-
ways shifted her face, angling her good side into the car
windows. While Chuy could guess nothing about this
woman, Silvia of course was no illusion. She had a past.

In some centuries Silvia would have been burned for a
witch, or revered as a seer of sights. In other cultures, she
may have been drowned at birth for the double wham-
my of her eye and her vagina. But Silvia was born in
Mexico, where the days are hot and the wind thin. Too
much trouble to work up a case against a little girl with
an odd eyeball. An oddball.

Silvia and her sister Ana grew up on the Nayarit coast

near the main road traveling between Puerto Vallarta and Mazatlán. Their cinderblock home was built on a cliff overlooking the Pacific and fronted with an open-air *palapa* kitchen and scratch-dirt yard. The chickens were free range, skinny and boastful. As were Silvia and Ana. Their father worked construction in Puerto Vallarta and only came home on weekends, pockets full of tamarindo candy and necklaces of plastic beads. The girls had no idea they were poor. They didn't know they didn't go to school because they did. Right in the front yard on the tables with the benches, Mamá taught them. About the Bear Prince and the Gypsy Queen. All the stories. Silvia's favorite book was not Mexican faerie tales, but those of Hans Christian Andersen. The Little Match Girl.

At night Silvia most often slept outside in a hammock surrounded by the ficus and busera trees. Wild orchids reflected moonlight like monkey faces, high up in the trees. The night wind was full of the smell of the ocean, of things alive and things dead. When the wind jostled the dried palm fronds of the *palapa* it sounded like the whispered arguments of parents behind closed doors. The white-nosed coati raccoons sometimes played with the pots and pans in the kitchen, causing the chickens to roost for protection round Silvia in her hammock, leaving their feathers in her hair and, once, a brown egg in her lap.

One very early morning Silvia walked out to the steep point that overlooked the ocean. It was that time of day when a green light illuminated the depths. She saw a trolling great white shark, dark oblong in the sea, the shape and danger of an unexploded missile left over from a war before her time. The shark slowly moved its

danger elsewhere as the rising sun threw glitter across the waves, obscuring the depths, colluding with the ocean to keep its secrets. Silvia could hear her chickens calling her home, demanding breakfast, potato peels please! Gallo doodle doo.

Silvia's mother posted a wooden sign out on the main road printed in both English and Spanish: *Lobsters by the Sea. Home Cooked. This Way*, with an arrow through the jungle to their cinderblock house. Mostly gringos came. Her mother served up whole red-faced lobsters, rice and beans, fried plantains, and remarkably iced beer for a price she did not know she could triple. Ana's job was to serve the guests and shoo the chickens. Silvia's job was to wash the dishes and not look directly at anybody. Ever.

Between customers their mother taught them long division and how to read the stars. They learned how to pull their dark hair into Spanish braids, and that if the jungle ever falls into silence you better run uphill, fast. Their mother told them of Pancho Villa and Emiliano Zapata, assassinated heroes of Mexico. Silvia pictured screaming horses and the released souls of great men mistaken for gunsmoke rising from a mortal wound. Silvia knew the names of all the trees and four different words for rain.

There came a night when Silvia was sleeping in her hammock and awoke to the sounds of the *palapa* whispering sweet nothings. No. It was her parents. It is delicious to eavesdrop, like a lime tart. She knew her mother was uncomfortable and hoping for a boy. She knew her father was worried about money. She believed this to be the way of parents. It was not alarming. But her father kept using the word *maquiladora*, which she did not

recognize, and talking about moving to their *tia*'s house. Did her mother's sister Juana have a new baby, Maquiladora? Silvia would call her Dora. But would they move to Tia's house up where the rosewood grew and there was no ocean? No lobster or great white? Her parents' voices drifted over her and out into the jungle, where the words were overcome by the chirp of a single night bug. Silvia was asleep.

In the spring the baby boy was born! Dominico, but they called him Pepe because he was so cute. And before summer they had left their cliff above the ocean not for Tia Juana's house but for the great city by the wall, Tijuana.

"You know you are like syphilis," said Gómez as Chuy hoisted his newest Jesus onto his shoulder and headed out for the border crossing. "You finish one and start another. Endless Jesuses."

Chuy looked at his friend, nonplussed. He often did not understand what Gómez was talking about. "Sisyphus," he said at last, "You mean Sisyphus, rolling the rock up the hill of eternity."

"That's what I said, syphilis," confirmed Gómez as he picked up Queenie and got on his bike. Chuy closed the car door and rolled down the window. "What are you doing with her?"

"Taking her to the hypermarket so she can pick out treats. Vienna sausages from the imports aisle, I think. I took the money out of your coconut monkey jar." Gómez was referring to the carved coconut that collected change on the dresser in Chuy's bedroom. Gómez arranged Queenie's red blanket in his basket and then placed Queenie inside. She was used to this. The blanket

helped to stabilize her for the wobbly ride, but she knew enough to stay awake in case she had to jump out or was forcibly ejected.

"Okay. Stick to the small roads. I don't want her to get run over."

"What about me?"

"You, my friend, will dent the car with your bony knees and survive unscathed," said Chuy as he drove away, Jesus staring out the back window. This was Chuy's third day on the border crossing without the sale of this particular Jesus, which was a record for a nonsale. The purpleheart crown usually secured a sale on the first day. Gómez did not comment on Chuy's lack of sale, as he did not want to be rude, but Gómez wondered if Jesus was losing popularity with the gringos in America. He thought since Trump won the election that Jesus would be through the roof. The truth was that Chuy could have sold his Jesus five times over at five times his regular price. But he didn't want to sell. He wanted to have a reasonable reason to watch the girl with the Picasso eyes.

Gómez headed out to the Soriana Super. As he had had his morning nap, but not as yet drunk his midmorning beer, Gómez's trajectory was tolerably straight for the little dog and she dared to raise her head and enjoy the view. Arriving at the hypermarket, Gómez tucked Queenie into his always-present sweater of questionable heritage. She snuggled into the pocket of the shirt beneath the sweater and had no problem breathing through the fabric. She liked Gómez and his old-man smell, like flour tortillas that had been in the garbage for, say, two days. Plus, it was cozy. She felt like a taquito inside the food warmer at OXXO.

In his youth Gómez played baseball like he be-

longed on a box of American Wheaties. Now he could barely reach any shelf above eye level. This meant that he was usually stuck buying sugar cereal like *Choco Zucaritas* with that silly tiger on the box because the stores stocked the kids' cereal on the lower shelves so the children could point and howl at their parents. Gómez reached for the box and changed his mind. He didn't want sugary cereal. He wanted *panqueques*. Pancakes. With that Aunt Jemima syrup.

Gómez headed over to the syrup aisle, stopping to grab a few dusty cans of Vienna sausages that had probably been on the shelf since the war on drugs started because no self-respecting Mexican is going to eat Vienna sausages. Queenie loved them. He didn't show her the cans, because *No dogs allowed in the store*, but he did give her a little pat through his sweater. She knew not to come out. When he reached the syrup aisle it perturbed him to see that the Aunt Jemima syrup in her Negro lady bottle was on the top shelf. Gómez was determined. He climbed up onto the edge of the second-lowest shelf and reached as high as he could, feeling the joints in his shoulders snap-crackle-pop with the movement. He ignored the pain, climbed one more shelf, and reached higher. At this point a young woman rounded the aisle and moved to help the old *abuelo*, but Gómez did not see her because of his diminished peripheral vision.

Gómez's left foot dragged across a lower shelf as he climbed, dislodging several glass bottles of syrup, the cheap Mexican brand, all of which broke upon landing. Gómez turned to look at the mess on the speckled concrete floor, green and pink, which he noticed for the first time and felt was rather festive before this thought was lost as his heart mimicked a dramatic contortion-

ist's twist. Gómez felt a POP in his heart the likes of which he had never previously experienced. All the blood in his heart squeezed out, the last note of a sad accordion. Gómez fell. He remained aware of Queenie and managed to land on his back. The syrup spread slowly around Gómez, looking just like the rusted color of blood one might expect to come from such an old person, sort of an anemic, age-spotted shade of blood. There was also a good-sized piece of glass in his butt, but due to the tonnage of pain coming from his heart, his butt declined to comment.

"Great," said Gómez, but only in his head. "I'm lying in a puddle of syrup and it isn't even the *Tia Jemima* kind." But it smelled fantastic.

The young woman moved in close to Gómez, stepping into the syrup and bending down. At this moment Queenie, intoxicated by the sugary smell, burst out of Gómez's old sweater. The woman, bending over Gómez's chest had not expected a very small, virtually hairless creature with rather large eyes to jack-in-the-box out of the old man's chest. Her first thought was that an alien (outer space, not illegal) had just exploded from the carcass of the *abuelo* and that the syrup really was blood. She screamed and lurched back, which caused her to slip on the syrup and join Gómez on the floor. The alien began to lick up the syrup, inducing the woman to faint. Gómez had fallen unconscious some moments before, listening only for his heartbeat, *Where is my heartbeat, have I lost it?*

At the end of the long aisle, a checker could see that some kind of mess was going on at the back of the store. He calmly picked up his speaker and said, "*Limpiar en el passillo siete.*" Clean up on aisle seven.

Everyone in Mexico knows about the great white street sharks, the trolling Mercury Grand Marquis. Steel and guns and drugs and girls in stilettos in the back seat, cocaine snort that shit right off the skin of the prettiest girl. Sinaloa cartel, Tijuana cartel. And those American-grown boys from Logan Heights in San Diego, paid assassins, cross the border and shoot-em-up gangster style, think they are cowboys, think they are Pancho Villa, think the Wild Wild West still lives in Mexico just because it's dusty. Nothing but a bunch of Mexican jumping beans. The Chiclet girls sell gum to the tourists and watch the drugged-up girls get out of the Marquis, thighs and long black hair, and why would you be a schoolteacher if you could ride around all day in a car like that? If you could curl your hair and ride around in the sleek leather belly of the shark?

Chuy was born Xavier Jones to a Mexican-American Catholic girl who hid her cross behind her back and uncrossed her legs for the captain of the football team in her senior year. Of college. San Diego State. It wasn't so bad. Lola and Doug got married in 1969 and Xavier was born on January 2, 1970. Their real mistake was buying a house in Logan Heights because the price was low. Six years later Doug was shot while getting the mail out of the mailbox on his way into the house from work. Logan Heights Gang drive-by, wrong place at the wrong time, said the police. "How can the mailbox of our own home be the wrong place?" asked Lola, and the policeman held her while she cried. She kept the mail, a Sears bill and a loud flyer for a sale at a car dealership, *Friday, Saturday, and Sunday Too*, American flags flying in the corners. It made no sense, but all Lola could think was

that she wished there had been a love letter in the mailbox, that she had sent him a letter. If Doug had had a love letter in his hand, it would have been a better death. After that, she put a note in Xavier's lunch bag every day. *Mommy loves you to the moon.* But by the time he was in high school, he didn't even read them, threw them away with the apple. Rotten to the core.

It isn't hard for a young man to join a gang. It can start for little boys in a tree house with a wood-handled penknife and a couple drops of blood. A teenager might take the next step. A dark romance that takes place under the overpass, the sound of the cars, the art of the graffiti, the starlight of cigarettes. A gun. The heaviness of that gun. Xavier always thought the soul was the exact same weight as a Colt 45. Whiskey is a pretty color and cocaine is angel-white. Xavier was part of the Logan Heights Gang easy as ink. A tattoo to mark the event.

It was a game of Chutes and Ladders for Xavier. Thanks to Lola he had dual citizenship and the looks that could shift at the border to match the scenery of either side. People see what they want to see. He ran drugs for four years and had money to burn. But he didn't burn it. He locked it away in a safe-deposit box along with a large portion of his morals.

On May 24, 1993, Xavier was sent with a number of the gang to the Guadalajara Airport to assassinate Joaquin Guzmán, *"El Chapo,"* the Mexican drug lord of the Sinaloa cartel. The Logan Heights boys were hired by the Tijuana cartel. Good money, half in advance.

No one ever really knows what happens in Mexico. The sun is too bright. The dust obscures. History is a shiftless cowboy. Juan Ocampo, archbishop of the see of Guadalajara, and a cardinal of the Roman Catholic

Church, was at the airport that day. There he is in his white Mercury Grand Marquis. And he is a sort of drug lord, is he not? *Opiate of the masses.* Stepping out in his black cassock with a cross on his chest as large as a heart, could he be mistaken for *El Chapo*? At two feet away? Apparently so. The authorities said it was a case of wrong place, wrong time, mistaken identity, what with that car and all. But everyone knows Ocampo was a heavy opponent of the drug cartels.

It was a holy mess. Xavier never even knew if Ocampo or *El Chapo* was the real hit. He never heard so many bullets at one time, a mad staccato concerto he would feel forever on the back side of his eyelids. A sound tattooed to his soul. Six civilians died. The image he could not obliterate with all the holy water in the Guadalajara cathedral was the sight of a young woman in a blue-flowered dress, an old fashioned suitcase without wheels, the way her body blew back and folded in at the same time. The way the flowers turned as red as Flanders poppies. Six civilians died, they wrote in the paper. "Civilians?" thought Xavier. "Humans."

While Ocampo was departing his body, and *El Chapo* was lighting a cigar, Xavier was running away. Everyone was running; gun tucked, it was easy to blend in. With every block the sirens faded until finally the circular wail sounded like the theme song of a cops-and-robbers show on a black-and-white TV. Xavier walked into a clothing store and bought middle-class clothes. He checked into a by-the-hour motel that did not require ID and took the longest shower of his life. Then he put on the new clothes, walked out of the motel, and hired a taxi to drive him the hour's ride to Ajijic, the expat town on the banks of Lake Chapala. When he stepped out

of the taxi, he was no longer part of the Logan Heights Gang. He ate a roasted chicken and drank a heavy beer. That night, he threw his gun far out into the flat waters of the already highly polluted Lake Chapala and made a very Mexican prayer to the goddess of the lake. And although she is a goddess of fertility, it couldn't hurt.

Silvia and her family moved to Tijuana and her father went to work at one of the many *maquiladoras*, building electronic parts that would be sent back to the United States. Her father had not adequately anticipated the costs of rent in such a city, and they were forced to live in the slum at Los Laureles canyon. The houses were built onto the side of a hill, which gave it a nice terraced look from a distance. But the construction was corrugated tin, thick cardboard from discarded packing boxes, home-poured concrete. Rebar stuck up everywhere like broken bones. The garbage washed away when the rains came, or at least was buried in mud. Chickens flourished. Silvia was relieved to hear they spoke the same language as her old chickens.

But where were the monkey-faced orchids and the scent of trees? She could see the ocean in the distance, but it was flat and gray and wordless. She knew that America was on the other side of the border wall, but America was a mean aunt who made cookies, then slapped your fingers if you reached for them.

It soon became apparent that Silvia's mother would have to work in a *maquiladora* as well. And so for the first time in their lives, Ana and Silvia went to a real school. Silvia's mother sewed a pink velvet patch for Silvia to put over her eye and told Silvia to tell everyone her father was a pirate and she lost her eye to an octopus

in a battle at sea. Who doesn't like a pirate? Silvia told
no one anything.

Over time her mother sewed patches from scraps
of serape, embroidered Otomi, and once a large appli-
qué hibiscus flower, but that was disconcerting because
the stamens looked like tentacles coming out of her eye.
Perfect for the Day of the Dead. Every single one of the
patches made Silvia silently seethe. The patches might as
well have been a burqa. She had two perfectly good eyes.

Silvia grew up a private and quiet girl. Well, it was
hard to read her face. On the day she graduated from
high school she privately and quietly threw away all the
patches. They gave her headaches and weakened her eye.
Why should she suffer to make others comfortable? It
was liberating. But no one would hire her. Even if she
could type like a spray of bullets from an M16 and do
complicated word problems with one hand tied behind
her back. Even if she was kind.

Chuy, carved Jesus in the back seat of his car, arrived
at the San Ysidro Point of Entry to the United States.
He parked his car, hoisted Jesus, and made his way out
to the many lanes packed with cars inching their way
across the border, the slowest parade on earth, like ele-
phants. Chuy joined the other entrepreneurs who sold
things through the windows to the bored and captive
consumers in the cars. He was looking for the girl.

Silvia was there. She positioned her tray with the
crisscross straps across her back and balanced the stacks
of tamarind candies, just like the kind her father used
to bring her in Nayarit. She made the candy herself and
painted the small white boxes by hand. Each box had a
little donkey and the script said *Tingalao's Sweet Noth-*

ings. Since Silvia's oddball was on the right side of her face, she always worked the left-hand side of the cars. She developed some knotty neck muscles from the bandolier straps of her tray and keeping her face turned out. But all in all, most people did not notice that she had one eye closer to her nose than the other until they had already reached for their wallets and by then, Silvia knew, almost no one was so rude as to retreat.

It was the boxes that sold her product. The script was in Spanish. Little boys and girls in the back seats wanted the donkeys, pink saddle blankets for the girls, red and blue stripes for the boys. Silvia would look into the back seats and see the children strapped into their protective booster seats, feet sticking straight out. TV screens. The children looked like designer purses to her. Sometimes she felt like the Little Match Girl, peering into other people's impossibly beautiful, air-conditioned lives. Sometimes she wanted to open the door and quietly slide herself in, go right through the wall. She knew they knew it. Because while they rolled down their windows, the doors were always locked.

But they liked her donkeys, and at the end of the day she could pay her rent and eat a couple of tacos.

About an hour into the morning she saw him. There he was again. That Jesus guy, looking at her. She wasn't blind. And it's hard to miss a not-bad-looking, not-too-too-much-older man carrying Jesus on his back. She could tell he had been watching her these last several days. Most men who were interested in her wanted something she was not interested in giving, so Silvia had grown wary of men. But he did have that Jesus . . .

Chuy saw she was coming straight toward him! He was sure of it. What was he going to say to her? Obvi-

ously she had caught on to his surveillance. Could he tell her the truth? That he wanted to know the color of her eyes. He dreamed they were paisley. That he wanted to paint her face, that he was certain she would be his Mona Lisa. Was that too much to tell, on the San Ysidro lanes, with the dusty cars, the horns and hawkers, the seagulls' haughty laughter? Too much?

His phone rang. Truly there is something demanding about a ringing phone that makes you answer it, even when your personal muse alights. "*Bueno*."

"*Hola*, this is Amanda Sánchez and I have your dog, Queenie?" Amanda said it like a question, but Chuy's heart fell. For all his years of abstinence from crime, his first thought was that Queenie was being held for ransom. "I work at the Soriana Super, and there was an accident? The old man, they took him to the hospital, I think he's dead, but I have the dog, and this is the number on her collar . . . ?" For while Gómez never carried identification, luckily Queenie did.

Moments before Silvia reached Chuy, Chuy turned and sprinted away.

"Well, he's not the first one to see my face and do that," thought Silvia. She took the rest of the day off.

Chuy found Gómez at the new Scripps hospital. "Oh, Chuy," said Gómez upon the eventual arrival of his friend. "I died."

Obviously Gómez had not died, but Chuy chose to ignore the facts. "What's it like?"

"No, no, I know I'm not dead *now*," said Gómez. "I came back."

"What *was* it like?" Chuy amended.

Gómez was thoughtful for a moment and then

said, "Augusta National," and that seemed explanation enough. "But when I came to, I didn't know where I was."

"The hospital?" Chuy asked. "It's so nice here." It was a new-fashioned hospital with healthy shades of paint and artwork of landscapes and soft abstracts. A garden with a reflection pool, a piano in the foyer.

"Too nice. The last hospital I was in when Maria died had those pea-green walls and you could be certain to die there. I woke up here and thought I made it to the next level of heaven. Sandals, All-Inclusive," said Gómez.

"How are you feeling now?" asked Chuy.

"I could use a beer, my friend, and where is Queenie?" Chuy pulled them both from his overcoat.

It was but a few days later that Chuy made it back to San Ysidro. He had forsaken his Jesus and came alone. Silvia accepted his offer of coffee without hesitation. He carried her tray of candies. As so often happens when one is both sure and fearful at the same time, Chuy felt he had to tell her everything about his past. A confession. He felt his soul was a bucket of water in the bottom of a deep well and he had to haul it to the surface, hand over hand on a rough rope.

Xavier told her about Guadalajara and Ajijic, and how he changed his name to Chuy (Jesús) Rodriguez; it's not hard to get a new identity in Mexico. He got ahold of his mother and had her get the money out of the safe-deposit box. He told her to take what she needed to move out of Logan Heights, something he should have done for her years ago. They set up regular trips for Lola to come to Tijuana. For years it had felt too

dangerous to actually meet or for Xavier to try his passport at the border, but when she was in the line at San Ysidro, she would appear to be interested in his goods. They would exchange letters and she gave him wads of his money, until he didn't need it anymore. They carried out a mother-and-son reunion once a month right under the watch of the U.S. government and the cartel.

When he was finished hauling up the bucket, he asked Silvia everything about her. But he never commented on her eyes.

And now, this is how things are. Silvia is the new artistic face, the new Frieda Kahlo of Mexico. Silvia's oddball eye is as recognizable as Frieda's mustache eyebrows. Xavier's paintings are uncompromisingly straight on, his choice of colors startling. The backgrounds are always of Mexico. Monkey-faced orchids. Monkeys. Donkeys and tamarind trees. Also harsher things like Trump's new section of wall, the slums of Tijuana and Guadalajara, Chiclets. But it's all about Silvia's asymmetrical eyes.

Silvia, her parents, Ana, Ana's husband and children, Pepe, Lola, Gómez, Queenie and her red blanket have all moved to San Miguel de Allende, where in the summer the air remains cool as a linen sheet. Lola and Gómez got a thing going on. Silvia and Xavier have a spacious, white-walled gallery with their house on the second floor and a studio out back where the light is as golden as a Del Sol beer. They give away boxes of *Tingalao's Sweet Nothings* to any child who walks in the door, and all the local children know it.

Most days Gómez makes the ten-minute walk from his house to theirs, two doors down. If the workshop is

open when Gómez arrives, he joins Chuy.

"Chuy, would you like a beer?" Gómez asks, offering up a now warm Del Sol which he has brought with him.

"I do not drink, my friend, but thank you."

"No? I did not know that or I would have brought Coca-Cola," says Gómez.

And the two men smile small smiles, for they are the best of friends.

Epilogue

Please recall the Soriana Superstore girl who saved Queenie, Amanda Sánchez. While everyone else was shouting over the fallen woman, the apparently dead man, and the overall mess, she calmly pulled the Chihuahua from the syrup and and took the poor dog into the ladies' room to wash her in warm soap and water. She fed the little wet dog three-milk cake. Then Amanda called the number on Queenie's collar and returned the dog safely home.

About three weeks later Amanda was pleased to see the old man come back to the hyperstore. Of course the old man did not know who she was, but Amanda watched him as he made his way back to the syrup aisle. On the speckled linoleum, below the still out-of-reach Aunt Jemima syrup bottles, he placed a statue of Our Lady of Guadalupe and a small bouquet of glorious flowers. It was, she realized, a holy shine of thanks. Satisfied, the old man turned and left. Amanda found this beautiful. But she also knew it would only be a matter of minutes before she heard, yet again, *"Limpiar en el passillo siete."*

Later that night she got an idea. It took her about two years, an unnamed financial backer, three trips to

China for bottle manufacturing, and the lucky intro-
duction to an independent Vermont syrup farmer with
a sense of the absurd for Amanda to finally bring her
idea to the hypermarket shelves: *Our Lady of Guada-
lupe Wholly Syrup* in a bottle shaped like the Virgin,
full-body-length Mexican-style halo and all.

Our Lady of Guadalupe is outselling the *Tia Jemima*
brand two to one.

The House of Naan and Saffron

Marigolds and smoke, hopscotching monkeys.
It is impossible to see clearly in Varanasi.

I was born in the north where my mother stirred her morning coffee with a twig of an alder branch. It was inadvisable to go out in winter without gloves. When the northern lights appeared, I knew it was the light of angels. My father said it was an effect of the solar wind but he's an idiot, not to know an angel when he sees one. He of all people.

My parents lived in a cabin, loaned to them by the parish church. They counted their blessings on my toes, their only son, Kristoffer, born in the year of Our Lord Jesus Christ 1994. Our cabin was snug with braided rugs and a large stone fireplace. My boyhood room was up a ladder to a loft with one window that looked out on the village creek and beyond to the forest, where the gunny wolf lived. I had a blanket made of rabbit fur and slippers the same. At bedtime my father would bring me a toddy of brimstone. Then my mother would come sit by me and tell me stories of the Norwegian faerie cat that could fend off the red fox and The Lad Who Went to the North Wind.

Beyond our little garden of root vegetables and marigolds is our church. Not a stave church, but a fair Norwegian structure built of pine and a whitewash of good intentions. Behind the pulpit is a large, hand-painted

glass window of Jesus bearing the cross, knees buckling, crown of blood and thorns. A Jesus too tired, it seemed to me, to care so much for us. I thought it nearly obscene, a sort of snuff film, this almost-dead Jesus.

To the west of the little church is the graveyard, most markers covered in moss and tilted. To the east, a flagstone path leads out a rusty-hinged gate and down into our village of a thousand or so souls. Our village is on a mountainside, in a large meadow bowl with a silver creek that runs through, and a surrounding forest, whispering ancient tree tales into the wind.

When we moved to India, I think I missed the winters most. The smell of snow. Early winter storms hold the scent of pine. The snow is pure and lighthearted, filled with air and antiseptic. But toward the solstice all the pine needles freeze into tiny icicles and the layers of snow compact into a strata of storms. Now I can only recall enough to say it smells like winter, the death of smell. Come spring the snow melts in the day, freezing again overnight. By morning there's a top crust, easily broken with footfall, releasing a slush of sunshine and the scent of damp earth.

In summer, by the time I was eight or nine, I was allowed to walk the three miles from our village down to the fjord and the port town. I was known to the fishwives on the piers. They would send me on errands or I would clean fish for a few kroner and go home smelling of smelt and herring. Once a Russian vessel came to dock; I was curious and inclined toward the ship. But Elin, who is my mother's childhood friend and has eyes in the back of her head, called out to me, "Kristoffer, leave those Russian boats be." "Why, Elin?" I asked. She pushed out a hip in consideration. "Because they drink

a different vodka than we drink," as if this explained the difference and the danger. And somehow it did. I kept to my kind.

I came to know the seasons by the colors of the sea. In deepest summer when I raised my gaze to the horizon I found it difficult to discern the difference between sea-sparkle and sky-sparkle, but I know an angel-light when I see one. Then on toward October the sea is of colder colors, emerald and darker still. That's when the whales come and I know winter soon will follow.

I spent my kroner on squares of chocolate or soda and felt a little guilty for it, because I knew my father would consider it wasteful to hand my money to the dock vendors. It would not be fair to say my father was stingy so much as frugal. He taught me to fish, not for the joy of the sound the twine makes at cast, but because fish is food. He taught me to build a fire, not because it's almost an incantation to call to life such an elemental thing as fire, but because it's expensive to run the radiator. Thus it was that all my pants were purchased too long and worn until too short. Same with boots.

It's true that my mother gave me honeycombs and wild flowers. But the centerpiece of our kitchen table was always a bottle of clear table booze. Mostly my parents had a shot together after dessert. But sometimes, in the winter, when my mother said the days were too short to bother with, she sailed into that bottle and my father made eggs for dinner until she tumbled back out.

The year that I turned thirteen everything in my life changed. I remember that as the year autumn stayed so long the forest iris were confused and started to bloom early. I had spent the summer apparently doing nothing but growing. I barely fit in my bed. I had grown out of

my rubber boots. My mother told me to put talcum powder in them to help slide them on, but by the time the rain finally started to fall, the powder trick was clearly failing. Reluctantly my father agreed to new boots. My mother never learned to drive, so he drove us to town in the world's oldest Saab. I chose beautiful Wellies of shiny black with red plaid wool lining. On the first real day of rain, I put them on and showed the mud puddles who's boss. In the evening, I set my Wellies by the fire to dry. But I put them too close and the fire melted the face of the boots.

I was a boy without a future.

I hid the boots until my father left the house and then I showed the pathetic melted things to my mother. I would forever forgive her any infraction because she got out her cookie-jar money and walked three miles into town and three miles back with a new pair of boots. They were navy and the plaid yellow, but my father never noticed and my mother never told.

If my father was a stingy moralist and my mother an occasional drunk, they covered for each other, and under that cover I was safe.

As winter set in it was my job to build up the fire in the church an hour before the congregation arrived. Then, during the service, I was to stand by the stone fireplace and add in logs of oak and birch. Our church was from the 1800s, and although it had been retrofitted with a heating system, it was always on the brink of despair and my father cared not to spend the money to fix it while there was a perfectly good fireplace at hand.

Jorgen Munsen carried a loaded pistol. Everyone knew it and he wasn't the only man to do so. When he came to church he treated the chapel like his living

room. This Sunday, as usual, before he sat down Jorgen took his pistol out of his shearling coat, unloaded it, and set the gun and the bullets on the stone mantel of the fireplace. He left a tin of chewing tobacco and a few coins as well. Jorgen thought it disrespectful to carry a gun in church, but disinclined to leave the weapon at home. So be it.

After Jorgen had settled into his pew, Blind Ingrid tap, tap, tapped her cane across the rough floor and, for reasons unknown, this day ran her hand across the mantel as she crossed in front of the fire. It was an exceptionally cold day and I had built the fire wild-high. Perhaps the strength of the flames had alarmed Blind Ingrid and she wanted to make sure of the distance between her skirt and the embers. Her hand pushed three bullets into the flames. I was the only one to see this.

Before I could even find my voice, the first bullet went straight through the Jesus window, shattering the glass. The window just slumped and fell like a landslide. The immediate shared thought was Second Coming. There was a stunned silence as the last pieces landed with a tinkling sound. And then a warbler, that littlest of birds, flew through the open space. I would almost like to say that the second bullet shot the warbler, just for the thrill of it. But that bullet was stopped by the pulpit and stays there still. We all stared at the bird and the sky like we had never seen such things.

(Later the window was replaced with a solid sheet of wavy blue glass, which was just as well because ours was a Lutheran church and the painted glass affair was a leftover from a fifty-year hostile Catholic takeover, resented, but not enough so that anyone would take down perfectly good glass. There were those who felt that

particular bullet was God-sent. However, the blue was somewhat ill advised, because when the northern sun pushed the watery color onto the very white Norwegian skin, the congregation looked like Nordic Smurfs. But that was later.) Back to the third bullet . . .

Then I remembered the third bullet and my voice and screamed, "Duck!" Some idiots thought I was calling the warbler a duck and stayed standing, but most had now caught on and knew good advice when they heard it.

The third bullet was marked for my mother. While others went down, she stood up and turned toward me, reaching out her arms, climbing over the pew. I don't know why she did this because I was the safest person in the chapel. Standing to the side of the fireplace I was the only one who couldn't get shot. My father slid behind his pulpit like a lump of lard. But Arne Erikson, the village butcher, perceived my mother's danger and threw himself up into the air. Arne looked so courageous I swear he could have stopped that bullet with his teeth. But he didn't and his head kind of blew off and onto my mom. She held on to him, this big, kind of headless ragdoll. I don't know how she had the strength. No one wanted to move because no one but I knew all the bullets were spent. The warbler flew back out into the forest. Finally, Jorgen took Arne from my mother and laid him down on the broken pieces of colored glass, which was a sort of shattered shroud for the poor man as his blood ran over the pieces of Jesus.

My father came to and collected his hysterical wife and told everyone to go home and pray for Arne. Some people stooped to pick up pieces of glass as souvenirs but my father said, "This house of prayer shall not be made

a den of thieves," plagiarizing Matthew, but effectively shaming everyone into leaving without the Catholic relics.

Of course no one but she knew, but in that moment my mother lost her lover. At the funeral, it would have been unseemly, the amount she cried, but it was excused because he had, in fact, died for her. Well, maybe I knew, or suspected. During the funeral I remembered when I had seen my mother and Arne together a few months ago in the early fall ...

Each September my father would go hunting for a few weeks. He would bring back boar and deer to hang and cure in the smokehouse. It was a time of some small reprieve for my mother and me. We would eat late and leave the dishes in the sink, watch movies on our grainy TV, or dance to the radio. She would sleep in and I would read comics on the porch, something my father forbade as a ridiculous waste of time and money. The last late daisies nodded to the meadowlark.

One day during this time my mother and I walked into the village. Usually she just wore knee-blown jeans and her hair pulled back. Today she wore a summer dress that showed the outline of her thighs when she moved. Her hair was curled and pulled up in some different fashion. She wore her wedding earrings, large hoops of thinnest silver with weighty dangles of aquamarine. We stopped at the library and I checked out a book of Rudyard Kipling short stories that would change my life, although I did not know it at the time. For now, it was just a book with a dusty green cover and gold letters. We bought produce and then surprisingly went into the butcher shop. We usually had our own meat, but it was late in the season. Arne, the (soon-to-be-dead) butcher with beefy arms and an always-clean white apron, came

out from behind the counter to talk to my mother. He called her Liv, but her name is Livinia.

Arne's shop stocked one-kroner candies displayed in an old trunk made to look like a treasure chest. Sugar booty. I loitered by the candy while my mother talked to Arne. I saw her head go back in a small laugh, her white neck, her earrings a-jangle. Then one of the earrings fell loose and into the top of her dress. This jewelry was the only exquisite thing she owned. She must have been able to feel that her bra would not stop the heavy piece. Arne's floor was cold cement, easy to hose. My mother had no choice but to spread her legs just a little bit and squat just a little bit, so she could reach down and catch the aquamarines in her hand. I knew this would humiliate her, the unfeminine act of an earring coming out between her legs. But Arne broke into a fractured laugh when decorum would have been to turn away and pretend it had never happened. Then my mother laughed too. I was confused by the intimacy but quickly distracted by a pyramid of red-yellow-orange gumdrops.

Yet perhaps I knew that my mother liked Arne. He was a nice man. Not as straight-lined as my father, not as full of pastor-words and rules. Arne gave me the gumdrops for free. When we left, I hardly noticed that we had no paper-wrapped packages of meat.

Father came home from the autumn hunt. I helped him butcher and hang the carcasses. Mostly I just carried the innards out. When we were done, the forest was completely removed from the animals and they smelled of salt and smoke and were dry to the touch. I hated them. These things devoid of face and fur. My friend Fredrik and I would sometimes walk through our smokehouse with our eyes closed and allow ourselves

to knock into the hanging carcasses, set them swinging, let the legs and heavy middles collide with us. Meat to meat, I would leave the smokehouse bruised and feeling brutal. I don't know why we did it.

The book I brought home from the library was not as expected. I thought it would be like the Just So stories I had previously read. But it was a collection of adult stories and I set it aside to be returned to the library. Father picked it up: *Plain Tales from the Hills*, set in India—British India in the hill station town of Shimla. He read that book to pieces.

And then he wanted to go to India to preach.

"Are you kidding me?!" my mother shouted, her voice climbing straight up the ladder, under my rabbit blanket, right up the back of my spine and into my heart. "India! What are you? Some hero-preacher, some walker-on-water? What are you thinking?!"

My father's voice was low and even. He wanted to do this. It was his calling. She had to come; she was the wife.

"Calling? It's a novel, Nils, it's a novel."

Through the autumn this argument went on. Then came a night in late November when I heard my mother's footfall in the dark. I heard her pull her shawl from the wall peg, the blue wool one, I knew, the one with edelweiss embroidered on the edges and yellow fringe on the hood. She opened the door and stepped out. I couldn't help myself; I climbed out of bed and opened my window. The run of the river silvered under the moon. The night wind pushed the smell of pine into my hands. I watched my mother walk away and thought I would never see her again.

That night the first snow came, sudden and hard. But in the morning the sky was pure blue. I dreamed of

the gunny wolf and when I woke there were slender icicles hanging from our roof, like prisms against the blue sky. When I went downstairs my mother was making oatmeal with apples and her shawl was in its place.

My father kept up his argument and kept making his plans. My mother kept shouting and taking walks in the night. But then, after the shooting in the church, she suddenly stopped her night wandering. On the day of the funeral I thought she would climb into the table booze, and she did. For three days. Then she started to pack. For in the spring we would go to India, soon after my fourteenth birthday.

My father was not assigned to Kipling's hill station of Shimla, where the air is Himalaya-shaded and tea-plantation-scented. There you could live like an English teapot with pink roses on a silver tray with biscuits. Every foreigner wants to live there, even the Dalai Lama. They made room for him.

Instead, we were sent to Varanasi, four hundred miles south of New Delhi, built on the holy, wholly polluted Ganges River. My father was given leeway to pick the country, but had no control over his parish assignment, nor was the church ever known for explanations. When my mother read "Varanasi," she was shocked. "What a bunch of addlebrained muddlers! Of all cities. How will you get a congregation?" The letter fell from her hands onto the table. I knew she was not concerned about saving souls so much as eating dinner. My father's stipend was limited; his livelihood was dependent upon donations from his flock, like tips for good service.

"It's the holiest of the seven sacred cities. The birthplace of Buddhism," explained my father, like this would help his case. "The spiritual capital."

"It's like sending a Zoroastrian to the Vatican or a Jew to Mecca." She was really worked up. "Like all the Hindus and Buddhists in Varanasi are standing up on tippy-toe, looking for a new God!"

"There is no new God," said my father, the literalist, and my mother had that *what-was-I-thinking-when-I-married-you* look on her face. She decided to pack all the preserves in our larder. If she could have put a side of venison in a suitcase, she would have.

But I was excited. The farthest from home I had ever been was three miles.

Nils's Point of View

So what does Nils think of this state of affairs? He lies in their bed, and when Livinia joins him she is in flannels when she used to be bare and burrow into him like a forest animal. Now she sleeps on the razor's edge. They've known each other since the time before they even knew their own names.

Nils remembers when Livinia ate his crayons. He remembers when she fell in the blue creek on an ice-cracking day and he let her walk home in his boots. How she looks in May. When she was the taller one, and then she wasn't.

Nils knows he is a man who always wants to do the right thing. He went to seminary school to learn how, and the Bible is his primer. He wants a simple life. He wants guideposts and the hope of a miracle. But now it's come to this. His heart is the wolf running under the full moon.

When Arne was killed by the church-bullet, so help him God, Nils was happy. Arne had been butchering his marriage for the previous six months and just in that in-

stant Nils allowed himself to think God put that bullet just where it was most needed. But Nils is not that kind of man, or won't allow himself to be that kind of man for more than an instant, and so he let that thought drown like a bug in a bog. Livinia thinks Nils is following Rudyard Kipling into India. But he's not. He's taking his wife on a far-away adventure, in hopes of bringing her home.

Livinia Speaks for Herself

My childhood was daisy chains and ice skates. But nothing lasts forever. At seventeen I ripped my childhood to shreds like a paper doll. I wanted to go to Oslo for college, not so much for the education, but to get the hell off the mountain. I was crazy for it. But my parents told me there was no money for such a thing; there would never be money. Suddenly the forest around me was a pine box.

On a May day of thin sunshine I took Nils up to Mink Creek and seduced him to punish my parents for being poor. Nils asked me to marry him that very afternoon, but I did not agree until the fall when I found I was pregnant. Don't doubt that I loved Nils; I still do. The first time he asked me to marry him we were six. I wanted to marry him. But ever since he came home from seminary school I've felt like I'm in a three-way with Jesus and one of us has got to go.

And now I'm supposed to follow him to India? For Christ's sake!

For Kris's sake. I'll go.

Kris

I don't think a Norwegian can be prepared for the heat of India. Heat in the north is stones by the creek hold-

ing on to late afternoon sun. The closest comparison to heat in India would be staying inside a Finnish sauna and sweating until your heart fell out. That's what an "Indian" summer feels like.

My first impression was that Varanasi was a mirage rising out of heat and dust. A sky without the hope of blue. The sun a twilight disk at noon. I could not clearly see the far side of the river and the water was the color of a speckled trout, gray-green and impenetrable. From somewhere there came fire smudge and ash, and at the time I did not know that it was burning bodies.

We secured long-term quarters at the Ganges View Hotel, an inexpensive riverfront tourist retreat. We had a dollhouse suite of rooms, but it didn't matter because the lodging had three floors of open verandas lined with bougainvillea and pots of lemon trees. There were secluded, shaded areas with teak floors and silk pillows on dusty couches. My favorite outdoor room had an orange-feathered chickadee in a willow cage who could sing the light fantastic. As long as I was respectfully quiet, I had free roam. From the verandas I could play an endless game of I Spy.

And I spied everything. Everything is for sale in Varanasi. It's like a caravan.

My father was given a small space for his chapel just off the main street by the old market. It was whitewashed and had a ceiling with wood beams and not-bad lighting. The floor was covered with old wool rugs of a thousand colors. There was a large cross on the wall and a desk for a pulpit with a glass jar full of flowers gone to seed. My father pondered his lot. How to build a congregation in a city that thinks Jesus pales next to blue Krishna?

Next door was a family of Momin Ansari, part of the

silk weaving community of Muslims who wove the silk in their parlor and sold it by the yard right out the front door. Once, my mother went in and I trailed. The father/merchant offered us tea in small glasses while his son threw down bolt after bolt like magic carpets at our feet. My mother grew embarrassed, thinking of the labor to reroll the bolts, so she bought a single yard that was the same white-yellow of her hair. No doubt the merchant's worst sale, because brides are the main business of the famous Varanasi silk merchants.

My father paced his chapel. My mother laid the silk out on the pulpit-desk and refreshed the flower jar. How to bring people in? We left him to it and explored. The old city market was a dark warren of small stalls and cookeries. We began to buy our staples from the vendors. Dried apricots and naan, tandoori and coriander. My mother learned to roll her eyes and get a lower price. My father thought of Jesus while my mother thought of new recipes.

There is commerce in Varanasi. In silk, in tourism, and in the business of death. In the university and in the Bodhi tree, which isn't the original Bodhi tree that Buddha taught the dharma from, but it's an uncle, or a relic, like the shroud of Turin or a saint's knuckle. Pilgrimage-worthy. I learned these things during the monsoon season while my mother home-schooled me and the rain was so loud the chickadee didn't even bother to try and sing. But in the afternoons, when the rain was done for the day and the air was cooler, we would walk down to the eighty-seven ghats, the riverfront steps that start at the base of fantastical buildings and end in the water. The ghats belong to religious sects, and some to private people who should give them back. They all have differ-

ent characters of colors, symbols, statues, meanings that flew around me like mockingbirds.

On our daily walks we were splattered with garbage and smells and sounds and humanity Rudyard failed to prepare me for. During the first few weeks, even at fourteen, I would not let go of my mother's hand.

Shit from the wandering cows, spices from the cauldrons of the street cooks. The high-mountain scent of Darjeeling from the passing tea-wallahs, and the dry smell of bone and sandalwood from the pyres of the crematorium ghats. The sounds of thousands of people moving in thousands of directions. The Muslim call to prayer. The rooftop monkeys, the little boys selling marigold wreaths and paper lotus flower candles to set afloat in the Ganges. Tourists climbing into wooden boats to be rowed down the ghats in a voyeuristic journey. Their clicking cameras, so many of them, sounding, if you really listened, like gnats. "Ghat gnats," my mother said. "Disgusting."

We walked, never taking the boats. But the boys still tried to sell us flowers and once she let me buy a necklace of wilting orange petals and I tossed it into the Ganges and watched it float away.

I always thought we were poor, as a pastor's family should be. A thin-soup life. But we were not poor. Near our hotel and in many other places, lines of the poorest women sit on the ground with tin bowls set on thin mats in front of them. Their children are set loose to play close by like tumbling puppies, while the women beg. It is daily work. At first I strove not to look at the women, to make them invisible, to make the uncomfortable way they made me feel invisible. But still I looked. Out of the corner of my eye.

My mother noticed that people came every day

with bags of uncooked rice. They walked the line and hand-poured rice into the pans, never stopping, never talking, or really looking, not worrying if it fell into the pans or on the mats. But giving. And the givers looked about twenty-five rupees wealthier than the beggars. My mother took to joining this ritual.

"You're wasting money," my father complained. "They never change their lives. They always beg."

"The poor will always be with you," my mother said, quoting Jesus without a discernable smirk. I expected a banter, but one of those cartoon light bulbs exploded over my father's head. He went down to his chapel and named it: The Church of Loaves and Fishes. This was a reference to the miracle of Jesus feeding the multitudes with only five loaves of bread and two fish. A Muslim might know this reference, but it would be lost on a Hindu or a Buddhist. No matter.

My father wrote up a number of handouts that said in essence that if you came and listened to a sermon, you would be fed. He passed these out to the women in the beggar lines. Most of them can't read. A lot of them don't speak English.

But some can. And some of the marigold boys can.

My father waited in his chapel. My mother set up a brazier and a pot to cook rice with a handful of spices, if anyone showed up. It was really hot in there and I took off and wandered the ghats because I wasn't afraid anymore, nor my parents for me.

Often, I couldn't help myself, I went to the burning ghats of Manikarnika and Harishchandra. There is a brick crematorium where bodies are disposed of on the cheap. But the lucky dead are slathered in ghee and marigolds, men burned face up, women face down on a

sandalwood pyre at the burning ghats. Three hours later they are swept into the Ganges, *moksha*, free and clear from the cycle of reincarnation. Nirvana-bound.

The Doms, the most untouchable of the Untouchable castes do the work. I came to learn that the cost of sandalwood is high and mighty, the price set by the Doms. If you can't afford enough, grandpa will go into the Ganges partially burned, to be eaten by specially bred snapping turtles. Nobody wants that.

The fires burn day through night. The remains are swept into the Ganges with brooms made of hurly-burly sticks that make a scratchy noise. The Doms keep rings, money, gold teeth, whatever the ashes yield. Fire-hearty items that make the Doms relatively wealthy. But disdained. Like sin-eaters, my mother said.

Sometimes in the winter, when the temperatures are lower, the holy cows stand by the fires to warm themselves and eat some of the fire-starting straw. They poop right there, and I think that's where the term *holy shit* derives from.

Some weeks passed before the brazier needed to be lit in the chapel. But then one day Sanjita, a beggar girl, showed up with her one-year-old daughter, Neera. The preaching restaurant was launched! Sanjita was twenty-two and beautiful, of course she was. Her black braid reached her waist, and how is it a woman can wrap nine yards of material around herself and still have a bare midriff? Neera was a bowl of coffee-colored cream and my mother wanted to drink her up.

My father used an old Christian trick to peddle Christ. He told Sanjita that with Jesus there were no castes. She did not need to be a beggar; she could choose her own path. She said yes, she knew it, she was a Buddhist, but

that didn't matter because, wake up and smell the pa-
tchouli oil, there are still castes. So he didn't get her
there. But then he said, you can achieve Nirvana, only
we call it Heaven, in this lifetime. You can end your suf-
fering and go to eternal peace. She said she could do so
by being burned at the Manikarnika Ghat. And he said,
"Do you really think you can buy your way to Nirvana
with sandalwood?"

Sanjita kept coming back.

My mother fell in love with Neera and my father
and I fell in love with Sanjita. She brought seven more
women to the congregation and four of their husbands
joined, too. Pretty soon Sunday was a potluck. We be-
gan to tease my father by calling the church the House of
Naan and Saffron. My mother started a weekly women's
Bible study and daycare and I made Bible storyboards
for the kids out of felt.

My father began to feel successful. But I could tell
my mother was still discontented by the way she took
up Charminar cigarettes, the way she inhaled the smoke.

Livinia Speaks for Herself

I didn't expect to love it so. Such a cesspool. I missed
the clarity of the north. But the women in embroidered
silk saris look like movable gardens. My hands smell of
saffron, turmeric, and plums. I wash my hair with rose-
water. Roof tops are strung with bells and I can hear the
chimes in the last of the day's monsoon rain, or when
the hopscotching monkeys shake them.

I don't remember when it was that I first climbed
into Hari's boat and paid him to row me to and from
Dashashwamedh Ghat. He said not a word. I was un-
comfortable, both with him and because I had joined

the shore-voyeurs, an activity I thought rude. But it was done. Many, many boats carried tourists. He must have thought it odd that I didn't have a camera. I came back and soon enough Hari realized I lived here and knew to look for me at dawn, because I couldn't sleep, or didn't want to. Occasionally I went at dusk. He would find me, if I waited. We spent an hour together two or three times a week. I learned he had been rowing for twenty-five years. It showed in his arms. We didn't talk much, but he told me that his wife had died in childbirth and his son was one of the boys who sold wreaths and lotus flower candles on the shore. At some point he shook his head and declined my rupees.

I told him about snow.

One morning when it was cooler and the city too wet to kick up dust, Hari left the shore and headed across the river, well over halfway. It was deserted. He anchored the boat, stood and took off his clothes, revealing skin the color of cassia bark. Hari's intent was clear, but it was an offer, not a demand.

The boat has many seats, so it wasn't possible to lie down. No matter. There are always options. I took off my own clothes. Bare, I barely breathed. Then, for the first time, I jumped in the Ganges. Surfacing, I turned toward the boat and pulled my shoulders and arms up on the smooth, green-grained side and anchored myself to the boat. I smiled up, met his nut-eyes, perhaps seductively. He smiled too, jumped in and came behind me. He put his arms over my arms, and I felt like I was filled up with ash and bone and marigolds. With the holy Ganges.

I don't know why I did it. I think it is the river dolphins that make me think I could stay in India. If some-

thing of the sea could belong here, why not me? But most likely I am just a monkey. A fool.

Kris .
The Ganges is filthy. It's full of dead people. Really you can't get around that. My favorite mornings came to be when I awoke to a great commotion with the dawn. Getting up and looking over the veranda, the ghats were swarming with excited people: a holy day. A day to bathe in the Ganges for purification. Can a sinner be made pure by putrid water? If you believe it, you can.

Thousands of people worked their way down the steps of the ghats to plunge fully clothed into a river of crap. Both upstream and downstream from the still-burning pyres. Well, religion ever was more pagan than pragmatic. There is always magic in water.

I would thread my way through the crowd until finally I just sat down. Because it was so beautiful. I was in a kaleidoscope. Inside the northern lights. Saris brushed by, the smell of cardamom-infused flesh. I watched the girls, even the old women, drenched, rise out of the river. Sari-soaked, a second skin of silk and color. Well, I know angels when I see them.

Bikinis are stupid.

Through the Clear Eyes of Sanjita
Sanjita sits on her thin mat receiving rice, looking out to the Ganges, singing to herself, *Jesus Christ. Superstar. Do you think you're what they say you are?* Livinia sometimes plays the Broadway score at Sunday dinner, and Sanjita likes the tunes. She had joined the Church of Loaves and Fishes to get extra food for herself and Neera, but now she brings as much food as she takes. She's not com-

pletely sold on Jesus, but she is on Nils, the sincerity of Nils. Some mornings, when Sanjita arrives early and the sun is red, she sees Livinia get into Hari's boat. She sees Livinia does not pay. She knows Livinia is a fool and will someday pay a full fare.

Sanjita keeps a half-eye on Neera, who plays nearby. God is good.

What Hari Thinks
"I am in love with that crazy *gori* woman." But he thinks it in Hindi as he slowly shakes his head and rows his boat.

Kris Tells the Hard Part
I've told almost everything now. I've put it off as long as possible. Sometimes at night I would lie in my bed listening to the hum of the rusted and useless fan above my head. I tried to recall the north and it came to me as very blue and white. India is every shade intensified. Hard to sort; you just can't organize it like a sock drawer.

So now I come to December 10, 2010, our second year in India. The Church of Loaves and Fishes had grown to a congregation of around forty people. But I'm not sure one could say they were converted. It is very comfortable for an Indian to simply accommodate an additional religion. Why not cover your bases?

That evening, as we sometimes did, my father and I decided to attend the evening prayers at Dashash-wamedh Ghat. My mother, reading on the veranda by the hibiscus tree, stayed home. As we knew there would be, there was a logjam of boats on the river and a thousand locals and tourists at Dashashwamedh as the sun went down and the Hindu priests started the nightly

Angi Pooja. A line of priests on a raised platform with neon umbrellas overhead sang prayers and did a fierce fire dance. Some faces in the crowd were in rapture, and some of those were from my father's congregation. We were used to that and waved hello. If it looked like silliness to me, what would a Hindu think of a Catholic priest in purple velvet holding aloft a thin wafer while ringing a bell and calling it the body of Christ? Seems about the same to me.

My father saw Sanjita sitting on the nearby Sheetla Ghat with Neera on her lap. He headed over to her and I wandered further.

At first I took the sound for fireworks.

Slowly I realized I had been knocked to the ground. I heard tinkling chimes and thought the roof-top monkeys were shaking the lines of brass bells. At last, or quickly, I opened my eyes and there was ash falling from the sky and I assumed I was near a burning ghat and the Loo wind was blowing. I tried to move and I had to concentrate very hard on each part of my body and tell it what to do. Finally, I sat up. There may have been screams, but I could only hear bells. People were running and I saw a railing give way and bodies fall, but still I could not hear the voices, thank God. I looked to where my father had been sitting with Sanjita and then I knew. It was some sort of terrorist pipe bomb. I still couldn't hear but suddenly I remembered how to run, and I ran, or stumbled, to my father and found him. He was a jumble with blood pouring from his ears and out of a large cut on the side of his head. Before I reached him, I was pushed aside as he was loaded on a stretcher. Sanjita was on a stretcher too, but all I saw of Neera was one small, pink shoe.

I ran for home. My mother wasn't there. I count-

ed myself nearly an adult, but in that instant I was but a child. I started to cry, and would have surely turned into a cub and howled, but my mother gazelled up the stairs and took me in her arms. Her hair was wet, but her clothes were dry. "Kris, where is Papa?" She shook me a little. Her words came to me in a whisper. "Hospital," I said, in a hummingbird voice.

We learned that it was the Islamist militant group the mujahideen who were responsible for the blast. The papers told us it was because Babur the Mughal emperor built a mosque in 935 on the site that was known to the Hindus as the birthplace of Rama. So that's a problem. By 1992, the Hindus had had enough and they demolished Babur's mosque. This caused Muslims to riot throughout India and over two thousand people died. Now, in 2010, on the anniversary of the 1992 incident, the mujahideen placed an explosive on a Varanasi ghat. In a milk carton. Religion is the dragon biting its own tail.

Many were injured, some critically, including my father and Sanjita. Neera died. Sitting in her mother's lap, a piece of shrapnel chewed into her like a snapping turtle, but her little body saved her mother's life.

When we found my father, he was in a small but private room with white walls and white sheets. There was a single light blub above his head, burning within a wire cage. It may have been the cleanest place I had ever seen in India. His head was wrapped up in a bunting that looked remarkably like a turban. He didn't know who we were, but he had his Bible in his hand.

This part I surmise, for I was not there: my father asked the nurse repeatedly to turn out the light, and she said, "So sorry, Sahib, light must stay on." The light began to feel like an interrogation of the Spanish Inquisi-

tion. It ghosted onto his retina when he closed his eyes. He began to think it was the Burning Bush. He was willing to sacrifice his firstborn son, even if he couldn't be sure he had one.

In the middle of the third night my father ripped pages from his Bible, stood tippy-toe on the bed and stuffed the pages within the wire cage to dull the light. The light dimmed to almost candle incandesce. With a deep sigh, he fell deeply asleep.

I often wonder which pages he used. I hope it was the Song of Solomon or some sort of little lamb story. Something soft and not of struggle. The pages, heated up by the bare bulb, began to smoke into a smudge fire. The hospital was not equipped with fire alarms and it was after all, the night shift. His door was closed. They told us he died from smoke inhalation, his body only partially burned, like a body on a pyre where the family could not afford enough sandalwood. No one else was harmed.

And so we finished the job at Manikarnika Ghat, buying a double load of wood, one for Neera. I sat next to a cow and watched my father's body burn. I watched the Dom scrape his ashes into the Ganges and hoped his *moksha* was over. I tried not to cry, as is the Hindu way, but was grateful for the light rain which lent me a disguise.

My mother was in a trance. She paced the veranda like the white tiger. For the first time in her life she was completely free to make decisions. We could stay in Varanasi. She could turn the chapel into a real restaurant—she had become an artistic cook with a palette of spices. Norwegian Fusion. Yet I think the freedom

scared her. It is easier to play the rebel of your own life than to actually lead it. I might have thought her heartless, pacing the veranda, smoking. But I also saw her sitting by the lemon trees at night, crying like a little girl, or a sad widow.

In the end she gave as much money as possible to Sanjita and we moved to Paris. She opened a used-book store and became a salon-style coffeehouse intellectual. She kept up the Charminar cigarettes and favored Darjeeling tea. It was at last the life that suited her blown-knee jeans and white linen shirts. But she ever kept a photo of my father by her bed with marigolds, when she could get them, in a small vase by its side.

I was the one who came to open the restaurant. With my French-Indian wife, in Montmartre. The House of Naan and Saffron. Come see us sometime; the food is divine.

The Franklin Avenue Rookery
for Wayward Babies
Katrina has a regard for nuns, and it isn't high.

"Some son of a bitch wet my bed!" That's me, wakin' up.

"Oh my God, Katrina, y'all wet the bed again?! You're nine years old!" That's my brother Beau, yellin' at me. But I don't wanna talk about it. So I climb right out of that pee puddle. Beau opens the curtains and the sun comes in. I don't know why my brother is in my room anyway. Where's Mama at? She's the one who wakes me up.

Beau tells me to wash up and come straight down for breakfast. Usually Mama does my hair. It's Sunday, so she could be hung over, lying on the floor of her bedroom, the French door with its peeling blue paint open for oxygen. I'll find her later and tickle her elbow insides. She hates that! But she never yells at me like Beau just did.

Beau sets out Cheerios and leftover fried chicken. Well, that chicken's from Willie Mae's Scotch House so I'm eatin' that. I don't wanna eat anything called Cheerios anyway. Don't tell *me* how to feel. Beau isn't talking, he's just shuffling around like he can't pick his big black feet up off the ground. "Baa Baa, why aren't you talkin' to me?" I ask and all he says is, "Stop calling me that." He is flat-out angry today. He slaps a glass of milk down on the table and Kitten Little jumps up and starts licking up the spillover. I pet her.

Charlie walks in and he looks at Beau, but he won't look at me so I know something shitty's going on. The two of them go over to the kitchen sink and turn away from me, facing out the window, kind of twinned together. My brothers. Baa Baa, I call him that because he looks like Black Sheep in my rhymes book, I don't know why he doesn't like that. He has woolly hair. And Charlie, pock marks stitched across his left check, he's Oriental like the drawings in my Marco Polo book. The two of them stand there looking like the black-and-white ying-yang tattoo Charlie has on his shoulder.

Well, I can't do nothin' about whatever's bothering those two. I share my cold chicken with Kitten Little.

Beau sends me outside to the garden, which is the size of a pea. The magnolia tree is in bloom—imagine being able to push flowers out of yourself—pink and waxy and smelling faintly like they just got out of the bath. We have a patio of old red brick mossed over and a statue of Saint Francis in the corner of the flower beds. Shreds of old Mardi Gras netting from the people who lived here before us still hang on the fence. I think about taking the netting down and wrapping it 'round my head like a sultan's turban, but it's probably got spiders in it. I sit down and start to color in my paper book of saints.

Color is what I do when things go wrong. If I want to pretend everything is all right, I stay in the lines and press softly. I make the gold halos see-through. If I'm feeling blue, I color everything blue. If I'm angry, watch out, that page is going to be so thick you could run a fingernail through the red wax.

I know I was born in the Superdome. My name's Katrina Theresa. Named after the storm and Mother Theresa. Not the good one. Just our mother, Theresa Chalfant.

Sometimes I imagine what it must have been like in the Superdome. Mama won't tell me about it. So I make the story up in my head: I picture the Superdome coming off its foundations, pulled out to sea. A slave ship. The weather is like looking into the round porthole of the washing machines at the launderette. Inside the Superdome, too many people. It smells like men, hot metal, fried chicken gizzards, people-shit. I picture my mom in labor, her hair tied up in her banana-print scarf, kinky hair coming out the top like exclamation points. She has to gulp down those smells. Her legs are spread and some old-men bastards sit on their cots and watch. Women coo around her, put towels on her dark forehead, but the water isn't cool and the rags smell like old bong water. At last I come out, white hair and blue eyes. No one hears me cry. The slave ship heads into the storm.

After the hurricane all of New Orleans is a rotting bayou. Alligators eat bloaty-floaties like it was lunch at Commander's Palace. What a feast! Water hyacinth and mosquito fern edge the streets of the Lower Nine. Mold blossoms in flower shapes inside, outside empty houses. Egrets land like angels, flutter their wings in released prayer, fly on. Motor boats putt-putt up and down the waterways, *Bring out y'r dead.*

I get bored imagining the past and read some of my Classics Illustrated comic books. Finally, I sneak back inside the house. Beau and Charlie are still in the kitchen drinking coffee. As I enter the room, Beau puts sugar into his cup and when he drinks it a few grains stick to his lips like glitter. Beau tells me to go straight to my room and put on a dress. Charlie is taking me to church. I say nothing. Charlie doesn't go to church. Mama does. Mama takes me.

I put on my blue check and head back downstairs. But my feet bypass the stairs and go into her room. I see her vanity with the Woolworth's lipsticks and the printed cardboard box of lavender powder, white satin ribbon on the puff. A box of Dark and Lovely. Her empty bed is unmade, her favorite old crazy-quilt askew. She is on the ground, toes sticking out from the far side of the bed. Wineberry polish. I watched her apply it just last week. I move a little closer. The French door is open and a slice of sunshine turns her skin two different shades of brown, like toast where one side is toastier than the other. She is wearing her Swiss dot nightgown, buttons all the way up the front.

Charlie is at the door before I see her face. "Let's go, Katrina, let her sleep."

Charlie and I walk through the French Quarter to the St. Louis Cathedral. I look in the windows of the shops we pass on Decatur Street. But I'm not looking at the gaudy displays. I'm looking at my reflection. My pale hair in too-tight braids and my clothes always too big because I'm skinny as a voodoo pin. My face of freckles. I look like a girl who lies. If I see a rainbow, that's all it is. I'm not going over it.

I beg for beignets every time we pass by Café du Monde but I never get 'em.

We pass the Presbytère, where Fats Domino's Katrina-wrecked Steinway lies in requiem. The Steinway took a vow of silence on the day I was born. Fats's house was in the Ninth Ward. On the day after the storm, morning light filtered through Fats's punched-out roof, spotlighting the underwater piano. A catfish slapped its heavy tail on the ivory keys and a slow cloud of algae rose instead of melody.

Church is church. Tourists, locals, and nuns. Kneel, stand, kneel, Jesus, Jesus, Jesus. This is the body of Christ; this is the blood of Christ. Yuck. I mostly look at the stained-glass windows depicting the life of King Louis IX of France. He pooped himself to death in 1270 during the Eighth Crusade, which somehow translated into making him a saint. Charlie, who hasn't been to church since his sixteenth birthday two years ago, listens to the priest and pays to light a long, sallow candle after the service. The little flame immediately blows out in the wake of a fat white woman and, against the rules, Charlie relights the wick. This time the flame takes hold and waves goodbye to us as we turn away.

Charlie doesn't make me go to Little Saints Sunday School and on the way home we stop at Café du Monde! Under the green-and-white-striped awnings I drink chicory coffee for the first time, and although I thought chicory was a type of horse like a pinto, it's not. Turns out beignets are sugar-powdered angels that you eat. The whole experience is holier, more gratifying to my soul than an hour in that cold cathedral with its roofline of three pointy black witch hats. Hecate and the other two.

As we leave the café the bells of the cathedral chide me, *naughty girl, naughty girl*. When we get home Beau tells me Mama is dead. Her body was taken away while we were at church and all I got to say goodbye to were her Wineberry toes.

Two Months Later

I have cried every day for two months. I look like a snowy barn owl, all big eyes. It is hard for me to under-

stand my brothers. Charlie is eighteen and Beau nine-
teen. They are old enough to take possession of me.
But they do not. They tried, and I tried to be good as
gold. But let's face it, I'm more like that rack of cheap
Black Hills stuff they sell at Woolworth's, they don't
even put it behind glass. I cuss, I wet the bed, I fling my
thoughts to the wind. Boys that age don't know what to
do with little girls. The laundry alone confounds them.
And there's no money. Even I know that. Even I know
what an Eviction Notice is. My brothers are joining the
armed services and I'm going to The Rookery on Frank-
lin Avenue. They promise to write. I know they will. I
nod to the magnolia tree and steal the Saint Francis stat-
ue, squirrels at his feet, puppy in his arms, birds on his
shoulders like Cinderella.

Kitten Little is lost to me.

On the day Beau and Charlie walk me to The Rook-
ery, my legs don't work. Head down, I see my skinny
knees below the hem of my yellow dress. My kneecaps
look like little brains. My knee-brains want to turn
around and run the other way. Plus, I'm so mad. A sum-
mer butterfly wings by like a sonnet and I cuss at it, call
it a shithead. Beau picks me up in his big dark arms and
tells me I'm twitching like I got that St. Vitus' dance dis-
ease. I don't know what that is, but yeah, I got it bad.
"Baa Baa . . . ," I cry into his shirt that smells like some-
thing I am going to miss and he holds me tight. I'm just
a bag of sticks.

The Rookery is a small Catholic orphanage run by
two young white nuns, Sisters Camille and Hope, and
an old black nun, Sister Lily. Sister Lily is so old she's
almost ashes and she's got a gimp. I meet them on the
front porch. They wear full-length habits and headpieces

that cover their hair, the fabric faded to a sad gray, and their hems are frayed. I'm not sure they would let them in at the witch-hat cathedral. Charlie tells me I am lucky—the Sisters only take in six children at a time, usually babies to be adopted out. I am clearly too old for The Rookery. I turned ten last week. I'm probably going to be made into a slave. If they think I am going to join them in nun-dom, they got another think coming.

I sit out on the porch in a wicker rocker and old Sister Lily gives me a cola drink in a glass bottle. Beau and Charlie go just inside to the sitting room and sit. It's a hot day and the windows are open. Everyone keeps their voices low, but Sister Hope has one of those traveling voices and I catch snitches and snatches. "What a tragedy..." "We are happy to have her..." "Y'll's mother..." "Y'll's mother..." "Heroin..."

Heroin! Those fuckers told me it was a heart attack. If I had my crayons and my saints coloring book right now I'd find a picture of the Virgin Mary and I'd make her black. I'd give her springy hair and dark eyes. Then I'd get my red crayon and put the flames of Hell around her so thick I'd use my whole stick. Right over her face. I hate her I hate her I hate her. She died and left me at The Rookery with a bunch of penguin kooks.

When I say goodbye to Charlie and Beau I'm crying so hard it's as if I'm behind a waterfall. They are wavery, already-gone brothers. Beau tells me he loves me more than football, but I don't believe him. Charlie tells me not to cuss in front of the Sisters and I tell him go to shit in a bucket. They both hug me so hard all my bones crack, or at least my heart.

*　　　*　　　*

Well, life goes on, doesn't it?

The Rookery is an old house with wood-plank floors that talk to each other constantly. The kitchen is speckled linoleum worn to the nub. It has nothing to say. I know the floors intimately because it's my job to clean them. The window frames are painted pink and there's houseplants everywhere, big Boston ferns that look like banshee heads at twilight. Palms, and purple coleus. Old Sister Lily plays a rickety piano, and all the furniture is comfortable. I am allowed to sit anywhere. The TV is larger than you would think. Both younger Sisters have laptops. Sister Camille is fond of '70s and '80s music and she takes me with her to Euclid Records, where, believe me, nuns don't usually go. With Sister Hope I go to the Crescent City farmers' market, where all the vendors know her and our baskets runneth over for free.

The Sisters gave me a room of my own! It has a small bay window with a seat that lifts up, and I keep my art supplies and Saint Francis in there. There are two twin beds, quilts thicker than I am. I have a trove of books— *Peter Pan in Kensington Gardens, Anne of Green Gables*, and my secret favorite, the baby book *Madeline,* about the little French orphan raised by nuns.

I don't want to say I like it at The Rookery.

The babies are the best part. Aaron, Sarah, Jacob, Charlotte, and Suzette. They don't know they are orphans, so they don't cry over that. The Sisters don't have to ask me to help. I like to give the babies baths, two at a time, bubbles, and powder their backsides until they look like beignets.

I have a regard for nuns, and it isn't high. I associate them with a lack of makeup and a ruler that seems to be

used for many things, excepting measuring. You don't need crayons to draw them; a pencil will do. The Rookery nuns are different. They appear to be people.

Of course we go to church. On my first Sunday I expected we would walk over to the St. Louis Cathedral but instead we headed two miles straight down our street to the Franklin Avenue Baptist Church. I thought it was a mistake when the Sisters started bouncing the baby strollers up the front steps, but the pastor came out to help us, calling everyone by name and asking about me, "*Who's this here, who's this here?*" His eyebrows shot up when old Sister Lily said, "Theresa's girl." The babies got bundled off to the nursery, and I assumed we would leave and go around the corner to a Catholic church. But no. We went in. I didn't think nuns were allowed to go there; isn't that against the law?

The only church I ever met was a cathedral. Gilt and guilt. This church looked more like a movie theater, full of wood and only one stained-glass window with a big white dove. Pretty much like the one on a bar of Dove soap. I'm familiar with a Jesus who hangs on a cross, all skinny, wearing some diaper thing, long dirty hair, face down, nails in his hands and feet. Nails! You better listen up! Look what this man did for you! There was no Jesus on the cross in the Baptist church. How am I supposed to feel bad if I don't see Suffering Jesus?

The younger Sisters from The Rookery and I were just about the only white people there. Certainly the Sisters were the only nuns. There were no tourists sneaking photos. Then the sermon started and, Holy Christ, what a commotion. That church could bust a move. At the cathedral I got down on my knees, head bowed, palms pressed tightly together to pray. I had nowhere

to look but inside. What am I going to see in there that I don't already know? The Baptists do it differently. I watched as those around me held open one hand, two hands, raised those hands to receive. The Sisters did it too. Hands up and open, they sang. I was a nervous little sparrow so all I could make myself do was tentatively hold open one palm, just barely, awkwardly close in to my body. But I left it open.

Maybe I felt Jesus there, just in the palm of my up-turned hand.

For a year or more I stayed in my room when I was sent to bed. Sometimes I would sit in the window seat and think of Charlie and Beau. They did write me, and sent me halvah and Persian nougat. I tried to picture them with bandoliers crisscrossing their chests, I tried to picture them killing people. I felt I would never know them again. In the worst of the summer humidity I would watch clouds rise right out of the cypress trees, like ghosts in the moonlight. In winter raindrops would catch in the Spanish moss and the night birds would stop for a drink. I would sit in the window and think of my mama and how she liked to pin a gardenia in her hair. Her beautiful fingers. She would sing me to sleep. I hate her I hate her I hate her. Mother fucker, heroin addict drunk fuck-up dead cunt.

Late at night I would hear old Sister Lily at the pia-no and the nuns laughing in a quiet way that made me think of crystal glasses. Always they were quiet to keep the babies still. Sarah and Aaron had been adopted out and now we had Justin and surely another baby would be here soon. I had to learn to think of the babies as puppies, something to play with that we couldn't keep.

There seemed to be no question of anyone adopting me.

One hot night I couldn't sleep and I listened to the Tinker Bell sounds of old Sister Lily at the keys. Soon I heard her climbing the staircase, headed to bed. I waited a stretch. Then I ghosted out of my room and down the staircase. I could have named each plank, I knew those steps so well from cleaning them; they would not squeal on me. I peeked into the parlor and almost peed.

The Sisters were playing cards. It couldn't have been poker with just the two of them, so maybe gin rummy. Their robes were huddled on the floor like loyal gray hound dogs. There was a bottle of dark wine. Candles. Sister Hope was in a red bra and black panties, Sister Camille in white, nothing but lacy bits. And they had hair! Just the fact of that!

Sister Camille lost the next hand and Sister Hope gave a pirate laugh. She held her cards up like a dagger. Sister Camille surrendered her bra but held Sister Hope's eyes so intently that Sister Hope could not break the stare. I was the first one to see Sister Camille's release of candlelit flesh.

I ran back up stairs.

Was that a hula girl tattoo I saw on Sister Hope's arm?

And so began the great spying game. Most nights the Sisters sat around in jeans and ponytails, shorts, a glass of wine. Books and laptop videos. Some nights Sister Camille liked to dress up like Madonna, wearing all her crosses at once, and she would dance to "Like a Virgin" and "Papa Don't Preach", and Sister Hope would applaud. On these nights they seemed like . . . sisters.

It was a hula girl tattoo. Additionally, between them

they had a constellation, a branch of cherry blossoms, and the pinup from the cover of the *Cars* album, which I came to learn was a Vargas Girl. One night I sneaked down and found Sister Hope with a tattoo gun, getting ready to use it on Sister Camille, who had a look on her face like that gun was as sexy as the Sex Pistols. The Violent Femmes.

In the morning they had on their old gray habits. Nothing was different. Breakfast, lunch, dinner.

Then came the year that Ella arrived at The Rookery. She was fourteen years old, one above me. She could match me for skinny, brown-as-bayou water, her hair an untamed Afro. She had bruises, layers of green and deep purple over her skin, under her eyes. She looked like she never cried. I must have looked like a candy apple to this girl. We shared my room. She didn't talk. She didn't want to read my Judy Blume books. When we went to church, she held her arms up high and wide. That part she got.

Three Months Later
With Ella there, I never sneaked down the stairs. Most nights I would open the windows, settle into the seat, knees tucked up under my nightgown. One night Ella came and sat by me. The moon shone through her stand-up hair. A teenaged boy rode his old red bike down our street, out at midnight. He saw us in the window and rang the little chime on his handlebars in greeting. We could hear the crickets until the next car came by. "Your hair is pretty," she said, touching my long braid. I had it in my mind I couldn't cut it or it would be bad luck for Beau and Charlie. I told her I liked her skin, because in

fact it was the same shade as my mama's. It doesn't really take that much for two little orphans to become sisters.

I called her Annie after Little Orphan, and she called me Madeline after *The smallest one was Madeline.* They were our secret orphan names.

Certain minds might think that I will now tell salacious stories, but the only ones I have are of solace. Ella was my Jesus. She suffered so much more than I did, she took all my suffering away. When we held hands, black and white fingers like a checkerboard, we were saints.

Beau died in Afghanistan on a bullshit *peacekeeping* mission. When I got word of his death, all the anger came back as swiftly and as unhesitatingly as the bullet that blew Beau off the face of the earth. I broke everything in the parlor. Old Sister Lily's porcelain chow dogs, the antique teacups, I pulled the Boston ferns down and cried like a banshee, smashing the pottery onto the floor. All the babies, who were in the kitchen, shut up in fear. Ella came running down from our room, barefoot, cut her feet on the shards and smeared the dirt right into the wounds to take me directly into her arms. I pushed her away. The Sisters came running in. I was screaming, "It's all my mama's fault! That fuck witch burnt-out heroin addict coward!" In my mind, if she hadn't died, Beau wouldn't have joined the Army and he would still be with me.

She would still be with me.

Sister Camille cut through my screaming with some screaming of her own. "What do you mean, heroin addict? Your mother wasn't a heroin addict! What's wrong with you?" She yelled this so loud all the babies started crying at once. It was louder than my heartbeat, it was

the trumpet of God. I stood in silence.

We soaked Ella's feet in lavender Epsom salts. She asked us to collect the pieces of porcelain and china; she would make a mosaic. We swept up the rest, repotted the plants. While we cleaned, the Sisters assembled the puzzle of my past and laid it at my hearth.

My mama wasn't my mother. Why did I ever think she was? How could a seriously brown woman give birth to a feather-white baby with blond hair and blue eyes? My mama wasn't Beau's or Charlie's mother. She didn't have a Chinese baby. She didn't have babies. She took poor orphans from The Rookery when it got overcrowded. Theresa didn't use heroin. She *was* a heroine. That's what I heard through the window, all those years ago. *Theresa was a heroine.* A goddess. But she drank. "A goddess can drink, Katrina," said old Sister Lily.

Did I never notice that Theresa was older than the other mothers at school? No I never noticed, because she dyed her hair and painted her nails and wore pretty headbands and lipstick. Because I was a child.

"Katrina, Theresa was seventy-two years old. She died of a heart attack," said old Sister Lily.

"Too much Willie Mae's fried chicken," tsked Sister Hope.

Old Sister Lily ignored her. "She got y'all from here, same place your brothers came from, so your brothers brought ya back."

I was so shocked I grew an inch. And old Sister Lily was just getting started. "Y'all might as well know it," she continued, "The Rookery isn't even a licensed orphanage. People bring us babies, we find homes. We're not nuns." She ripped her habit off her head, great waves of silvery hair cascading, little diamond earings. It could have been

the parting of the Gray Sea. I think I peed my pants. Not nuns!

"It's *impossible* to keep this up. That's why we stick with babies. We started wearing these god-awful outfits after Camille got robbed at knifepoint on our own street. While carrying a baby! Even crackheads usually don't attack nuns. And yes, Pastor Letur knows we aren't nuns. Everybody in that church knows we aren't nuns!" She stamped her foot like, *so there!*

"So those aren't your real names?" Ella asked, looking at Camille and Hope. Ella's eyes were bigger than her hair.

"Course not. Don't be ridiculous. It's a joke," said Camille. "I'm Diane. Pleased to meet ya."

"Jenna," said Hope, "and well, Lily really is Lily."

Well, bless my soul.

Five Weeks Later

Five weeks later Charlie came home. I knew he was coming; letter said today. I sat out on the front porch swing and waited, nervous as a mayfly. Ella and the Sisters left me to myself. Would I know him? Would he still have the little cross-stitch pattern of pockmarks on his cheek? Would he smell like Afghanistan and dust and guns?

When I saw my brother walking up Franklin Avenue, I ran down that street and clamped on to him like I was an alligator. I pulled him under and ate him in one bite. He was mine.

Charlie stayed at The Rookery for a week. He played with all the babies, *one, two, buckle my shoe* and Charlie Horse. He talked to me long and slow and we talked about Beau and Mama. We polished the stone of what we had, what we lost. On the third day he told me he

was getting married and moving to Arizona. I should come with him and I could grow cactus that blooms only at Christmas. I could see saguaro. The rain is filled with dust. He told me that Beau left half of his death benefit to him and half to me. I could go to college. I could buy a dress that wasn't secondhand.

But then Ella wouldn't have worn it first.

How could I explain that The Rookery and the Sisters and Ella, the Franklin Avenue Baptist Church, and the merry-go-round of babies had become my home? How could I say that in truth we had to work hard to recognize each other, our travels had taken us so far apart? How could I leave Ella, who cut her feet for me?

I told him I would think about it.

Three Years Later

Ella and I rent a little two-bedroom bungalow near Tulane. Garden District folk might consider our bedrooms the perfect size for a wine cellar, but a *room of my own* is orphan-speak for *luxurious*. Ella is majoring in law with a goal to work for women's rights. Her boyfriend brings beignets and there's always one for me. I'm majoring in creative writing. This is my first assignment.

On Sundays we go to church on Franklin Avenue and then to The Rookery to do a batch of cooking and take care of the babies to give the Sisters an afternoon off. In good weather we eat outside and when the magnolia petals fall, they fall right on us.

The Little Ice Girl

A reimagined faerie tale based on The Little Match Girl
by Hans Christian Andersen

On the morning of the summer equinox the sun rose
over San Diego as if drawn with a child's crayon,
flat and waxy. A low and roaming fog caught on har-
bor masts and drew ghost sails across the sky. The city
was cool and preparing to sparkle. But just south, at the
San Ysidro border crossing, the sun was in a different
mood, the sky already blanched by rising heat. As the
people of Tijuana came out of their homes, few both-
ered to look up, for the poor come to believe that they
deserve less, even when it comes to weather. There has
always been Auntie America with her pockets of pop-
pies in her green hills and Tia Juana with her dust and
dirt. Oh, there is color. The giant flag of Mexico flapping
over Tijuana like a bullfighter's cape. The strings of fili-
greed *papel picado* flags crisscrossing the tourist streets.
Rainbows of Chiclets in a little girl's hand. On this equi-
nox, San Diego would slip in and out of air-conditioned
homes, cars, restaurants. Tijuana would sweat.

There is a little house in the Los Laureles Canyon,
assembled from garage doors discarded in San Diego,
patched together with plywood and gumption. One of
the doors that is part of the roof has three oblong win-
dows over the kitchen, and a feral cat that Ana Maria
Bianca Aguilera is forbidden to feed sleeps in one of the

early morning sunbeams from the skylights. Ana calls him Pedro, but not in front of her father. She pets his rakish ears as she gets her ice chest together, then steps outside.

Her house is not so different from the others in the slum. The worst are made of cardboard, the thick kind used to box appliances that tend to blow away, come winter. The best are made of brick; even Mexican kids know the wolf can't blow a brick house down.

Ana caught the dusty bus down to the San Ysidro border crossing. Luckily Juan was the bus driver today; he waved Ana on. With other drivers she fiddles with her cloth satchel, pretending to dig for pesos until an impatient line forms behind her and the driver lets her on. Or kicks her off. But generally no one much minds when a wisp of girl, she barely takes up a seat, rides for free.

On this day Ana wore the dress her grandmother hand-stitched out of flour sacks; she looked like a faded, walking billboard for tortillas. A triangle of calico pulled her black hair back from her churro-brown face, and freckles daisy-chain across her nose. She has a pretty face; she doesn't know it, because it's been a long time since anyone told her so. Ana always wears a humble tin cross from her first communion and a small medallion stamped with the raised image of Our Lady of Guadalupe with her star-covered cloak covering her hair and flowing over her gown. A halo enshrines her entire body; that's Ana's favorite part. Ana absently pressed her finger into the Madonna while she sat in her seat, feet swinging well above the floor. She only had on socks. When Ana left home, it is true, she had her grandmother's slippers on. She had tried the baby powder trick to make her feet

slide into her too-small shoes. No luck. Her father says it's just the heat, the shoes are fine, but he's wrong. So Ana wore the slippers; her grandmother doesn't need them anymore, wouldn't mind if Ana wore them. The slippers had started out a hopeful pink, but quickly dusted down. Well, they are gone now. They were far too big for her feet and she lost them trying to avoid a truck that was trying to avoid a donkey that was trying to get the goddamn flies out of his eyes. She fell. One slipper was simply gone, the other carried off by an ur-chin, no better off than Ana, who thought his mother might like it for the new baby to sleep in. His little sister seemed as small as a slipper. Ana went on in her socks. She had tough feet anyway; slum soles. The important thing was that she didn't lose the Yeti.

Ana's father had stolen the Yeti from some American tourists on the Playas de Tijuana. When he opened it, the ice chest was full of Coronas, a pot of gold! He had the idea that Ana could make ice cubes and popsicles and sell them at the border crossing. Make money from water, for the popsicles add a little food coloring and a stick, that's all. The American imbeciles would buy anything.

But they won't. They will buy many things while trapped in their cars waiting through the long lines of the border crossing: tacos, cokes, toys for the kids. Ta-lavera plates. Huge patio pots with orange and green geckos painted on the sides. But not water. Never wa-ter, unless it's bottled and sealed. A very, very few, will give the little girl—what could she be but seven years old?—a few coins. Their leftover pesos that they can't spend at home anyway. Sometimes other Mexican kids will buy a popsicle from her. These coins Ana brings back to her father.

Ana worked the border on many hot days. Among the roving merchants she was known as La Pequeña Niña de Hielo—The Little Ice Girl. Sometimes she would be handed some food; there was that man who carried the wood-carved cross of Jesus on his back, he always bought her a lunch so big it's also dinner. But he was not there often. The lady with the funny eyes sometimes gave her tamarind candy in a pretty box with a pink donkey on it. But mostly people were concerned with themselves, and a little girl was below their line of sight.

Ana walked between the cars in misery. The sun was assaulting, coming up through her feet like the heated brick her grandmother used to place under the covers on a cold winter's night. Her hair an itchy blanket down her back. Nobody wanted her ice; nobody saw her at all. She had not one peso the whole livelong day. It was late afternoon. Most of the merchants had departed, it was too hot to be out. Mexicans know when to take a siesta.

Ana twined her way between slow-moving cars. She nearly fell several times. The air was pale molasses, she almost had to push through; any moment she would be caught, a bug in amber. Ana reached the edge of the lanes where the heat slightly receded, sat down in an eddy of luster. That Yeti, that glacier of ice, sat beside her. She reached her hand into the cool, touched a cube. A jolt of cold. She ran the ice up and down her arms, it made her shiver, her whole body shaking off heat like a puppy would water. Looking inside the fissures of the ice cube Ana saw a snowy mountain range, the Sierra Nevada. Imagined herself in the black-and-white photo of the mountains from her schoolbook. Black-and-white is so much cooler than color. A world of snow, a relief of white. The fever inside her quieted. But quick as melting ice, the cube was gone.

Ana refocused her eyes. Saw the low, gritty exhaust cloud radiating a wavy haze, tires Catherine wheels of heat. She stood up. She should go home. But her father ... Ana remembered the last of her parents' fights—half the slum heard her mother shout, "You so macho, hit a woman? You're as macho as a daiquiri." And he hit her again. No trusting that father.

Ana looked into a passing car, could see the air-conditioning lifting the fine hair of a little blond girl sitting in the back. The little girl was buckled securely into her booster seat and on her lap was a wide, white napkin illuminating a treasure of food. Ana saw bread fluffed up and buttered, circles of cheese in red wax, Mexican wedding cake cookies dusted with powdery sugar. Ana was so hungry. She pulled out another ice cube, it started to melt immediately, her fingers incendiary. Again she looked into the prisms of ice, and inside she saw a summer's picnic laid out on a clean white cloth. A whole fried chicken, if you please. But then the chicken hopped up and started reeling toward her, knife and fork in its breast. Poor girl! The ice melted, almost sizzled in her hand, and was gone, along with the food.

Ana was too fevered to care about repercussions from her father. She pulled another chunk out of the Yeti, peered into the prism. Deep inside the cracks she saw a tree, a winter pine covered in icicles, tinseling in the soft glow of a light falling snow. Under the tree she saw presents, wrapped in silver foil and velvety ribbons. As Ana watched, entranced, the icicles on the tree turned to candles and then the lights rose from the tree, higher and higher, she saw them now as stars in heaven. One fell down and a trail of fire burned behind.

"Someone has just died," whispered the little ice girl.

Her grandmother, the last person to love her, had told her that when a star falls, a soul ascends to heaven. Ana did not know that she was now back on the ground, that her knees had deserted, soldiers giving up the fight. She looked up into the sun and in the wavy luster stood her grandmother, radiant, with such an expression of love. An expression Ana had not seen for so long.

The ice cube was fast melting in her hand. Almost gone. "Oh, Grandmother," she called, "Take me with you. You'll go away when the ice melts, like the snow, like the feast and the presents. Take me with you!" Ana knocked open the Yeti and gathered all the remaining ice up into her hands. The melting ice ran down her arms, dripping into the ground as if couldn't wait to get it over with, to evaporate and reincarnate into a cloud that drifted over the border and rained in a benediction on San Diego. Ana looked for her grandmother in the fissures of the ice but couldn't find her. She looked up into the sun and saw a woman in long robes, a cloak embroidered with stars covering her hair, cascading over her shoulders, coming toward her. The sun made an aura all around the woman, shimmering and silver. "Our Lady of Guadalupe," whispered Ana, knowing the Madonna had come to take her to her grandmother, that her prayers were answered. She dropped all the remaining ice from her hands and raised her dripping palms up to the Madonna.

What might this Madonna ask the people of the San Ysidro border crossing about this girl in need of charity? If all the gold and silver crosses of the people who made their living or drove across the border were illuminated, it would be a constellation, a Milky Way of holy crosses, representing people professing Jesus's little lamb ways.

But it was not Our Lady of Guadalupe appearing out of the dusky sun. No one called the Catholics, the Christians to task. It was only Huda, who had managed a brutal escape from Syria; Huda, who had scars both skin-deep and beyond the bones. Who thought she would never have to see a child die again. Huda had made her way to Mexico, land of plenty, to make a life selling harissa chicken and mashed fava beans in shallow foil bowls from her halal cart on the border. The woman with a hijab draping her head and shoulders in soft folds, reached down for the crumpled child. The woman had kind eyes, the kind you want to look at you. "Don't worry, little one," she said. "I will find help for you."

The little ice girl was never seen on the San Yisidro border crossing again. Her Yeti was found and recognized but where was the girl? No one had the slightest suspicion of what Ana had seen, they could not dream of the splendor in the ice, or with what joy she ended the first day of summer.

Good as Biscotti

Emboldened with silk lingerie and a pomegranate,
Vittoria is on her way to becoming Joan of Arc

It could be that only prostitutes are free of their past, able to discard each day like a Goodwill sweater. Every lover I have ever had sooner or later makes me into an archaeological dig. Tracing a finger up a scar, on my thigh, or in my heart. They poke, poke, poke at my past. No man would ever do that to a prostitute. She is held in a suspension of time that is seldom extended to me. They always want *to know*. What am I, *Show and Tell*?

I only told one time. It's in the court documents...

Rome, Italy 1990
Once in my lifetime there was a spring snow in Rome. Mamma still wanted to paint. So we left our flat in Trastevere, shut the faded green door, Parrot squawking behind us, "Hey, big boy." One red tail feather caught in the draft and followed us, landing on the white snow. I looked over our small piazza formed by our building and several others clustered in a loose rectangle. The buildings reminded me of elderly, afternoon-limoncello ladies, tending to lean on each other.

The corner grocer was open, baskets of onions and eggplant covered in burlap under the awning, the wake-up smell of espresso coming from the tiny Café Stella d'Italia. Signora Bianchi had left her laundered sheets

hanging out overnight and now they were stiff, drifts of snow forming on the lines. Just last week Parrot had flown up to those lines and shit on her bloomers. "*Hey! Sacco di pidocchi*—you bag of lice," yelled Signora, shaking her fist at the bird. Parrot looked down at Signora Bianchi and called, "Pretty boy, pretty boy." Pooped again.

Mamma and I headed into town. The snow continued to fall. It seemed we were walking through baby angel wings as we crossed over the Ponte Sisto, the water a dull silver. It snowed so seldom in Rome, even the birds were shocked. They sat stone-still on the fountains and statues we passed until they themselves appeared carved. When one or another took flight, snow trailing from wings, it was as if the statues had come alive and flown away. It was so quiet. All the Vespas stayed home.

By the time we reached the busier streets and jumped on a tram it was obvious the snow had no chance of survival under the weight of city traffic, which was slowed but by no means stopped. The snow could only stick to the rooftops and monuments. We passed by the filigreed coliseum and made our way to Piazza Navona. Most of the artists and vendors had taken the day off, but the cafés were open; surprised tourists in too-light sweaters drank hot chocolate with their hands wrapped around their cups. The fountains were running, cold and clear. My mother retrieved her big umbrella from the back room of Angelica's Gelato. Angelica's sign is a cherub eating a cone of pistachio.

"I didn't expect to see you today, Lia," said Angelica, as Mamma dragged the umbrella out.

"I guess neither of us will sell much," agreed Mamma. "But the snow! I want to try and paint." I helped Mamma carry the heavy umbrella out and set it up toward

the Fontana del Moro. She did this without me most days, but on weekends I tended to go with her. Liliana used our house for work, and who knew which room she would end up in. It was better for me to be out.

Today Mamma didn't bother to lay out her table with her finished paintings, instead setting her easel up just outside of the protection of the umbrella and clipping a thick piece of rough-press paper into place. She let the snow fall on the paper and I wandered off to visit Signor Cacibauda.

"Vittoria," said Signor Cacibauda, stretching out my name like soft nougat. I wish I had his musical accent; Mamma is from America, arrived not much ahead of me. We basically learned Italian together, never quite getting the sound quite right. "Why are you here, in the snow, an April snow?" asked Signor Cacibauda, putting his hands out to catch a surprise of flakes. "It only snows in Rome when Mary is crying." I could smell the olive oil and garlic, the vinegar he used to marinate the eels. *Anguille Tevere Fritte* said his sign in bright red script—Fried Tiber Eels. He handed me a paper cone of hot bites. Signor Cacibauda's son was one of the last eel fishermen of Rome. It was possible I was eating mercury and sewage, but Signor Cacibauda had found a way to bread and fry the Tiber itself; he served up little pieces of the silver river.

"Mamma wants to paint," I said with a shrug. He motioned me to stand on the scale he used to weigh pails of fresh eels for the Piazza Navona restaurants, where tourists could pay three times as much to eat the same thing Signor Cacibauda sold, but overfried and soggy. He was lucky to have a stand in the touristy Piazza Navona, because we all know locals will not buy food

from a *Siciliano sporco*—the cooks sent the dishwash-
ers to his stand so the cocky cooks could pretend they
didn't know where the eels came from. Idiots.

"Let's see if you weigh forty-five kilos yet," he said,
and I climbed up on the scale. I was a wisp of a girl,
like a sentence that fades from hearing. At fifteen I was
most often mistaken for a thirteen-year-old boy. I had
hope. My mother was beautiful, at least I thought she
was beautiful, but I was about as attractive as an eel in
a pail of muddy-bank water. This week I weighed forty
kilos even with my boots on. "Forty! That's up from last
week! Five more kilos and that twenty thousand lire is
yours. Eat up!"

O Dio! I wanted that money.

When I went back to Mamma I saw that she was
working with snow-dampened paper; she was adding
streaks of watercolors that washed down and spread in
plumes. It was mostly out of her control, but I saw an up-
side-down forest in blues and grays, and when she turned
it over it was so evocative I could feel the Gunnywolf
peering round a bend of a faint forest road. A whisper
of his eyes, the folktale of him. It was perfect. A painting
based in snow.

The next week was warm and Signora Bianchi's window
box colored with violets and periwinkles. The burlap
was off the grocery baskets and the oranges presented in
green waxed paper. Parrot was out again, Signora shout-
ing at him, Parrot parading across the courtyard like a
peacock. Alberto was sunning himself in his wheelchair,
calling, *"Pappagallo, vieni da Papà!"* But Parrot did not
consider Alberto his papa, only a mate whom Parrot
was happy to join when Alberto had apples or grappa

or limoncello on a hot day. Or best of all, when Alberto went about town and Parrot could ride on his shoulder and pretend Alberto was a pirate and the wheelchair, shaking over uneven pavement and cobblestones, was a ship at sea. Parrot would say, "Shiver me timbers," in Italian-Parrot, which no one understands. But I'm sure that's what Parrot wants because he keeps trying to poke out one of Alberto's eyes, so that Alberto would have to wear a black leather eye patch.

Honestly, though, Alberto can't afford to lose the use of any more body parts.

Parrot flew over and joined me on our balcony. Our apartment is really quite nice. We have four bedrooms and a large kitchen with a farmhouse sink. Leaded French doors lead to a tiny, walk-out balcony looking over the piazza, big enough for two folding chairs and a little chipped mosaic-topped table that always sports an overflowing ashtray. We have blue silk curtains so old they might be made of dust and an overstuffed couch of faded brown velvet. Alberto lives with us, and he has the only downstairs room, because of the wheelchair. Mamma and Liliana each have a room upstairs and I have the smallest room, a converted linen pantry that still smells of starch and mothballs. I sleep on a long, fairly deep shelf and it's not going to work much longer, but for now, as long as the door stays propped open, I am content to pretend it's a bunk bed.

While I idle on the balcony I try to come up with a plan. Everyone knows the devil lives and breathes in Rome like no other city on earth. I want that twenty thousand lire. I'm getting tired of falling into the *Quattro Fiumi*.

On the following Sunday, as with most Sundays, I go with Mamma to Piazza Navona. Today we go as a

family. I push Alberto, Parrot sitting on his shoulder, talons digging into Alberto's sweater. Alberto's legs are supported straight out in front of him, so sometimes Parrot walks the plank of his legs. Mamma and Liliana follow a little behind, arms looped. Liliana has short, dark curly hair and bouncy boobs in an off-the-shoulder dress, high heels. I am jealous. My chest requires no sanctuary. Mamma is shorter, dressed in rolled-up jeans and a white linen men's button-up shirt, her brown hair in a high ponytail. Mamma used to dress more like Liliana, more like most Italian women, but she says she is a feminist and "it's hard to be a feminist when men keep pinching your fat." So she switched to the painterly look. And why not—it's what she's selling. Liliana says, "If you're going to wear something it might as well say *hello*." That's what she's selling. I'm in shorts and a faded T-shirt that says *When in Rome* that Mamma bought secondhand because she thought it was funny. I have spare clothes in my satchel.

After we all help set up, Mamma's watercolors laid out like daydreams of paper, Liliana, Alberto, and I wander off on our own. Alberto pulls out his old red-and-silver Illy brand coffee tin and starts to push himself through the pigeon-flocks of tourists. Alberto's legs are as skinny as the word *Illy* and he has several scabs on his face. His clothes are ill-fitting, mostly because it's just hard to get dressed. He is only in his forties, which makes the fact of him even sadder. Habitually burning *Fortunas*, but seldom inhaling, the long coils of ash fall in a heap in his lap. And then there is Parrot. Parrot is certainly an attention-getter. He shits on Alberto's sweater, plucking threads with his beak when he's nervous. And Parrot steals leftover food from café plates be-

fore the busboys can clear them and then eats the food while perched on Alberto's shoulder. Crushed chicken bones cascading from his parrot beak litter Alberto's chest. It's not hard for Alberto to earn money. People just want him to get away. He makes his weekly living in a day. Besides, he's a solicitor during the week, but that's mostly gratis for poor people. And addicts. He used to be one himself.

Liliana finds a wall where the old terra-cotta of the building is complementary to her outfit. She just looks and waits. She says it's all in the eyes. She's a daytime lady-of-the-night. She calls herself a day lily. She says the hours are better and the clientele behaved. She only does hand and blow jobs, and I should not know these things, but she told me because she wants me to think better of her. She is quite beautiful in a Gina Lollobrigida way. Apparently she can also do it just with her boobs but I am not quite clear on the details. Sometimes I think there must be sperm all over our house and I wonder if I got one of those black lights if the mess would show up in a purple glow. Honestly, I should probably avoid the couch. Liliana tells me she's saving money to move to Iceland because she is certain the northern lights, the sky fields of greens and blues, are the exhales of the ancient Behemoth and she wants to see it for herself. But I know that's a faerie tale.

I don't want her to leave. I know she spends some of her nights in Mamma's bed, and if that would make her stay, it's okay with me. I want them both to just be what they are. If they could be in love, she could stay and I could have two mothers. And then, also, I would get my own room. If they came out of the closet, so could I.

I might look as if I'm wandering through Piazza Na-

vona, but I'm not. I make my way over to the *Fontana dei Quattro Fiumi*—Four Rivers Fountain—and climb up on the edge and balance. This is not allowed. I know it; everyone knows it. But I have the persona of a boy in a tourist shirt. Boys will be boys. Some tourist moms are glancing about, wondering where my mother is. I see Mamma. She sees me. Ignores me. I have the choice of the Nile, the Danube, the Ganges, or the Rio de la Plata. Like Moses, I go into the Nile. I go all the way under and start picking up as many coins as I can while I kick my feet so the choppy water will obscure my hands. I can't get much. If I stay under too long some American hero will jump in to save me. I pop up, all smiles, and climb out of the fountain. The tourists are relieved. Just then I see Giorgio, the security guard, coming my way. He's watching me like I'm a monkey with a monkey wrench going to pound that fountain to dust. What does he care if I grab a few lire? No time to change clothes. I run out of the piazza.

I've got to come up with a new gig.

First things first. The following weekend Alberto is outside drinking espresso from a little red cup across the piazza at the Stella. Parrot is reading *La Repubblica* over Alberto's shoulder, tsk-tsking the most recent shenanigans of Presidente Cossiga. While they are thus occupied, I go into Alberto's bedroom. He has a sort of footlocker by his bed where he keeps this and that and his pot. His Venetian blown-glass bong. I know there is a metal cross in there, over a foot long, heavy, Jesus's face the color of old pewter, his hands veined in gray. I put the cross in my satchel and run up to my room.

When we get to Piazza Navona I go over to see Si-

gnor Cacibauda. "Vittoria, Vittoria, are you here for your weigh-in?!" He hands me a cone of salty-sweet eels and I eat them first, as I always do to put on the extra weight.

"Today's the day, Signor Cacibauda," I say, "I feel it right over my heart." I climb up on the scale, the metal cross tucked into my tightly belted jeans, Jesus's arms stretched across my chest, secured by a thick Christmas ribbon tied around my body. How much does sin weigh? Apparently about eight kilos.

"Vittoria, you did it! Forty-eight kilos! You are a woman now! *What* have you been eating?!" He hands me the twenty thousand lire and I want to hug him, I really do, but I can't, because he would feel Jesus come between us. I give him a Mona Lisa smile.

In the summer, I turned sixteen and Liliana made me three-layered lemon cream cake. I blew out all the candles. Nope, no boobs.

Rome was on fire. Parrot lost enough feathers to make a half a dozen shuttlecocks; he pulled them out himself. He only went outside to walk under the cool water pouring from the little *fontanella* in our piazza. Parrot begged Liliana to take him with her to Iceland. Mamma took pity and bought him a personal fan and plugged it in by his perch. When Parrot felt the soft wind he reached up with one talon and petted her face.

Alberto was writing a novel set in the Himalayas. Something with snow leopards and avalanches. His words were cooling him down. Mostly he stayed in his room, going over to the Stella when he hears Liliana's heals clicking on the cobblestones. She steps hard as she gets close, code for "Go out the back door *now*." She al-

ways fumbles with her purse to find the key to the already unlocked door.

Mamma goes to work almost every day, selling her watercolors, anything in shades of blue and green selling like bottles of water. In the evenings we walk to the Lungotevere—the night markets—pop-up summer bars and restaurants along the banks of the river, illuminated by strings of bistro lights and hot-colored neon. We can't bring Alberto because it's a long staircase down to the embankment from the Ponto Sisto, but we bring him back half bottles of cheap, garnet-shaded Chianti and fabric bags full of biscotti so light they almost fly away.

During the days, I am free. I kiss a boy from my class and he squeezes my flat chest. I will my boobs to pop up like those pop-up children's books, fast as that. We are behind the Basilica of Santa Maria and when the bells go off, so does he. I see the wet through his pants. We both feel silly. We used to play cops and robbers together. We don't know yet how to grow up. I don't know if we will tease each other, or maybe we'll try it again. Maybe I'll write his name, Roberto, in a heart with a lacy border drawn in pink-wax crayon.

On an early morning I joined Liliana on the balcony. It was still cool out and the air smelled of lavender and thyme coming from the Stella kitchen gardens. Pepi, the black cat, lazed by the fountain. Liliana lit up a smoke and I drank milk straight from the cold glass bottle I brought from the kitchen. "Liliana, why do you want to move to Iceland?" She inhales and does not look at me.

"Because it's uninhabited."

"People live there."

"Sure. But when they die they get buried and that's

that. Here, they keep digging them up, or putting up statues, or painting portraits. Nobody dies in Italy, the past never . . . passes. In Iceland I'll be young and that will count for something. Here you practically have to be dead to be remembered." She takes another drag. "Iceland is windswept on a regular basis."

I picture a land where the wind is a broom made of twigs. I push further. "Why do you put up with all those *teste di cazzi*? Why not go wait tables or go to night school?" I know she has a drawer full of lire; she really could afford her own place.

"I did once, wait tables."

"Why'd you quit?"

She watches Parrot and Pepi have a chitchat out on the piazza. "There was this boy, Luca, same age as me, nineteen, but retarded. Well, slow. He was the busboy. The state paid his wages, so it was free labor for the owner. I worked hard, *Cara,* I was in a hurry to make money. I wasn't going to be a waitress forever! Luca was costing me tips—he was slow as potatoes. I resented having to work with him and I guess he could read emotions better than menus. One day he handed me a wadded up paper napkin. On it he had written in pencil, *Ti odio* Lili.[I hate you, Lili.] Oh, he shamed me, Vittoria. I realized this was the best job he could hope for. Waitressing was only a twirl for me, but busboy was his aspiration. I gave him all my tips and quit. Luca deserved better than a cartoon like me."

Liliana lit another cigarette and continued. "That was right after my mom died of breast cancer and my dad married that whore who probably is a really nice person, but it had only been maybe four months, and it made me feel, I don't know. Replaceable. So one night I got drunk at a bar and this man came over. I thought

he was going to offer to buy me a drink because I was *all that*, but he leaned in and said, "How much?" And I said, "Let's go, big boy; I'll be your blow-up doll."

Liliana had been living with us for three years now. "Did Mamma know you were a blow-up doll when she let you move in?" I'd never wondered this before because by the time I realized her profession, she was just Liliana to me.

Liliana glanced at me. "I know what you're thinking—how could she let someone like me be around her daughter?"

I tried not to blink; it would be a judgmental blink.

"Sometimes in the summer I was sleeping in the plaza. I'd take showers in the fountains at godforsaken hours."

I pictured her, a nude marble statue, sluiced by the rush from some ancient, carved water urn. Beautiful, really.

"Alberto was the one who noticed me; you know he collects the little lost souls. And your mamma? Well, judging by Alberto and Parrot, so does she."

I think she forgot I was there; her eyes were in her heart. Then Liliana shook herself back, looked at me, and said, "Three true things about me—I'm twenty-two years old, I'm technically a virgin, and you're right, I need a new gig."

"Movie star?"

"Movie star."

We giggled, I took a puff of her Spanish cigarette, and she took a swig of the milk.

The following morning, I fell off my shelf. I really need a bed.

There was a turn in the weather, a shading in the air.

Mamma took the day off and we walked together to the Vatican. On Via della Lungara we rummaged through the outdoor book stalls and moved on with the scents of mold and faded ink on our fingers. We drank espresso under the shedding bark of the plane trees, mottled green-and-gray patterns that remind me of paint by numbers.

Of course there were tourists in St. Peter's Square, but we waited. I knew why we were there. Last night Alberto had coughed and coughed and left a small trail of bloody saliva that plumed his bedsheet like a lost tail feather of the Firebird.

We weren't there for a mass, or to climb the steps of the dome, or even to get on our knees and pray, although we knew how. Mamma turned directly to the right when we entered the basilica and we slowly made our way up to Michelangelo's *Pietà*. A crazy geologist attacked Mary with a rock pick in 1972, condemning her ever since to solitary confinement behind a bulletproof screen. Every time I see Mary and her fallen son, I long to be closer to the single most beautiful, most human thing ever made by the hand of man.

"That's how Alberto looked," Mamma whispered. She wasn't really talking to me. Jesus, skinny as a Treblinka Jew, held in the strength and grief of his mother, who is somehow still a young woman. He did look like Alberto.

"This morning?"

"No, no. Back then. When he overdosed and almost died. You were there, but I know you don't remember." I didn't. I was two. I knew Mamma was asking Mary to save Alberto again. To have pity.

It was at that moment that I had my epiphany. "Mamma, I want to be an altar boy." She looked at me with one raised eyebrow. I decided to go for broke.

"Also, is Alberto my father?" Mamma took my hand and we found our way to a quiet café where all of Rome was our backdrop.

I always knew my mother was an American. Not the Lia she was called now, but Amelia Watkins from Gary, Indiana. In 1975, most Americans were watching helicopters dangle people over Saigon or wondering what Patty Hearst was doing with a machine gun. The '60s were a fading peace sign in the rearview mirror. But Mamma had just graduated from high school and she wanted to be bigger than Maple Street, more than an apple pie. She considered herself a feminist and an artist, but all she had done was burn her bra and sell one landscape to her grandfather. So she took her graduation money, bought a backpack and a one-way ticket to Milan. She was going to make herself into the things she chose. These were my bedtime stories, knitted into my growing bones. She taught me about America. If ever I get there I am going to eat Nacho Cheese Doritos.

We ordered *pompelmo* ices. "When I arrived in Milano, I knew it was too big for me," Mamma began. "I took the train to Cinque Terre on the coast, where the five tiny villages are stacked like a jumble of children's building blocks. I can't begin to tell you how I felt. The color of the Mediterranean—I mixed up whole new color wheels of blues and greens based on that water. And the buildings grafted into the cliffs—I learned umber, ochre, vermilion. I would never have become an artist in Gary. Plus, basically I was starving, and I'm telling you, when you are hungry all colors take on a watery, intensified hue. I wanted to dip my fingers into everything. But I had to eat. I really had to eat. Because I was pregnant with you when I left Gary."

Oh, I let out a gasp! "Before you left home?!"

"No. Gary. Well, yes, and home too. My boyfriend was Gary Petersen."

Gary Petersen. That's my dad's name. Sounds like he would wear a football jersey.

"He was cute, Vittoria. Wore his baseball cap backwards and he was going to be a farmer. He was all *yes, ma'am* and haystacks. And I just couldn't do it, Vittoria, I couldn't put that apron on. So I got on a plane, four months pregnant, and I never told him. Just said I was leaving and don't come lookin'."

"That's why I was so hungry. You were stretching out your legs! Alberto found me in Vernazza and he took me in. He was already a successful solicitor. He was taking a summer vacation on the coast. He fed me every shape of pasta and huge slabs of tiramisu. He was kind to me. He took me back to Rome with him when the summer was over, and then you were born."

I already knew the story of Alberto's accelerated quest for drugs and cocktails that came out of the stress of his big-city job. The paper said he was destined for politics! The people loved his crusade for the working class, his Armani suit, his Fabio hair. "But it was too much for him," Mamma reminded me. "One morning I found him looking like Jesus in the *Pietà*, and I saved him. Mary and I saved him. As best we could."

I was getting so much information; I couldn't stop now. I really wanted my own room. "Mamma, are you and Liliana in love?"

"Oh my goodness, no! Why do you think that?"

"She goes into your room . . ."

"Oh, Baby, Liliana is just a lost little girl! Sometimes she just needs a mamma too. She climbs in and we sleep.

We are not in love like that."

There goes that idea.

We fell quiet and the buzzy sound of the city's Vespas reached us like swarms of killer bees. There was the clink of silverware and the smell of grapefruit and ice. "So, now tell me about the altar boy thing," said Mamma.

"Why can't I be an altar boy?" I asked in a guileless, innocent tone. And I knew I could get her. I knew the feminist in her, the bile of repression would burn her heart to pieces. This entire city is filled with women in black muumuus while the men wear red-and-gold-threaded gowns with lacy collars, big-stoned rings, embroidered, pointy-toed shoes. I knew she loved Jesus and Mary, but she was always uncomfortable with the discrimination against women in the clergy. I saw the conflict in her body language; she sat back, folded arms. Could a professed feminist let her daughter deny her sex? She leaned in.

"Well, of course you can be an altar boy. How dare those pious shits say you can't? Joke's on them, at least until your boobs come in. Let's go cut your hair even shorter."

I didn't tell her I wanted to be an altar boy so I could pilfer coins from the collection baskets. Why spoil a really good day?

I took my comforter down from my shelf, folded it in half, and started sleeping on the velvet couch. Once I woke up with Parrot standing on my chest, three small, downy-white feathers in his beak that he had pulled out of my quilt. "What are you, some sort of cannibal?" he said with his eyes, then spit the feathers in my face.

Mamma took my quest for altar boy service seri-

ously. But it was my job to do reconnaissance. I went to masses of masses. I took notes:

Basilica di Santa Maria—Too rich. Altar boys look like they are in prep school for the University of Bologna.

Santa Cecilia—Locked collection boxes / slot on top. When did that start!?

Chiesa di San Francesco d'Assisi—Too many nuns / sharp eyes.

There are so many churches in Trastevere that if I walked in the two o'clock shadows of the bell towers I could make it all the way to the Vatican without stepping out into the sun.

Then I found Santa Bernadette. Santa Bernadette's is not a tourist church. No thirteenth-century gold mosaics, no baroque statues. Just cool stone and a wash of blue color from high stained glass windows. There were a lot of Marys but only one depiction of Jesus, and he did not look you in the eye. Best of all, there were only two altar boys and the collection was done with open baskets. Best, best of all, Father Nicola looked about twenty-five and I was going to marry him. I threw away all my childish Roberto hearts.

Mamma took me to Santa Bernadette's and waited until after mass to talk to Father Nicola. I stayed in the pew. I knew her plan was to explain that we lived in the neighborhood and had been going to Santa Maria. Lately I had fallen in with some Sicilian immigrants and although she knew we were all lambs in God's eyes, these boys were smoking cigarettes and had tattoos. I was sixteen years old, but looked young for my age. Santa Maria was perhaps too (and here she played on what she hoped would be Father Nicola's vanity) interested

in, well, *history*, and maybe not so much the problems of its congregation. She thought I would do better at a smaller church devoted to Mary. Could he use another altar boy? Vittorio knows all the altar boy rules.

I was in!

Autumn came with a fading grace. The stone pines withstood the season's change, but here and there a birch or aspen ignited with color and burned in effigy. I divided my time between school, Piazza Navona, and Santa Bernadette's.

The only problem with pretending to be a boy was I didn't know boys are such idiots. I became Sunday friends with Mario and Daniele, the other altar boys, but everything was *fica*-this and *cazzo*-that. I'm surprised those two could get through a mass without masturbating. I had no interest in these *children*. I put on my bright red cassock with my white surplice edged in lace on the hem and sleeves and was dedicated to my duties. Now that there were three altar boys, Mario, the tallest, carried in the cross and Daniele and I carried lit candles. We proceeded through the smell of beeswax, silver polish, and damp stone. The service was as choreographed as a performance at Teatro dell'Opera, and in my opinion just as daffy. Maybe Liliana is right—nothing dies in Rome. Not even poor Jesus.

I did get to carry a basket for offertory collection. What a golden goose! I watched the lire pile up in the basket and thought about this going on in every Catholic church in Rome. What a bunch of beggars. They say they are collecting for the poor, but there's a translucent life-sized Carrara marble statue of Mary and the candlesticks have rubies. It's like a rich man panhandling on the

corner, you can see his polished Berluti shoes, and still you put lire in his hand. It was easy for me to block myself from view with my wide cassock and long lace sleeves as I made the turn at the back of the nave. I self-identified as one of the wretched poor. I was just taking out the middle man.

Mario and Daniel, the service, the censer with its billow of incense that is supposed to be a symbol of prayer rising to heaven (but we all know it is to cover the smell of the unwashed and the farts)—none of this was my true concern. Not even the money, which was really more of a bad habit and only a few lire a week just to keep my hand in the game, since I gave up my Four Rivers gig. My true concern quickly became Father Nicola.

Father Nicola looked like the cover of a romance novel. All the sexy saints are men. Think Saint Sebastian with the arrows. Sebastian's the patron saint of athletes, but I think he might also be the patron saint of masochists, tied to the tree, a look of transcendental ecstasy on his face.

I hung around after mass, after Mario and Daniele left, pushing each other down the church steps. I went to the cleaning closet and got out cloths and lemon oil and polished the wood of the altar, refilled the large rack of cheap candles in the red glass jars, thirty lire to light a candle and increase the potency of prayer, or buy an indulgence. I prayed that Father Nicola would indulge *me*.

Autumn yawned into December. Days ended abruptly, but Rome is ever a city strung with café lights and candles melting over Chianti bottles. Father Nicola added a late afternoon mass on Sundays because when Christmas draws near, everyone's a Catholic in Rome. Christmas lights crisscrossed the alleys of Trastevere like star-

crossed lovers. Signora Bianchi put a twelve-meter tree, heavy with twinkle lights and strands of popcorn, out in the piazza by the Stella. Parrot took to sitting on top, gaudy as a Vatican Swiss Guard, eating the popcorn whenever Signora Bianchi wasn't looking. When she caught him she would shake her fist, but honestly I think she strung that popcorn as Parrot's Christmas gift.

On Christmas morning we overslept and then drank dark cups of espresso and exchanged our presents. Liliana gave me a lace-edged white silk bra and matching panties so soft they slipped through my hands. Madonna, they were beautiful! And at last I had some itty-bitty-bit of boobie to put in them! I was certain their emergence was the result of my months of lusting after Father Nicola. Thoughts that intense were sure to change a body. My breasts were not visible under my surplice, but the way Father Nicola sometimes glanced at me, he saw them. I thought he saw them.

We lazed through the morning and then had ham in a pecan sauce, cordial glasses of ice wine from the Aldo Adige and chunks of chocolate and pomegranates. When we could eat no more, Alberto wheeled round the table to Liliana and offered her a small velvet box. Liliana held out her hand but said, "Alberto, we are done with gifts."

"This is one more small thing for you, *mia dolce*. I am so proud of you." Liliana had started working in Alberto's solicitor's office; she had a gift for making uncomfortable people comfortable. She had quit her daylily job. We all leaned in. Inside the box was a folded-up piece of paper. A check! "For school, Liliana; it's time to go back to college. This will get you started," said Alberto. Liliana and Mamma both started to cry.

"Don't cry," said Alberto to Mamma. "I have one for you too, *il mio cuore.*" He placed an identical box on the table in front of her. Midnight blue velvet.

"Alberto, I'm not going back to school!" But she took the box.

"Open it, Mamma!"

We all leaned in. Inside was a slender silver ring, runed and tarnished. A star sapphire. "Lia, will you have a poor excuse like me?" Alberto asked. He could not get down on one knee. Liliana and I couldn't breathe.

My mother bit her lip and looked at Alberto with watery eyes. Did she see the albatross? She did not; or she only saw him in flight. "*Si. Perché ci hai messo tanto tempo?*" [What took you so very long?] Now we all were crying and laughing and hugging like Italians. Mamma and Alberto kissed and I realized that although Alberto was not my father, at least from time to time he had been my mother's lover.

Alberto turned to me. "So. Now, something for you, Vittoria." he said. "A puzzle. What won't fit in a box, but is a box?"

I threw my hands up in the air. "My own room!"

"We will decorate! Everything new," declared Alberto. And then he handed me a slender ring of twined silver and said, "For my daughter."

God, what a day! And it wasn't over.

Everyone had meant to go with me to the late afternoon Christmas mass, but when it was time to go, they were in the Christmas coma. I didn't care, in fact didn't want them. I put on my new silk *lingerie,* pieces so fine they were a dictionary away from the word *underwear.* As I layered my black slacks and black top with the buttons on the boy's side, I felt for the first time the power

that a woman feels when she puts on back-seamed fish-nets, stilettos, cat eyes. Two little pieces of silk opened that door for me. And out that door I went, to Santa Bernadette's.

Now this part is hard to tell. Memory is smoke.

After mass I returned my cassock and surplice to the closet. I waited until everyone had gone and followed Father Nicola into his study, nervously inhaling the smell of stone and books and coffee. He looked up from his desk to my face. A smile. "Vittorio, go home now. It's Christmas, be with your family."

"I have a gift for you, Father."

"Oh, no need for that," he dismissed. But I had al-ready taken my hand from behind my back and brought forth a pomegranate. No one could say no to such a sim-ple gift of edible rubies. So he amended, "Thank you, Vittorio," and put out his hand. But I came round his desk. His desk was old and scarred but his chair was wide and new and swiveled toward me. I did not stop. I climbed right up into his lap, legs wide, and held the pomegranate between us like a third, exposed heart. I leaned over and kissed him in a way to match my linge-rie. A very grown-up kiss that tasted of communion wa-fer. This was the extent of my bravery. If he had repulsed me, I would have flown.

He kissed me back.

He took the fruit and let it drop to the floor and I pressed into his chest. This, I was sure, was the kiss of two people who had been thinking about it for seasons. Neither of us intended it to end in a kiss. It wasn't as if we could go out on a date. Our breathing was wild. I feared I would break out in hiccups and ruin every-thing. Father Nicola unzipped my pants. I thought he

would start with my shirt, as lovers do in movies. But then I remembered *The Godfather*, where they did it standing up against a wall half undressed, and this only excited me more. His hand went inside my silk panties.

Then his hand came out of my silk panties.

Father Nicola pulled back, a horse running full speed who had reached the edge of a cliff. "Vittorio, you are a girl." It wasn't a question. He almost whispered it. He got up so quickly I fell, landing awkwardly on the pomegranate. He was a completely different person. All sexuality had drained from him like dirty water down a stone sink. He started to say he was sorry, or words I will never remember. He reached out a hand to help me up. It was then that I knew Father Nicola had always believed, until his hand was down my pants, believed I was a boy. He was rejecting me only because I wasn't.

I was shamed, in that moment embarrassed and humiliated. I was a child who had played at grown-up and lost. I ran from the study as fast as I have ever moved, tears destroying my vision, my heart on fire. Father Nicola was shouting after me and I turned to his voice. As I did I slammed into the votive candle rack, every candle burning on this Christmas night. The rack tumbled with my force and burning candles flew from the many red glass containers. I fell into a confluence of iron, shattering glass and tiny fires. The tiny fires took quick hold on my cheap polyester clothes and suddenly ... I was Joan of Arc.

* * *

I had a dream of white. Perhaps a snowy winter morning. Completely quiet except for faraway cathedral bells or maybe children in a music class playing triangles. Or angels. The lack of color was a comfort, for without col-

or, there is no emotion.

The worst of the burns were on my inner thighs, where the flames had traveled up the seams to the tightest part of my pants. There would also be a scar under one of my new breasts and along a single rib. The other scars would be the remains of flicks of flame, eventually fading to random freckles. I had cuts from the glass on my hands and knees. The pain was bad but the drugs were good. I'd like to blame my behavior on the drugs.

As the days of my recovery went on, it became clear that Father Nicola, who had doused my flames with holy water and called the ambulance, had only said that I had knocked over the candle rack. He said it was his fault; he should have had the rack secured to the ground. The Church would pay my hospital bills.

But we are a family of suspicious people. Liliana of men. Alberto of authority. Mamma of anything that hurts her child. All three of celibacy. The rack was heavy. If I had simply walked into it, it would have shivered and settled. *Was I running? Why was I running? Who else was there? Was I running from Father Nicola? Did Father Nicola do something to you?* I just wanted to sink into the white. They kept picking at my scabs.

I am ashamed to this day that it was preferable for me to say Father Nicola tried to rape me, almost raped me, than to admit that he declined my offered love and my beautiful silk panties. So I lied. Give me another one of those pills. I'll say anything.

Alberto filed a lawsuit against the diocese but the only action was that Father Nicola left Santa Berna-dette's. I heard they sent him to Lake Como, where the air smells of flowers.

Life goes on, and so much of it good as biscotti.

With summer, Alberto and Mamma got married. Liliana and I were bridesmaids and Parrot stood best man—on Alberto's shoulder. When Mamma said, "I do!" Parrot said, "My, what a big boy are you!" Signora Bianchi hosted the reception at the Stella and the party filled the whole piazza. Angelica brought gelato of many colors. Signor Cacibauda brought his fryer and buckets and buckets of eel. By the end of the night, Signora Bianchi and Signor Cacibauda were looking like they were sharing more than recipes. I hold this image of all of us, glasses of Prosecco in sweating flutes, a thousand café lights, everything watercolor soft, pastel. We are happy.

My burns healed and became a part of me. When eventually men did trace their fingers, their mouths over them, I told a different story every time. Never the truth. You think because you sleep with me you have earned my past? Men. They like to possess. My scars are not on the outside. I married the only man who never asked, who never lingered on a mark of me.

July 15, 2006
Dear Vittoria,
All these long years I have been wanting to contact you. Really, I should have sooner. But I think I felt you needed to grow up to understand this letter. I have often worried that you might think that what happened was your fault, as you instigated our contact. I am sorry for allowing you to think that, if you did, for even a minute. You were a child. I the adult. And I doubt you would have approached me if I had not given you signals that made you bold. The biggest thing I must confess, and I believe you know this,

is that I would have gone forward if you had been a boy. I know it was embarrassment and rejection that made you accuse me, but I am guilty of your accusation. That's what I want to tell you. I am guilty. I attacked you.

You changed my life for the better. A few years after the Church sent me to Lake Como, I finally realized that I was a joke of a priest. I had become a priest because I am a homosexual and I thought it was the only way to save my soul. Jesus could not love me. But then I realized He could. It was as easy as that. I quit the priesthood. I am still religious.

My partner Joe and I run a small bar in Bellagio. It's called Birds of a Feather and we have outside seating with a view of the lake. It's very beautiful. I hope that maybe someday you will stop in for a drink and I will kiss your feet.

I'm sorry for all the scars I caused you.
Geno Nicola

Around the time I received this letter, the Father, the Son, and the Holy Ghost were looking like the Three Little Pigs in a house made of sticks. The sexual abuse scandals were going to huff and puff and blow that house to kingdom come. I didn't think much about it, but Alberto did. He refiled my lawsuit.

About a year later he and Mamma came to our house, two streets over in Trastevere. It was normal for them to knock on our door and come in, wine and Parrot in hand. But tonight the Prosecco was already open, riding precariously in Alberto's lap. Mamma handed me an envelope. I opened it and inside was a check in my name for 1,357,000 euros. We called Liliana, *come over*

now, bring Matteo and the kids! It was undoubtedly bad for Alberto's system, but that night we partied like millionaires.

The next morning, quick before I changed my mind, I sent half to Geno.

Pink Flamingos and
the Good Friday Massacres

Inspired by a Smithsonian magazine article.
The Klondike. Small-animal taxidermy.
A girl with a plaid accent.
And are those pink flamingos out on the iceberg?

Los Angeles 1985—Evan

E van Sterling-Gutierrez wanted to move to Alaska be-
cause Los Angeles was too shirtless for him. He had
a bit of a pigeon chest. While he would never deny the
beauty of L.A. women in bikinis, all that sun-spangled
flesh tended to give him asthma attacks. He conjured
a soft-edged hope of a dark-haired girl (no chemical
blondes, please) in an Eskimo coat, bare on a bear rug.
Fire in a stone settle. All fur and flame, forget the bikini
wax. He was self-aware enough to know this stereotype
erotica was probably a Prudhoe pipe dream. And it was
just a sidebar anyway. His primary goal in moving to
Alaska was to be near the northern lights and to com-
pose, not a concerto, but a singular piece for violin to
be played only by polar light or, alternatively, in view of
the extremely rare Alaskan pink flamingo. Evan chose
Valdez because a certain Dr. Eloise Holden, renowned
violinist, retired, lived in Valdez, and had agreed to tu-
tor Evan for a startlingly large monthly retainer.

Evan began to build his bridge to nowhere.

One Hundred and One Years Previous
Isle of Skye, Scotland 1884—Grace

Grace Budge was born on the Isle of Skye in 1884. Her mother died during that event. Dougal Budge had survived many an indignity in his twenty-three years, including acne and poverty, but losing Clare was the saddest bagpipe song of all. He submerged himself in a gallon of Talisker's that tasted of peat and rot and matched his mood until Clare's closest friend, Geillis, slapped his face and the drink from his hand and re-placed it with a baby bottle. And a baby. "*You're an em-barrassment to Clare! And I've my own to-dos. She's your bairn, get on with it!*"

Bless the man, he did. Nappies and smashed peas, bedtime stories—*The Cattie Sits in the Kiln-Ring Spin-ning.* Pink indulgences. Dougal loved the wee girl. None would say otherwise.

Because her father was so often afield with his sheep, Grace grew into a solitary soul. They lived in a white-washed croft inherited from Clare's father near a loch in Elishader. When Grace looked out the wavery window glass onto the small waves of the loch and out to the vast sea beyond, she believed she would always dwell in the meadows with the faeries and could never see her future otherwise.

At about age four a confusion came to Grace that cleared with time, but she chose to keep. On Sundays she and Dougal would attend the stone church with the clear-sounding bell and bend the knee to God. It was one of the few Catholic churches still in Scotland and did not sound its bell but five quick rings each Sunday

to keep attention from itself. When the congregation recited the prayer *Hail Mary, full of Grace, the Lord is with Thee,* the young girl would look to the small plaster statue of Mary set in a corner alcove. Grace would recall what her father told her when she asked, as every child eventually does, *Where did I come from?* and Dougal provided the usual answer, *Your mother's tummy.* Thus it seemed to Grace that Mary, who was *full of Grace,* must be her mother. This confusion gave her great confidence and power. She never told anyone that she was Mary's daughter; she would never brag. But when she wanted her mother's advice or closeness she would say her rosary, skipping the Our Fathers, as her father was in the next room, and in this way talk with her mother.

The Holy Mother was Grace's invisible friend.

Dougal hated sheep. The way they smelled when they were wet, the insipid bleating. The fact that sheep are morons. He felt he was meant for greater tasks, for he was of Viking stock and a sheepherder's staff is no long sword. Sometimes while fire gazing, he wished to have lived a hundred years before, to have been a Jacobite, even to have died in the ravage at Culloden. Dougal could have taken the at-hand adventure of a new wife. Some liked his red hair. But Dougal was cheap. He was saving, thinking on a grand escape he knew not yet where to.

While Dougal made and discarded plans, Grace had the luck to attend an exceptional school in Elishader thanks to Professor Wolcott, an English transplant and true Victorian. He was a man of science and a naturalist of independent means. He purchased a two-story croft with a large farmhouse kitchen and opened his doors to the local children three days a week to run experiments

and generally amuck. He shared his library, although the children were required to wear white cotton gloves and sit very, very still when reading. Sometimes he would do watercolor paintings of them while they read. It was basically a home of free thought, and some were not allowed to attend the queer school, which perhaps was justified, as Wolcott was at heart a pedophile. But like many an Englishman of his day, he was never one to take action. To paint Grace in the easy chair, legs slightly parted, Audubon's tome heavy in her lap, her hummingbird eyes. To paint little Jesse, mouse in hand, face of a fox. That was enough for him. His paintings were quite good.

Wolcott was fond of the Grand Expedition! They tromped Mealt Loch clear to its suicide leap over the basalt cliffs into the oblivion of the ocean. The wind blew the explorers back from the edge. Below them the water was so clear they could see the boulders beneath, all of a similar oblong shape. With her wind-teared eyes, Grace felt the boulders looked like a school of dolphins on their own expedition come to see the strangers who lived in the aerie. They tromped through the meadows with the wildflowers and every shade of green that ever lived. The students found real dinosaur bones, which Wolcott sent to Edinburgh for classification. Wolcott had the students build cages of sticks and they caught otters, pine martins, mice. And once a red-winged faeriewren, but the children let her go when Wolcott wasn't looking, she was so far from home.

Wolcott brought the captives back to his house, and depending upon the animal, they dissected, skinned, tanned or stuffed with cotton wool, boiled down to study bone structure, or ate. The students found all this deliciously gross or, sometimes, delicious. Blackbird pie

in a rosemary crust. They even did Ouija, as Wolcott also considered the spiritual world a science, but only once when the rain was so heavy the day was gray as a ghost. Wolcott lit seven candles and played the séance as a joke and told the children to keep it secret.

The students read Dickens and Darwin and never talked of God except to agree that Scotland was a godly place and that church on Sunday was his due. Grace still said her Hail Marys, still chose to believe her mother was the Lady in Blue with sad eyes and lily breath.

On the days that Wolcott kept for himself, and Grace's father was most often at work, Grace was prone to hiking on her own through the Highlands just outside their croft. In spring the meadows greened clear up to the distant tops of the Quirang, where clouds would catch and fray like spider webs. She found the faerie glens where folk had built up circles of cairns for a thousand years. In August she walked through the bristly heather, as tart a color purple as purple can be, in bloom for miles. She collected the tiny flowers for tea and saved some dried in cotton wadding simply for the joy of smelling the color in damp September. October turned all seeds loose, willy-nilly, never giving up hope of a new year even while the month dulled to brown and gray. January brought snow and the whisper of *hush, mend your clothes, rest.* Smudgy peat smoke in every chimney.

Through the seasons and years as Grace grew older, she became more adept at the things she learned at the Wolcott school. She caught her own animals, mice and small birds, skinned them at home, stuffing them with seed-pod wool and straw. Then she took a skill she leaned from Geillis (who saw to the more mundane schooling of Grace) and sewed tiny clothes for the ani-

mals, giving them personalities. Minstrel mice. An otter in a sea-green dress and wire glasses holding a tiny book with the first line of a Robert Burns poem written with a straw for a pen. *Wee, sleekit, cow'rin', tim'rous beastie.*

Grace, of course, did not invent the attribution of human traits to animals. She had seen examples of this in Wolcott's periodicals and knew that even Queen Victoria, queen of lace and violets, loved the little taxidermy tableaux. Dougal, ever one to seek a profit, took Grace and her anthropomorphics to Portree and, to the delight of both of them, sold the animals at Highlander Gifts and Biscuits. They did quite well. Dougal pocketed most of the proceeds with Grace's approval, but she did buy a wheel of Isle of Mull cheddar, her grand indulgence.

It was in Portree that Dougal met his destiny in the form of a penny flyer that made its way to Isle of Skye one knows not how:

VALDEZ TRAIL: THE ALL-AMERICAN TRAIL TO KLONDIKE GOLD!!

The flyer was caught in an updraft, pushed down the street in a wake of dust and almost fluttering into Dougal's fingers. The ink was travel-weary, the paper veined. But the words may as well have been ablaze. *Klondike!*

When Grace walked out the door of their little croft for the last time she was fourteen years old, worldly belongings winnowed down to a few traveling cases. Oh, to have taken such a thing as Scotland for granted! She turned and faced the wind that smelled of salt and sheep and meadow muck. Grace was a slight girl with a whiskey-red braid to her waist and a face covered more in

freckles than not. How could she belong anyplace else? She had never thought the world need be bigger than Elishader. Professor Wolcott came in farewell, handing her a book on North American wildlife. *"My, what a fine expedition!"* he encouraged, seeing she was about to break under the weight of her own history. Dougal picked her up like a wee bairn and placed her in the wagon.

All the schoolchildren had come with Wolcott, but they had closed ranks on Grace weeks ago when the croft went up for sale. They didn't truly come to say goodbye so much as to solidify their collective memory of Grace Budge, *the girl who went to Alaska*, for if they thought of her at all it would be in that way. Geillis brought them food for the day's journey, her husband taking them on the first leg south where they would ferry off the island and then train to the port of Southampton. Geillis gifted Grace her best bonnet with the heather-sprigs embroidered on the ribbons. *"Make ye mum proud,"* she counseled. Grace never knew that Geillis had begged Dougal to let her keep the girl—*"You're going to a place for men!"*

Good-bye! Safe journey!

They would never return.

But, then, a new horizon is an intoxicant. Who could not be entranced by the sound of a train at night, red leather seats, food in a box? Breadbasket fields. Cities of stone and soot. And at last the ship, *Good Hope*, a flexed muscle ready to take on the vast Atlantic.

First class may have been a murmur of music and crystal, beef Wellington for lunch, but third class was an enclosed pen of human livestock. Within a week the stench was enough to make a soul believe in original sin. When allowed on deck, Grace looked over the railing

and considered jumping, a mercy to die with nothing but the scouring smell of salt water. She resurrected Mary, her old childhood invisible friend, and then embodied her in the Statue of Liberty when at last they arrived at New York harbor. *Hail Mary, full of Grace.*

Still they traveled on. Now by train, always rocking. Grace looked for buffalo, that symbol of the American West, but by 1898 there were fewer than a hundred left in the wild and she never saw a one. Nor an Indian. But she did see wild mustangs and the fractured ribs of a Conestoga carcass. It was a vast land with haughty mountains—yes they were purple, lakes of salt, basins of alkali. Forests thick as thieves. Rivers too wide to understand. It was a land that would *just as soon kill ya as take ya captive.* When at last they pulled into the Oakland Pier Station, San Francisco glittering across the bay, Grace and Dougal were exhausted. It was September. They would stay until spring, maybe they would sleep till spring.

Dougal took cheap rooms in the Bowery. It was honkytonk at night but Grace could hear doves in the morning. Dougal found work on the docks. Grace reached the Mission District in her wanderings and there it was: Woodward's Gardens. Garden, amusement park, museum, art gallery, zoo, and aquarium built by Robert B. Woodward with his forty-niner gold. Look what gold can build! Grace imagined going back to Scotland and building such a place. She became a ticket girl. But after her shift she once again became a naturalist.

Such animals she had never seen. A tiger. Monarch, one of the last wild grizzly bears on the California coast and poster boy for the state flag. Monkeys always ready for a game of Monkey See Monkey Do. Cormorants. A

conservatory of butterflies in silk-sari colors. Three pink flamingos from Florida, a mother and two babies brought in just this summer, high-stepping a cattail pond.

One day in October, Grace garnered her courage and showed Mr. Woodward her anthropomorphics. Three mice made up as forty-niners, little picks and pans, sour-dough box. *"You made these, girl?"* the great man asked; she nodded, her face a full blush. *"Hum hum hum, let me think on this,"* he said, nodding his head, and walked away. Three days later he set her up a taxidermy shop and fur did fly.

There came a December night when the wind blew in from the east with a story to tell of the Great Plains. Those who listened, all the birds and the little beasts, headed into the trees and under the doorsteps. There was a general burrowing. But people only heard the pia-no and the beautiful sound of Champagne. They never heard the hoot owls' warning.

In the morning when Grace woke up there was an un-precedented six inches of snow on the streets of San Francisco. And the flamingos were dead. Grace stuffed them.

Come spring, Grace packed the pink flamingos in a special trunk and took them with her when she and Dougal headed to Valdez. If Mr. Woodward had fore-knowledge of the flamingos' northern migration, it is lost to history.

When Dougal and Grace stepped off the steamer and into Valdez, Dougal realized he had made a grave mis-take. He should have left Grace in Scotland or at least in San Francisco. Valdez was a made-up city, made up by the penny-flyer men; there was no city. It was a hubbub of tents with a few raw buildings. It smelled of pinesap

and shit. Everybody was scratching something. Dougal and Grace walked bewildered between the rows of canvas. It was quite clear to Grace that she would not be able to make a living selling anthropomorphics in Valdez, but her eviscerating skills might come in handy.

Eighty-Seven Years Forward
Valdez, Alaska 1985—Evan

Evan Sterling-Gutierrez rented a bungalow on Klutina Street in Valdez and took a job at the Eskimo Pie shop, which didn't sell ice cream but actual pies. Salmonberry and blueberry with a Sitka spruce kicker in the crust. No vanilla here. Uki Begay owned the bakery and she hired Evan because she felt sorry for him. He looked like he would freeze to death come winter. Uki was always one to tend a broken wing. Evan knew he had that effect on people; he knew it was because he was too thin and because his pupils were just a bit larger than normal. But Evan wasn't weak. Within a month he had introduced quiche to the menu with an imported Isle of Mull cheddar baked right into the crust. Next up: frittata.

Three days a week Evan left Eskimo Pie at the afternoon closing and rode his used scooter to Dr. Eloise Holden's house, violin case bandoliered to his back. He arrived smelling of fresh air and flour with an eggy back. To Dr. Holden, Evan began to look like Lolita.

Evan was born on November 12, 1966, on the Sunset Strip, Los Angeles. His mother, Evangeline Sterling, had come to L.A. on the hippie caravan—that great western migration of Volkswagen buses converging on the California coast. She didn't want to be a Baptist anymore. Evangeline joined a commune on Mulholland

Drive, which was just the house of some Richie Rich kid whose parents were spending the season in Europe. By fall they would all have to clear out. Maria the Mexican maid kept them in line with her feather duster and black eyes that easily conveyed the message to not even think about sitting on the Elvis-blue-suede couch. She kept a silver ice pick in her apron pocket and wasn't afraid to use it. Maria had a habit, almost a tic, of making the sign of the cross while she vacuumed around the stinky sleeping bodies at two in the afternoon. Evangeline would wake to this sight, and although she would not admit it to herself, it gave her comfort to see that benevolent gesture, a reminder of home. Sometimes Evangeline would get up and help Maria clean, and Maria would make her green banana–mango smoothies.

Evangeline spent her days trying to get signed at modeling agencies. God knows the longer she spent in L.A., the more she looked like Twiggy. She spent her nights on the Sunset Strip at the Whiskey a Go Go or the purple and gold Pandora's Box built on a traffic island. Meeting the dawn walking down the avenue of tall, narrow palms on her dance-weary legs, the high-up pom-pom fronds waved to her. *Hello, goodbye*, she never could tell which.

At summer's end it was obvious to Maria that Evangeline was pregnant. Evangeline knew who the father was, but he had left for Mendocino to grow marijuana and whale-watch and there was no forwarding address. Neither of them had known she was pregnant when he left. Maria took Evangeline to live with her in the barrio on the Eastside. On November 12, 1966, Evangeline was seven months along but she wanted to go to the rally at Pandora's Box—it was all over the radio—to pro-

test the new curfew and loitering laws aimed at getting teenagers off the streets. A thousand people showed up.

That night Sunset Strip smelled of patchouli and pot, pre emission control exhaust, and teen spirt. Music pulsed. Kids in tie-dye and fringe—*Isn't that Peter Fonda?* It was beautiful. But the police showed up with their bullhorns spouting the blue-hair bully-pulpit line. With their bully sticks. Pandora's Box turned the music up louder, outside speakers vibrating. The kids moved in a psychedelic wave. No one would think that L.A.'s Finest would hit a pregnant girl, not that girl with long black hair and the little bangs, the one with too-big pupils, right in the stomach with his pig-stick. But he did.

No one could hear Evangeline's scream, or they did hear it, but everyone was screaming. Her water broke. Her baby began to follow the exit signs. It's hard to go upstream in a riot. She made her way to the back of Pandora's Box and gave birth to Evan behind the trash bins. The first song Evan ever heard was "19th Nervous Breakdown." He would have had one himself if he wasn't so busy learning to breathe. Evan's birth certificate lists his birthplace as the Corner of Sunset Boulevard and Crescent Heights.

By the time Evan got out of the hospital, all five pounds two ounces of him, Evangeline was gone and Maria was his mother. *Dios mio.* It wasn't easy growing up white in the barrio but Maria was a saint. Evangeline was nothing but a single black-and-white photo of a young girl in a peasant dress with sunglasses so dark Evan couldn't even make out her eyes. Evangeline became a piñata for all his angst.

While the neighborhood *chicos* learned to play with switchblades, Evan learned to play scales on his garage-sale

violin. He was first chair by his freshman year. When he played, eyes closed, he saw wavery colors. An aurora borealis of music. Perhaps this was not such an amazing thing except for the fact that Evan was completely color-blind when his eyes were open. The ophthalmologist conjectured Evan probably had color sight at birth but had lost it, a not unknown medical event. Thus he was conjuring, with the aid of music, his color-memory. Synesthesia.

When Evan was around ten years old he made a little boy pinky-swear promise to himself that he would go to Alaska and see the northern lights. Would they be nothing but stingy shades of gray? Or if he played the perfect violin piece, eyes closed, and then opened his eyes, would the sky show its true colors?

At age ten, regaining his color sight through an act of the heart had seemed possible; at nineteen, improbable. Likely impossible. But he had graduated from high school and college was financially beyond him. He had the small proceeds of the savings bond Maria had bought him when he was an infant. Call it a gap year, an adventure. Plus, in *Theories and Oddities*, a magazine that appealed to him, he had read about the extremely rare sightings of the Alaskan pink flamingo last seen in the vicinity of Valdez, Alaska. Where Dr. Eloise Holden, renowned retired violinist, lived. A trifecta.

Valdez may be the perfect place for a color-blind person. The Prince William Sound flows through the Valdez Narrows into a glacier-fed alluvial bay. Come winter the surrounding Chugach mountains shoulder more snowfall than any other single place on earth. An obliteration of color. Orcas and eagles, Eskimos and black bears. A landscape of darkening shades quite simply too beautiful to be in full color—the human mind

would explode. It's a very Buddhist place: The sky is the color of sky, water the color of water, the pines and mountains dare no other tones. Here live the elemental colors of the earth—the rest is frivolous. The whole landscape could be reduced to black ink on rice paper in seven serious strokes.

Until the northern lights show up and the polar sky turns Berserker. Who cares why? Whatever scientists say, they're wrong. Everyone knows true art needs no explanation.

Uki Begay was built like a totem pole. She could tell a story without opening her mouth. A mix of Copper River Delta Eyak and Tlingit, she carried her stout body with the dignity of the disenfranchised. She wasn't interested in living in an igloo or whale fat. She just wanted her slice of the American pie and to that end she sold it, a piece at a time. Uki was twenty-five when Evan came to town. She really wasn't intending to stay in Alaska. She was toying with college admission and student loan forms. Perhaps vet school; all those broken wings.

Evan was changing Eskimo Pie. Next he added green chilaquiles. He taught Uki to make homemade tortillas. Pretty soon people were showing up for breakfast and Uki had to buy some tables and chairs and put in an espresso machine that made a sound like a whale's blow. Tablecloths. It was nice. The days lasted all night.

On one such day Evan and Uki were sharing a piece of chokeberry pie after closing and he asked if she had ever heard of the Alaskan pink flamingo. "Sure, everybody has," was her casual response. Evan's heart felt anything but casual.

"What do you know about them?" He pushed his

fork into the lemon-zest crust. He acted like it meant nothing to him.

"Well, it was that self-made naturalist Grace Budge who first took photos of them. Out on the ice floes on the Beaufort Sea. She and her husband photographed and collected Alaskan birds. She kept eggs and wings and, I don't know, all sorts of body parts. I think she stuffed them. They still have a lot of her collection over at the museum." Uki paused. "Nobody really goes there."

Evan did. All those pretty little feathers.

Dr. Eloise Holden was surprised at herself. She was a renowned violinist who had played the Vienna Opera House and the Scala in Milan. The Roxy when she felt like wearing fishnets. She'd slept with Warren Beatty. Taught a child prodigy from North Korea. At fifty-nine, what was left to do? She had come to a point in her life where all her passions had passed out. Time to Garbo. Valdez would do. She bought an acre of land up on Blueberry Hill and built a Craftsman in the Sitka spruce that looked like it was a hundred years old. Slate roof with moss. Stone fireplaces, a (faux but quite well-done) polar bear rug. When she received the first letter from an Evan Sterling-Gutierrez asking for violin instruction she tossed it in the fire, where it burned in green and blue. By the fifth letter she felt forced to respond. She named an impossible price for anyone named Gutierrez. The boy agreed! Well, why not take him on then? She was bored.

Eloise thought not much of Evan when he arrived. Skinny, surprisingly white, effusive but not nervous. He held his violin with excellent posture, his gut strings of high quality although the violin was not. There were teeth marks in the wood of the bow; well, she could un-

derstand that, who didn't want to destroy the exquisite?

Eloise decided to take Evan through the ten best violin pieces known to man. Saint-Saens's Introduction and Rondo Capriccioso with its stormy arpeggios. Bach's Partita No. 2, Chaconne, with the serrated chords and agitation. No matter if he had played some of them before. He must play them *her* way to *her*. It was rather exhilarating to watch the pressure of this young man's style. He was good. She would *not* tell him so, only yell, *Again!*

Eloise began to dress for Evan's lessons. Oh, still the black stretch pencil pants and flats, but perhaps a falling-down up-do? She wondered if there was a decent colorist in Valdez or if she would have to drive to Anchorage.

Evan loved his lessons with Dr. Holden—now *"Call me Eloise."* The woman was intense. Later in the long artic twilight he would work on his own original piece, *Score for the Northern Lights.*

Evan made his way to the Valdez Museum and Curiosities, which was only open when a cruise ship was in port. Mrs. Shelton was the curator and owner. She had everything from Eskimo baby moccasins with seed beads to nineteenth-century flocked wallpaper from the Valdez Hotel. She had purchased for $10,000 a totem by the great carver Frank Steward. In the dusty back was the Grace Budge and Henry Wilson Room.

It was quiet as a nesting bird in the Grace-room.

One Hundred and Three Years Previous
Valdez 1898—Grace

Timing is everything.

The truth of the matter was that there was no "All American Route," no easy passage linking Prince William Sound with the interior. It was a hoax promoted by the steamship companies based on inaccurate descriptions by U.S. Army Lieutenant William Abercrombie. The stampeders who reached Valdez in 1898–99 were faced with the options of going back, staying in Valdez, or heading out to the Klondike over the Valdez and Klutina glaciers, twice as long and steep as the Canadian route. A year later the Army would cut a trail through Keystone Canyon and over Thompson Pass. But Dougal was a year early.

"Puss-in-boots, I want you to go back to San Francisco," said Dougal over their campfire.

"Dad, don't call me that. I'm fifteen. I'm not going back," said Grace, stirring the beans. "We can stay here and try prospecting in Copper Canyon."

The fire did all the talking. "I came for the Klondike," Dougal whispered at last.

"No you didn't! You came for gold. Who cares where?"

"Grace, don't cry." Dougal could see that his daughter was breaking down.

"I'm not crying," Grace said, standing up. "I'm deciding. I'm deciding for you. I know you think it's too dangerous to take me but you're afraid to leave me here. I'm afraid too! That you're going to get scurvy or fall in an ice crevasse." He couldn't deny it. "But, Dad, just go. I'll wait for you."

"How can I leave you?" asked the father.

"How can you not?" asked the daughter.

Dougal dished out the beans and a braised, white-tipped rabbit Grace had trapped. She was good at that. "What will you do?" Dougal had accepted her proposi-

tion.

"I've been talking to Mary Kate," said Grace. Dougal pictured the young woman and her husband from Texas. "Jared's going too. So we decided. There's a lot of mountain berries just about ripe. We're pickin' 'em before the bears do and making preserves. Every stupid miner in this place is going to the Klondike with Mary Kate & Grace Scurvy-Cure."

So Dougal went. He never did come back.

Day by day Grace watched the slow stampede climb over the first ridge. Many would die. A paltry few would become gold-pan-and-pickax rich. Some, pickax murderers who got away with it. The majority would come home with nothing but a Great American Story for their grandchildren. When Dougal joined the exodus he so quickly blurred into the single-file line Grace had no choice but to wave goodbye to all of them. *Godspeed, late snow!* Then she and Mary Kate set to the bushes like furious squirrels. They put preserves in every available canister. In a sad act of release and acceptance, Grace filled a long-empty perfume bottle of her mother's she had carried from Elishader with pure juice and a single seed. She called it Heart's Balm and sold it to a young prospector for a good price. She was never going home. To the most pathetic, the girls gave their preserves for free.

That first winter was harsh. Six hundred inches of snow and nights that lasted all day. By now Grace and Mary Kate had managed squatters' rights on a one-room cabin with a potbelly stove that a prospector had quit. There came a night when Grace awoke to a commotion; most probably a bear in town, poor thing, it would go *from shot to pot* by dawn. She looked outside. *The northern lights had come!* Grace and Mary Kate put

on their boots, blankets over their heads and shoulders, and went out. To Grace it seemed a thing almost worth losing Scotland for, maybe worth the beating of all the faeries' wings on the Isle of Skye . . .

Come spring the prospectors started coming back with horrible stories of deprivation. Prospectors began to move sick people out of the interior and back to relief cabins in Valdez. Mary Kate's husband came back on his own two legs with just enough gold to cover their expenses home to Texas. He wasn't broken, but he was done. "We got separated at Hell's Gate," said Jared to Grace, soon as he could bring himself to break embrace from Mary Kate. Grace knew he was referring to the Klutina River rapids. "It was like we were salmon being grizzly-slapped . . ." Jared stopped. There was no kindness in going on. "I just don't know what happened to him, Grace. I just don't know." Jared and Mary Kate left on the next steamer to Vancouver. They wanted Grace to go with them but she could not bring herself to give up on Dougal. As the steamer pulled away she had a terrible feeling that the foghorn emptiness would never leave her.

Grace spent her summer making edibles out of anything she could forage or trap. Rabbit with sorrel, salt-and-sage flatbread cooked in her potbelly stove. And she found little pieces of gold herself, one pea-sized nugget in a cold stream. Every day she watched the black line of prospectors coming home while others headed out on the new route being cut through Copper Canyon. No matter how many times she thought she saw Dougal, it was never so.

Two years went by and Grace began to wonder if she should leave. But she had come to love the rough place. It wasn't the boomtown that interested her. It was the clar-

ity of light, in the sea and of the sky, the reaction of the
forest when the bear padded through, and all the birds
in their cacophony. It was the northern lights and their
wavery message she was still trying to interpret. Every cul-
ture has a mythology for the aurora—slain enemies rising
in revenge, spirits of the harpooned beluga sounding the
night sky, or even the Scottish version of Merry Danc-
ers engaged in deadly battle. But through the long nights
that Grace watched the bolts of color she found herself
drawn more to the Norse legend of the Valkyries, the war-
rior women on horseback leading fallen soldiers to rest at
Valhalla. She came to think of the lights as comfort for
the lost miners, to catch her father's wink in the deepest
of the greens. She knew Dougal was gone. Who was left
for her? How could she leave the place closest to his lost
bones? She sat a quandary through another season, an-
other six hundred inches of snow.

Henry Wilson of Old Lyme, Connecticut, came
back from the Klondike with pockets full of nuggets.
He had stayed gone a long time; had moved from stake
to stake on a whim or a whisper of a strike. He never
struck a vein, but he struck it rich enough. Not for Nob
Hill in San Francisco or even to buy a tin-can goat farm
back in Connecticut. But it occurred to Henry Wilson
that it wouldn't take much to live well in Valdez. If he
could find something worth staying for.

Henry was twenty years old, and what better sight
than a red-headed gal with a plaid accent. Prospector
pants, don't-mess-with-me knife strapped to her thigh.
Henry bought a potpie from her and along with pay-
ment put an empty perfume bottle in the palm of her
upturned hand. And shortly after asked for that very
hand in marriage.

They were never officially married. Grace lost faith in the power of her invisible friend when she saw the Klondike-riddled bodies come back from the interior, when her father failed to come home. It wasn't a conscious decision. It just seemed that Nature was enough of a mystery; she sought no additional obscura. They went into a grove of aspen, song sparrows for witness and a white-tailed bunny that Grace momentarily thought of catching for supper.

"Grace Budge," said Henry, taking her hand, his atremble, "I take you for my wife and I promise to never leave you unless you want me gone. I promise to be kind and to give you everything you ever ask for."

"Henry Wilson," said Grace, "I take you for my husband and I promise to be kind and to give you everything you ever ask for. And I will never ask you to leave." A small wind trembled the aspen leaves in a kind of applause when Henry leaned in for his wife's kiss. He was tentative; Grace was not. She had lost her mother, Scotland, her father, and Mary Kate. For once she wasn't going to lose.

The rest of the season was spent building a *sung* up on Salmonberry Hill. The small cabin had a wraparound deck in a wraparound forest. On the second floor they positioned a telescope ordered from Seattle, pointed over the horizon to the tidal flats and the long fjord. They bought Pendleton blankets. At night they drank tea, or whiskey with tea, or whiskey, and played the game What Shall We Do with Our Lives? Henry had enough gold set aside that this was not a faerie-lark. Alaska was their oyster.

Grace went back to making her anthropomorphics. She pored over her Audubon *Birds of America* book

gifted to her by Professor Wolcott in long-ago Scotland. She lingered on the drawing of the Eskimo curlew with its cinnamon wing lining, this tundra shorebird. One night, when the sun refused to set, it occurred to Grace that while she could never be an artist like Audubon, she could do a photographic book on the birds of Alaska. She ordered a Kodak Brownie from the Sears catalogue and set off to the rest of her life.

Oh, that the world had all the film of Grace Budge! There's that photo of Henry, about forty, out on the ice fields by the Beaufort Sea with the sled and Husky dogs, all eyes hand-colorized, barely blue. Just blue enough to convey the cold. The tufted puffin with his orange nose insisting he wasn't a laughing matter. The good posture of the bald eagles who seemed to know they were a symbol. Sometimes it was what she left out. The Eskimo curlew flying out of the frame, on her way to extinction.

Grace also had those infamous pink flamingo shots, five or six different locales, the last surviving photo hanging in the Valdez Museum and Curiosities. A mother and two babies on a tabletop iceberg, floating away on the Arctic sea like it was a party on Miami Beach.

Sixty-Six Years Forward
Good Friday, Valdez 1964—Grace

On Good Friday, March 27, 1964, Grace was eighty years old and Henry eighty-four. Yes, they were old, but rustically elegant like antler chandeliers, or reindeer. Grace delivered a set of new prints to The Cannery Gallery and the couple walked down to the dock to watch the supply ship S.S. *Chena* unload. It was always a bit of an event, and a few of the sailors were tossing oranges to

the kids. There was a certain pure light on the sea from the late afternoon sun that drew Grace and Henry into its halo. Grace's long gray braid sparked silver in the kind light; Henry took her hand. He never let it go.

Halfway between Valdez and Anchorage, fifteen miles deep into the Prince William Sound, great slabs of the earth got up and moved around. A 9.2 magnitude earthquake, the second most powerful ever recorded, struck at 5:36 p.m. The Seattle Space Needle, 1,200 miles away, wobbled. There was a great heaving of underwater landslides that muscled the ocean into tsunamis. Valdez was always a temporary town built on sediment and dream. It took only seconds for the unstable ground upon which the dock was built to cruelly plunge into the sea. The *Chena* rose on a wave some thirty outrageous feet into the sky and landed where the dock had been. Everyone on the pier was lost as well as three of the poor sailors who had been tossing oranges.

Of Henry and Grace: the ocean ground and polished their bones to sea glass and their hearts to aquamarine. That's all we know of them.

Twenty-One Years Forward
Valdez 1985—Evan

Over the long summer days Evan continued to work at Eskimo Pie, study the ten top violin pieces in the world, and work on his original violin piece. When his eyes were closed and music was rippling off his fingers, color soaked his mind. When he opened his eyes the world was chalk and ink. He still had the admittedly childish hope that if he played the perfect piece, his interior color memory would finally leak into his open eyes.

Through the summer evenings and into the fall, Uki taught Evan to fly fish on the Copper River. They packed a blanket, a cold-chicken-and-beer dinner. For dessert, she tried to get him to eat *akutaq*, made the traditional way—moose fat swirled with cloudberries. "Come on, try it," Uki said holding out a spoon like Evan was a baby. "It's the real stuff, not the knock-off crap made with Crisco." How could he say no?

Uki taught him to cast the line rather than the lure, the transfer of *influence*, the beautiful waves that travel through the line as it unfurls. Dry-fishing in the heavy reeds to keep the lure on top, wet in the open stream. The funny little lures with bits of feathers. It rather fascinated Evan—kids from East L.A. don't fish. Uki gave him several back issues of her *American Fisherman* magazine. It was in the classified ads of these magazines that Evan found his personal bonanza.

Dr. Holden, *"Please, call me Eloise,"* was depleting his funds. She obviously had no sense of money or she thought she was Harvard.

Evan went back to the Grace Budge and Henry Wilson Room. Even with a cruise ship docked, the museum didn't get a great deal of traffic. Most tourists wanted to see Old Valdez, the city before the Good Friday earthquake, before the entire municipality was rebuilt on higher ground. They wanted to see buildings sliced open like dollhouses, the splintered twistiness of everything. Rotting wallpaper lifting on the wind like prayer flags. Everybody loves to rubberneck a disaster. Thus the museum at best only had a few tourists at any time. Evan had the Grace Room to himself. He looked at the flamingo photo. He could tell by the shading that Grace had colorized just the tips of birds' feathers, a whisper of

pink. Evan went to the huge wood cabinets and opened up the display drawers that held hundreds of her specimens. The drawers glided. Lying on parchment paper were disembodied wings. Feathers and feathers. Snow goose, blue-winged teal, ruddy duck. Five single (assumedly pink) flamingo plumes set in a specialty box.

Evan made his heist.

Come to find out there is a spectrum of fly-fishing angler who longs for the 1800s. Horsehair lines and Nottingham reels. Fly-tyers who insist on authentic plumes and will pay outrageously, even though the trout don't know the difference. For Evan, it was a mail-order feather Klondike. His customers found him through a small ad he placed in the classified section of the *American Fisherman*.

Christmas Day. Evan was sleeping in when the yapping of his neighbor's stupid Yorkie, Archie, woke him. The sun was barely up at 10 a.m., the sky a golden bunting. The dog was going insane. God, he hated that mutt. It's embarrassing to own a small dog in Alaska; Huskies don't bark. Evan opened his front door to yell at Archie just in time to see a massive gray coyote trot by with the poor creature in its jaws. Archie was wearing his Christmas sweater. *Jesus Christ*, Evan thought. *Someone should loose a coyote on the purse-dogs of Rodeo Drive.*

The sun would be going down around 3:30 p.m. Eloise had invited him up to her house for *a special surprise,* which he hoped was going to be money, some kind of Christmas bonus, although he knew that made no real sense. Then he was having dinner with Uki. The northern lights were expected and they were going to watch together. His original score was complete. This was the night.

There were lit candles set out in the snow leading up the stone path to Eloise's holly-wreathed front door. Evan let himself in, as had become their habit, and headed to the conservatory. The fire was crackling to itself about destruction in flames shot blue. Evan took in the room; he knew it well: ruby velvet curtains and a crystal decanter of claret. The (faux) polar-bear rug. But here was something unexpected: Eloise was lying on the pelt wearing a quite beautiful (not faux) full-length snow beaver coat. A naked thigh, a half breast, a patch of pelt exposed. Evan's body admitted that Eloise was quite attractive for her age, in this light, in this near approximation to his northern fantasy. He felt fizzy. Eloise patted the rug. A rookie predator error. She should have stroked it. The pat-pat summoned a memory of Maria inviting him to sit by her on the couch and watch *Happy Days*. Evan's body changed its mind and said, "Split, dude," and he did.

"Shit!" said Eloise. She downed the rest of her claret as she rose from the rug, catching her foot in the faux polar teeth in her hurry to leave the scene. Even though it was Christmas Day Eloise, still naked under fur, called her agent. She didn't say hello. "Fuck the Great White North, George. I'm coming home. Book me some gigs."

George didn't say hello either. "What took ya' so long, beautiful?" was all he asked.

One month later she was booked for the Sydney Opera and the Alaska house was up for vacation rental: *Pristine setting perfect for sport, solitude, or romance.*

* * *

Evan escaped his boy-toy adventure and made his way to Uki's house. Roast-goose-and-sweet-potato-pie later they drove about an hour north of Valdez to a little spit

of beach poking out into the sound. They had been here before; it wasn't a secret place. Some long-ago someone had constructed a heavy canvas tepee with strong poles and a potbellied stove venting out the top. While Evan tuned up his violin, Uki unloaded blankets for the floor of the tepee. It was packed dirt, pogonipped by the cold; her soft mukluks crunched on the filigreed ice. There was usually a small stack of logs inside the tepee and Uki brought more just in case, or to leave behind. She could hear Evan's scales. She put on water for tea, English Earl Grey. "What, no birchbark?" Evan always teased her. But she knew birchbark was for achy joints and rashes. She also had a silver flask of golden whiskey.

Evan set the violin close (not too close) to the stove to let the wood soak up the heat, and he and Uki sat in fold-up beach chairs just outside the tepee, an old itchy Pendleton on their knees. They sipped their tea and watched the stars come out. "Archie was eaten by a coyote today," Evan said.

Uki gasped. "That's awful."

"He had on his Christmas sweater, the one with Rudolph on it."

Uki turned to Evan. She started laughing. "Oh, that's awful," she repeated but she kept on laughing. She was his kind of girl. She was wearing her anorak with the bone buttons and fur-lined hood. "Well, here's to Archie," she finally managed, breaking out the silver flask.

At last the northern lights. For Evan it was only grays and ghosts. He took up his violin and played a melancholy piece that made Uki feel falling stars and whale songs. Eagles with their terrible talons. Things that rushed, water and the Arctic hare. Things that waited for spring. The booming of blue-bottomed icebergs.

It was a song of Alaska. Evan played with eyes closed, colors wavering through the notes of his internal aurora borealis.

His song gave Uki a great courage, a courage she had been waiting for. She quietly went to the truck, pulled a bundle out of the back, and went inside the tepee.

Toward the end of the score Evan prepared to open his eyes. He had done everything he could: He'd come to Alaska, studied with the master, practiced, stolen the wings of birds, composed his heart song and played it to the Wild. He wanted to see in real life the memory colors of his mind. Still playing, he opened his eyes to a beautiful sketch-study in coal and lead. Evan might have cried to lose his silly dream, but as he turned he saw Uki. She was just inside the open flaps of the tepee, backlit by potbelly glow. She was lying on some kind of white fur rug, minus the paws and head (actually a flokati wool rug she had ordered from San Francisco). She still had on her now-unbuttoned anorak and mukluks but was clearly bare beneath. Uki outweighed Evan by some fifty pounds. Her thighs were Vikings. She was an Eskimo Berserker, warrior of the North. She stroked the flokati.

Four Years Later(Exactly Twenty-five Years After the Earthquake)
Good Friday, Valdez 1989

The little sea otter, who didn't know she was an otter but thought of herself as something that might translate as Fur Ball, wrapped a dark ribbon of kelp around her middle to keep anchored amid the currents. Fur Ball floated on her back. Reaching into the skin-pouch on her chest, she pushed aside her foraging rock and

retrieved a bunch of thistly purple sea urchin she had just caught. She laid the urchins on her stomach and pulled them apart with her retractable claws. Breakfast done, she cleaned her fur like her life depended on it, then took a nap. She had no idea how cute she looked bobbing in the currents, her little paws crisscrossed on her gray-speckled chest, her long silver whiskers and her triangle ears.

While the sea otter slept, 10.8 million gallons of un-refined Alaskan crude oil poured into the Prince William Sound and inexorably spread to the shore waters. The otter woke up engulfed in sludge. In a panic she used her paws, her tongue to try and remove the oil, but with every wave she blackened. She shut her ears and her nose to keep the oil out. But the oil matted her fur. With her fur in clumps, water for the first time in her life penetrated to her skin. She had the thickest fur of any sea mammal; she did not know *cold*. The sea otter started to shake and she felt confused. She quit trying to clean herself. She let the kelp ribbon go and dropped her favorite rock. She tried to blink the black out of her eyes, to see something that she would recognize. It was so cold. Her heart slowed. Stopped.

Because the oil matted her fur.

The second Good Friday massacre took place on March 24, 1989, when the tanker *Exxon Valdez* struck Bligh Reef, twenty-five miles out from Valdez. The animals didn't stand a chance; they never do when it comes to humans.

In the years after the oil spill, scientists were extremely interested in comparing the DNA of the animals before and after the event. Thus the Grace Budge and Henry Wilson Room rose to great importance.

Three professors from Stanford University came to the Valdez Museum and Curiosities and Mrs. Shelton was quite proud to be able to show them Grace's life's work. She herself had not looked at the specimens in years (because really they were quite dull). But when she opened up the gliding display drawers she was shocked to find a great deal of the birds' wings missing. They had flown the coop. It was a feather-heist of horrific, national scientific loss.

No one thought to Sherlock the culprit in the classified ads of *American Fisherman*.

Some weeks later a large unmarked box arrived at the museum. When Mrs. Shelton opened the package she literally shrieked with joy which caused her to drop the box on her foot, breaking her big toe. Inside were not all but many of the missing wings. The willow ptarmigan, the coot and killdeer. The Arctic warbler and the yellow-eyed snowy owl. And a single pink flamingo plume the scientists were never going to figure out. A lot of the specimens had been plucked, but not completely denuded. Mrs. Shelton immediately called Stanford.

Not all was lost.

Evan finally got his first viewing of the extremely rare, some say legendary Alaskan pink flamingo. It was around the time of the second Good Friday massacre. Uki was going to college and Evan was on fire with the Phoenix Philharmonic. Maria lived with them and filled the adobe house with the dry smell of chili peppers and coriander. She was certain spicy foods would help bring on a grandchild.

The sighting was on the night of Evan and Uki's first wedding anniversary, it was in fact his anniversary gift. The couple were in bed. When Evan spread Uki's to-

tem-pole thighs to get at what he affectionately called her *Eskimo pie*, his line of sight was distracted. Carved in the smooth cedar of her inner thigh was a flamingo! Not in the ubiquitous position of a lawn ornament but in full, glorious, awkward flight. So there could be no doubt as to the type of flamingo, Uki had had the tattoo artist add a twist of calligraphy beneath the bird that spelled: *PINK*.

Evan was similarly tickled.

Silver

A quiet tale of loud events.

In late October or early November the first snow would fall. It always started at night, like a secret, a quiet descending. By morning the last of the autumn leaves would give up the ghost of color and hunker down to the serious job of mulching. Those still stuck on the trees, held by a last woody thread, would freeze and shiver, and when the sun came up it would strike the leaves silver.

It was the early 1930s and I was a young boy in Iowa. I loved the first snow, the promise of ice skates and mittens, warm milk. I would run outside and stomp through the drifts and pull the frozen air into my lungs. I would go to Jerry's house and his ma would give us that milk and maybe a cookie. I never asked. I never knocked on their door. I knew if I hung out on the street, if I just watched the leaves fall from the trees like pieces of silver, if I just watched the black cat pad across the ice, her paws doing the quickstep, I knew Jerry would show up. And all the quiet would shatter.

Here he comes now, red scarf, red hair, corduroys and rubber boots, a whirlwind of a friend. He made all my noise for me. "Louie, Louie, Louie, it snowed!" he would shout, like I didn't know it snowed until he told me. The cat ran away. Jerry knocked into a tree and snow sparkled on his head and he laughed and grabbed my

arm. We ran down the streets in the still morning, lace curtains drawn over ice-etched windows, milk out on the steps. We ran into the fields and beyond to the border forest, where we were alone and the only one who came before us on this cold day was the silver fox I saw loping ahead in the distance.

For Jerry it wouldn't do that the fox made the only mark in the snow. The fact that the fox prints were pure and made a kind of fretwork pattern didn't matter to him. Jerry peed in big loop-de-loops branding the snow. So I did it too, not because I wanted to, but because I did what Jerry did. We frittered the morning away, scattering birds, rousing the wind, breaking the fragile ice on the edges of the stream and sucking the pieces like cold candy. Then we went to Jerry's house and sat by the fire and dripped dry reading comic books and smelling our own smelly socks.

It seemed a good start to a winter. My brothers and sister are older than I am—Frank and Ernest, names to live up to, and Rose, a flower name. We are a team. We keep everyone but family away from our house. We keep an eye out. If Rose sees Jerry coming up the street, she sends me out before he reaches the door. It never strikes him as odd that I anticipate his knock and the door is open, my arms climbing into my coat, shutting the door behind me, before his fist meets the green paint. He's oblivious. I think he's oblivious.

It isn't as if the town doesn't know about us. Everybody knows that Pa left us and remarried and has a second family in Des Moines and even has a new son, also named Ernest. People talk. I worry about the day Ernest meets Ernest. Will it be civil or fisticuffs? I worry that Pa will have another son and name him Louis and then

I will become a ghost son. I never have the nerve to ask Ernest how he feels, but without talking about it we all take to calling him Ed and he never goes back.

I know because I hear the Aunties talk that Ma used to be a little girl with braids and ribbons in her hair and skin like summer milk in a pail. I know she worked for Quaker Oats. In Iowa, we consider the image on the Quaker Oats container a kind of Uncle Sam. I know that the doctor had to cut me out of Ma's stomach and I don't know what that means, except it makes me feel guilty.

Ma is straight of back and wears her braids pinned up crisscross. But she whispers to herself all day and forgets the chores and Rose does the Ma work and Frank and Ed take care of the Pa things. I'm still considered the baby so I get easy stuff like carrying the wood in and the ashes out.

When I came home that first winter afternoon from Jerry's house the light of the day was already on the wane. If there was a look in Ma's eye that afternoon, some shadow of what was in her mind, I missed it. I can catch the disappearing fox on the horizon, I can see the draft of the bird's wing, but I can't for one instant catch the movement of my own life. Had I known, I would have had an asthma attack for sure.

In the morning, Rose, Frank, and Ed go to work. Ed has a light step because he is getting ready to take a wife named Agnes. Agnes is a corn-fed Iowa beauty sure to go to fat, but not yet. Right now she looks a perfect pudding. We like her and the noise she brings inside our house. The tick-tock of the clock diminishes when she is in the room. Frank plans to have a corn farm and I plan to eat his corn straight off the stalk, just pull back the

husk. Rose wants to go to California, see the ocean and feel the sun on her shoulders even in winter, and eat an orange that does not come once a year in a Christmas stocking. These are the things I know about my family.

I wake up and expect to get ready for school but Ma is standing in my doorway with her faded red suitcase and a smaller valise which she hands to me and tells me to fill with a pair of jeans and a shirt. I do it and put in my favorite little blanket too; Rose calls it my baby blanket, but I don't. I assume we are going to see the Aunties. We go outside and the cold slams us back, but Ma steels her spine, takes my hand, we start walking. The Aunties live the other way.

I've never been to the train station before. It's sooty and all the snow is melted into gray slush and the sun has come out and turned the rails to mercury. A train goes by in a hiss of steam and the rails glitter like mercury. I stare after the train until it disappears. There's a lot of noise and rush rush rush. Ma buys the tickets and it's "All Aboard" for Chicago. I have no memory of the trip except I drank a grape soda. What a color to drink!

Chicago. I can't tell you what happened to Ma. I can't tell you how our hands became separated in the crowd, waiting for the light to change, walking through the valley of the buildings where there is but a slice of sky at the top and the doors open in circles that run round and round like a carnival ride. I can't say how I lost her. How did she lose hold of my hand? Did she just lose her grip on my woolly mitten, did the crowd shift as a herd against her, did a bad man jerk at her red suitcase and upset her balance?

When Ma's papa died the Aunties said Ma dried up like a tobacco leaf and they didn't understand it. They

would say, "Remember how pretty Emily was?" And then the next part was said in the lowest whispers, but I had really good ears before the war. The Aunties said that Ma was the pretty one, white like paper-whites. All the sisters slept in the same room so they heard when their papa came into the room sometimes at night when the owls were out, climbed in bed with Emily and he made sounds like the night owls and Emily made no sounds at all. At first the sisters were jealous because they loved their papa, loved to climb in his lap to listen to the radio and he would stroke their arms softly. It made them hate Emily a little bit. I did not understand this but I understood that now the Aunties hated their papa, a man I never did know outside of photographs.

I crossed the street with the crowd because it pushed me forward. I yelled for Ma but the streetcars, the horses, the automobiles, the horns of the automobiles, the paper boys, the very click of a thousand heels on cobblestones, the sounds bounced off all the silvered doors and windows and all of it jumbled together and no one even heard my voice. Not even me.

The Aunties thought Ma would be glad when her papa died, but she mourned something too hard. Like she had lost a husband, the Aunties whispered. So Ma's husband left too. I heard these coffee-cup stories told on visiting afternoons while I was too young to be taken into account. I knew Ma set up her own bedroom with a lock on the door after I was cut out of her stomach, then her papa died, and then Pa left us. I was pretty sure it was my fault. So now it must be my fault that I was in Chicago and I don't even know what Chicago is.

Except cold. I know Chicago is cold. There was a man selling chestnuts like in the Christmas song, steam and a

harvest smell coming from his stall. He gave me a wrapper of nuts, I held them to pull all the heat into my hands and then I ate them, but really chestnuts taste like mush. I don't know why people like them, but the song is nice. Rose wants to eat oranges fresh from a California grove. Well, I don't care if I ever eat an orange again because the rinds I pulled from the garbage bin were bitter and curling up and I can't eat an orange but I'll always think of those moldy bits. I slept three nights in the corners of buildings and watched the moon glint off the million windows. It was never really dark, and I pulled garbage around me, hid beneath it, pulled into a corner like a windswept pile of rubbish. In the days I walked just to bring on a warmth from the friction. Mostly I was invisible, but some people noticed me, handed me small things to eat. I wasn't the only urchin. Finally, a policeman found me and the Aunties picked me up. I left my baby blanket in the street.

At school Bob, who was a stupid bully, made fun of me, called my ma crazy. The teacher told him to hush and gave me a look of such sympathy it hurt even worse because it verified Bob's claim. She sent me out of the room to get some wood for the stove. Even I knew she was giving me a chance to regain my composure and cool my skin in the brittle air. But Jerry was having none of that. At lunch he found Bob out at the empty tetherball pole and Jerry's eyes were bulging with rage and somehow he pulled off looking like he meant business the way only a redhead kid can do. He made Bob lick the pole. Then we ran away because Jerry wasn't that big and as soon as his eyes went back to normal Bob would lose his fear and beat us both up. So we ran fast and hard and giggling. Besides, half the time we were friends with Bob.

Ma came home about six months later. They had her

in a Home, the meaning of which was not made clear to me. What was wrong with our home? I was happy to see her, but she was quiet and the Aunties and Rose took over more than ever. Rose took to sighing and I think she was sighing for the receding beaches of California. But she did make it there. After the war she lived there for the rest of her life.

Winter jumped the equator and I forgot about Chicago like a silvery flight of a dream. No one ever asked me about it and it became a memory of clamoring noise and hunger. Sometimes I really would dream of it, or more honestly admit that I remembered. I would see Ma holding my hand, I would see the light change from red to green. I am moving forward, and I would clearly see her. Just letting go.

Then came the summer of the lightning bugs. They made each long evening aglitter, and if there was a dust bowl down in Kansas, a stock market in New York that opened high windows, and an exodus of immigrants destined to starve in the very cornucopia of California, well, Iowa was having none of that. The corn was growing, the fireflies haloed the inky sky. They tangled in Maureen's hair; she was the field faery and I fell in love with her simply because she tucked silver-gold bugs behind her ears. We played kickball in the streets, hide and seek, king of the hill, anything that let us run. All of us, Jerry, Bob, Maureen, Sally, Joe. The lightning bugs blinked on and off and buzzed like neon, which wasn't even invented yet, all summer long.

One morning before the heat set in Rose saw Maureen coming up the street commanding a Radio Flyer. She had Jerry and Bob in tow. She looked on a mission. Rose sent me out quick, I pulled up my socks and we

headed down to the stream by the railway tracks to have a Morning Tea. Maureen came up with this thing and the only reason I could think she got Jerry and Bob to come along was because of the still-warm oatmeal cookies we could smell coming out of the cloth-covered basket set in the wagon. I went along for her green eyes.

She laid out the square of blue-check cloth, filled chipped china with Kool-Aid, and gave us the cookies. We played along, thanked her cordially, and ate with formal bites, even Bob. But then we had to impress her, reclaim our physical selves, so we took to racing on the rails to see who could balance the longest, run the fastest on the slender reflective steel. It was a hard thing to balance and run at the same time. Maureen laughed at us and we all stopped when the 9:15 came through loud as a lion and smelly too. I thought about the hobo life, I thought about Chicago. Maureen joined in the steel race and darn if she wasn't the best of us. I couldn't stand that so I ran all the faster and then we were parallel and the steel rails below me shone back my red socks. I slipped clean off the rail and smashed my head, and the only color I saw was silver. I buzzed like the lightning bugs. Then I wasn't anymore anything.

This part I know from later. I broke open my head and Jerry picked up my unconscious body and put me in the Radio Flyer. Jerry ran me back home and says, he swears it, that there were two inches of blood in the wagon bed and he could see my brains. Well, it was the Depression. Ma took me in and shooed the kids away, stitched me up with the same kitchen needle she used on the Thanksgiving turkey, but she did use her best white thread. I lay in bed unconscious for six days and Rose read the Bible over me and dripped water into my

mouth. I was expected to die. I do believe I dreamed of God and he had a halo of fireflies. There was the smell of grass and blood, his eyes on fire. He told me to pull up my red socks and get on with it.

I spent the rest of the summer in bed. No visitors allowed. Mostly I listened to music on the radio but sometimes just before the sun was completely gone and all the kids called home, Jerry would knock at my window and we would talk in the almost-dark. He would tell me what's new, and once he gave me a piece of Black Jack. He told me Maureen's ma washed my blood out of the wagon but Maureen was done with that wagon. He told me he kept a little piece of my brains so if I needed them back when school started I could have them back. You know how redheaded kids kid, yet the idea of it stuck with me. He brought me some fireflies in a Mason jar. Ma took that jar away, washed it out, and added it to the cupboard. But that didn't matter because all I had to do was open the window at night—in came the lights, like lanterns swinging on a pirate ship sailing a choppy sea.

Some years went by and my brains didn't fall out. Ed married Agnes and here came three little kids plop plop plop and a whole lot of diapers. Agnes refined the art of cooking goose-grease dumplings and greens and those little kids looked like dumplings themselves, all fat and white. Agnes took to wearing housedresses and aprons and Ed took to suspenders. Their life seemed on a fine tangent. Frank got his little piece of farm and planted his corn, but I came not to eat it because he ended up raising feed corn, as there's a market for that. Rose stayed home with Ma and me, and there came to be a little crease between her eyes. I knew she was just waiting for me to grow up a little bit more and she would go. I think I knew even

then that they were all going to leave Ma to me.

The Aunties were as yappy as ever talking about the I-talians taking over parts of town and then those Jewish families over on Seventh. Jerry's pa died, run over by a car with a woman driver, which started up the debate again that women shouldn't be allowed to drive. Jerry cried so hard at the funeral he got the hiccups so I just joined right in the crying with him so he wouldn't feel so alone about it. I knew Jerry's ma was worried about keeping their house, but as it turned out, Jerry's pa actually had a life insurance policy so his ma was okay. She took to playing Bingo at the Parlor instead of the church basement. In the summer she drank iced coffee down at the Good Morning Café. I do believe the Metropolitan Life salesman had a run on new policies that year; even the Aunties had a glossy brochure.

Bob dropped out of school after eighth grade, but many kids did. Time to go to work or learn their pa's trade. It was common. Bob would be a butcher because a lot of slaughtering gets done in Iowa and you don't need a Shakespeare sonnet to slice the gullet of a sow. I will tell you Bob eventually turned out some of the best sausage you ever tasted and his kids still use the recipe and sell Robert's Famous Sausage nationwide on the Internet. Maureen, well her eyes just turned all the more green, and I read up on all the sonnets just in hopes I could use those great words to win the damsel fair.

And so we slid quietly toward The Day That Will Live in Infamy.

What is Hawaii to an Iowa boy? To think of one day going to California, to think of going to New York City—those were possibilities. But Hawaii was unthinkable. Hawaii was the place where raindrops touch

ground and burst open in a splash of sunshine. Where women tuck Plumeria behind their ears instead of bugs. Where they eat poi and pineapple and pretty soon, SPAM. Apple pie and baseball are not a part of Hawaii, and the men there get tattoos of hula girls instead of MOM bannered through a heart. But everything changed with the attack on Pearl Harbor. In that moment, listening to the President of the United States on the radio, I was no longer an Iowan. I was an American.

Ma was silent as she clicked off the radio. I was perceptive enough to see the stories that Uncle Joe had told of the trenches flash in her stance, in the slight crumple of knee. I knew those stories too; I went with her to put tiger lilies on his grave each June. His mustard lungs did him in early. I could see her looking at me, courting the grave. She started to speak, I think she wanted to. But there was a knock on the door, insistent, and Rose was opening the door and there was Jerry, all red and blustery, actually in our house. He said, "Come on, come on, we're going to Florsheim's to make sure we ain't got flat feet!"

Everything changed, the war changed everything. The posters went up, Uncle Sam Wants You, and on graduation day he would have us. Without any formal announcement we seniors started staying after school for weight training. We jumped rope until exhaustion felled us, and then we started on the sit-ups since we were already down. We were smack full of bravado.

If Ma was mentally ironing her best black dress, she held her counsel. At Sunday dinners Agnes was teasing, telling me we were acting like schoolgirls showing off our going-steady pins. The comparison was emasculating, but she was right. We were thinking about how good our new muscles were going to look in uniform

and not beyond. Rose, who had been planning her escape, was thwarted by the war—if I left she couldn't. She boiled so hot she could wash dishes with her bare hands.

If I could have listened to Rose, to Agnes, heard even in Ma's silence the plea they would not fully voice, perhaps I could have stayed in Iowa. Perhaps I should have realized how momentous were the sound of summer crickets and the smell of grain in the silo, the sky bleached with heat, the sound of ice skates on the wintered pond. The silver fox running over the hill. I should have realized that a life need hold no more than that. A wife, a child, I could need no more. But I was having none of that.

Jerry and I didn't have flat feet and most of the senior class was joining up. And the girls knew it. They knew this was the end of the plans they had so carefully laid under the tutelage of their mothers. Legs crossed beneath the vanity, applying eye shadow, perfume to the wrist, all a sort of primer for their daughters. The girls had planned to emulate their mothers, and now all the men were leaving town. It caused a kind of madness in them. By Christmas they had turned from flirty larks into women. Those who got pinned by New Year's were lucky, and if they could get engaged by prom, the tiniest diamond would do, they would be saved. If not, they were destined to be typists, teachers, or nurses—just other words for Old Maid. They went on a kind of attack.

Jerry finally got up the nerve to ask out Julia Stein. The redhead in him loved the smoky darkness of her eyebrows against her alabaster skin and her absolute love of math. She did not giggle. Hers was a straight-on assault. He'd loved Julia since she was seven years old, never outwardly shaken by the racial taunts and slurs, never bend-

ing. She simply said she used the same Bible we did but only the first part. But I think "sticks and stones" was her litany. Her big-nosed brother Victor was an easy target. Bob worked him for years until eighth-grade gym, when he pulled the shower towel from around Victor's waist, triumphant to reveal to us all the circumcised Jew. But the joke was on Bob because Victor had the biggest putz we had ever seen and that was the end of the joking, right then and there.

Never in our town had a child baptized in Good St. Wenceslaus's church dated a Jew, but now, what did it matter? She's an American, ain't she? Well, Julia got the diamond in April and Jerry got laid in May and by June their baby Pearl was on her way. Julia was never the type to be a nurse anyway. That girl became a doctor. I stood best man and Maureen caught the bouquet.

On the best day of spring Maureen and I picnicked on the far side of Mr. Lesky's hay fields where a few aspens shaded a spot of grass with their triangle leaves. When a breeze drifted through the limbs, the leaves applauded, it was a day as fine as that. I pushed the cold fried chicken away and lay Maureen back on the same threadbare cloth she used for our tea party the day my brains fell out. I buried my nose in her hair and slowly unbuttoned her sweater, the little silver buttons. Bless the girl, she wore an under-smock with a ribbon and I slid it open and cupped her breasts in my hands. I moved my mouth to her, she smelled like flour and earth and she had freckles, which immediately won my love. I licked the space beneath the small weight of her breasts, dipped down toward the dell of her belly, glazed by the beauty of the sound of her rising breath. But Maureen was having none of that. She stopped me there and there

she would always stop me although I had a lot of fun trying to shift my hands, my face, lower. She swatted me away and I kissed her wrists. I gave her a silver ring and she did not begrudge me the lack of diamonds. When I left for boot camp she gave me a box of good parchment stationery and a silver-plated pen.

Boot camp was at the fairgrounds but that was fine, we were on our way. Jerry and I joined the Army Air Corps. I talked him into it. I didn't want to sleep on the ground and I just didn't think I could trust something as unruly as an ocean.

Rose surprised us all. She packed up the house and took Ma with her and moved to San Francisco. Our little house with the green door was empty quick as that. They took an apartment in the noisy city, but Rose said honking cars, honking geese, what's the difference? She loved the hustle and buzz. She went to the Embarcadero and dated sailors because they sure looked fine in their whites. But she married Pete the Junk Man who could fix up anything. They moved to Hayward with Ma and had a little girl named Debbie. That crease in Rose's forehead never did flatten out, but she gained a laugh that suited her. She kept a bowl of fruit on the kitchen counter and Debbie never had to wait on an orange.

No one can tell the whole of this war, any war. How can you snare that crazy essence? Inconceivably, the Jews were becoming landfill and lampshades, Russians were planting cabbages in front of Saint Isaac's Cathedral, the Swiss were remaining neutral with extended banking hours, and Mussolini was changing his mind. Pieces of bone still wash up on on the shores of Normandy, smooth as sea glass. The ocean can't swallow all the shipwrecks at Dunkirk, flecks of rust still copper the

shore. I have a pile of pity for those boys, both sides. But that was not my war, I was having none of that.

My war was taking place in Southern Italy, Cerignola, as part of the 756th Bombardment Squadron, 459th Bombardment Group of the 15th Air Corps. We piled into our B24 Liberators and nearly willed those beasts to flight. They had a habit of not actually taking off, and Omar, the only Muslim I ever met, told us if he died like that and not in honest battle he wouldn't get his forty virgins. I just wanted one virgin. I focused on her freckles, on the one freckle shaped like a little star.

We lumbered up and took our position in the squadron, two hundred planes or more, and flew over the Mediterranean like shoals of silvery fish. We crossed into France with the objective of bombing a bridge in Avignon and it could have been a milk run, I was hoping for a milk run. But the German fighters showed up taking sniper shots and the flak guns spit up at us. Formation could not be broken. There were no evasive maneuvers.

The little star-shaped freckle. Bombs falling on fields of sunflowers, a million yellow petals flung into the air. Bombs falling on lavender, singeing the wind with sulfur and sachet. Bombs falling on the Palace of the Popes, ruining Roman ruins. My mind flew through the air with the greatest of ease. I couldn't pay attention. I willed myself to pay attention. See that Luftwaffe going down? Who hit it, us or the flak? I started whistling Dixie.

Krauts jumped from the spiraling plane. Their parachutes clouded. I was the waist gunner so I shot one dead. I can't say I shot him out of the sky because his parachute still held him up. But he was dead. Blood coursed from his chest. I wondered if his blood would reach the ground first. I wondered if his soul would

slide out with the blood or if it would be stuck there for a while inside his muscles. Or had I shot a hole right through it? Or was his soul already rising, bobbing just within the parachute, passing through silk, no concern left at all? I had to pay attention. It was very hard for me. I had been in Italy for only two days.

We bombed the bridge and went back to base. Really I don't know anything about bombing fields of flowers or architectural sites. My mind just made stuff up, which I kept to myself. When we landed we ran our fingers over the pocks of shrapnel in our plane and went to find out who had failed to make it back.

Jerry made it back. We weren't assigned to the same plane and sometimes didn't go on the same missions, but we had a place to meet for nights of cards and cigarettes. Jerry liked to talk about Julia—if they had a girl they would name her Pearl after the harbor. There was a night we went one-over-the-eights and he told me intimacies about her, how once she had taken him in her mouth, and he too had tasted the very inside of her. I didn't want to hear it. She was his wife for Christ's sake, but I wanted to hear it too. Half the nights I couldn't sleep. I would think of Maureen and get heated up but I didn't want to be rough on my memory of her. So, God forgive me, sometimes I would borrow Jerry's wife and Julia would let me rise beyond her thigh.

I wrote letters to Maureen and told her not one true thing about the war.

The missions went by: Bucharest, Budapest, Brunswick, a synthetic oil factory at Odertal, Ploesti. Munich, where two B24s broke apart five hundred feet in front of me after accidentally brushing together when we were regrouping to head home.

I remember the night Jerry and I took a long walk around the field. We moved as far out as we could so the lights faded enough to see the Milky Way. The air was heavier in Cerignola than in Cedar Rapids. The stink of the planes, the gas and grease receded just a little. We could almost smell the wheat fields beyond. The clean smell. It was nearly unnatural, I had become so accustomed to the smell of war fought in planes. Jerry was excited. He had a new plan. When he got home he was going to become an airline pilot. He figured there would be a surplus of planes left over from the war and a boom in commercial aviation. He and Julia could move to Chicago and take vacations in Hawaii. I said who's going to want to fly to Hawaii in a B24 but Jerry said parts is parts—they'll build new planes out of the leftovers. When we got back and I sat down to write to Maureen, Jerry asked me to let him use my stuff to write Julia. I told him buzz off but he was so excited he sat there and kept on talking right over me while I finished my letter. Damned if he didn't keep it up until we went to bed. Those redheads are so excitable.

Munich. I am the turret gunner on this mission so I have an elevated view. It's horrifying and I keep humming the Viennese waltz and swirling my gun like a dance partner. The sounds of the plane, the bombs, form the bass. The air whistling through my oxygen mask is a silver tinkling bell. The flak, I see it leave the ground soundlessly, and then it explodes into the crescendo. I whirl my gun around like Elmer Fudd at the opera. I am a ridiculous soldier. We can't break formation; we never can break formation. I am the turret gunner so I see the flak forming and I feel it hit the plane, I see it break through my turret and little pieces of silver glance

by my chin, no, they hit my chin, and dislodge my oxygen mask from my face. I look down in my lap and pick up small chunks of metal, fallen stars, drop them in my pocket, and the waltz plays on. I adjust my mask and keep on shooting. Our plane is not compromised. The mission is accomplished, or not accomplished, but we are heading back to base.

We regroup like a flock of iron seagulls and maybe my shoulders relax. But then I see two Libs five hundred feet in front of me heading for the same space. I see them both shake, trying to shift but the wings collide and crumple like tinfoil, easy as tinfoil. I see the name of one of the planes, *Betty Boop*. I close my eyes, count to ten, feel each number like a boxer staving off the knock-out count because I don't want to see these planes fall. I count slow as that knocked-down boxer rising back up, leaning on the ropes. But it doesn't work because when I open my eyes it's as if no time has passed at all. I watch fury, smoke and flame.

Jerry wants to be a commercial pilot and he wants to tell Julia his plans. He wants to use my silver-plated pen and the watermarked paper that Maureen gave me. I am selfish with it. Ink is hard to come by. Last night he paced around me wound up with words, hands flying, ablaze with visions of the future. I pretty much ignored him.

I watch this junked-up piece of metal and I think of my friend, my whirlwind of a friend, my incinerated friend falling from the sky in his *Betty Boop* plane. I think of my stupid silver pen and the letter I didn't let him write. I see him at my window on a summer evening, trailing fireflies like sparks from the fire of his hair. Skinny. I see him running down the street on the first day of winter. I see his mother losing all her faith. Julia

with her growing belly wondering just what's she going to do now. I imagine the letter I didn't let him write, and I hate myself forever. The silver fox ran over the hill and just like that my friend was gone.

I could never bring myself to write Maureen again, which was just another unkindness. Later I heard from Agnes that at first Maureen thought I was dead, then she thought I fell in love with an Italian girl, then she got mad and quit the counter at The Good Morning Café, moved to Wisconsin to marry a goat farmer. Agnes told me she loved the little goats. She put bows around their necks because she never could have children, but her goat cheese was spectacular. She sent a round to Agnes each Christmas for some years, then that fell off too.

I developed a twitch in my trigger finger after Munich which actually improved my shooting and there was a part of my chin that never needed shaving again.

Down in Africa, Intelligence built miniature replicas of the Ploesti oil fields and the surrounding Romanian villages for our lead pilots to study so that when we made the strike on Hitler's biggest octane supply it would be just as familiar as looking down on our own hometowns. Except Intelligence wasn't intelligent enough to consider that oil burns like a son of gun. As soon as we started the bombing, black smoke concealed every possible landmark. And the Krauts might not have known when we were coming, but they sure knew we would come, and they were having none of that. We threw it down, they threw it up.

I think I was in the seventh ring of hell. The day turned to a cyclone of smoke and soot, cordite, yellow tracers from the flak guns, metal falling all around like meteorites. I saw Jesus in the silver clouds picking up

little lost soldier souls, gathering them in. My fractured mind sang along to Beethoven's Fifth, all symbols and percussion, my gun the conductor's baton. I was shooting pretty well, though. Then we were hit. The plane made a sound like a harpooned whale, so plaintive, as if that crate was sad to let us down. I tried to think of Maureen and her fine freckles, but she was lost to me.

Yet we did not go down. I don't know how it is that we limped our way out of battle. Maybe no one bothered to take another shot at us as it was clear we were already earthbound. But when the smoke cleared we saw farm fields below us. To no avail we dumped our guns and everything we could toss except our parachutes to try and lighten our load. We made it a good distance before we bailed, one at a time and miles apart, and I had my first visit to Yugoslavia.

I'd jumped out of a plane before, at boot camp, so I was ready for the stomach-wrenching free fall and the sweet, heavy tug of the parachute's release. The silk slowed me and delivered me down just like the baby and the stork. I bailed over farmland, rutabaga and beets—I know my crops. Instead of fences, low rock walls around neatly squared off fields, stone farmhouses, and groves of old trees. Plenty of open space for a safe landing. But a rogue wind was having none of that. Just before landing I was pushed hard to the side and down. I smacked straight into a stone wall and broke my ankle so severely it twisted out into a dancer's first position.

The parachute collapsed right over me, shrouded me in white, and for a moment I thought Jesus was an angel come to gather me too, but no such luck. I fought my way out of the chute and before the pain overcame the gauze of my shock I grabbed my foot and wrenched

it forward. There, that looks better. Then I passed out. But the pain was a dominatrix, whipping me back to consciousness. Through watery eyes I watched as a farmer and his wife came toward me across the fields. I was in enemy territory, unarmed, and I couldn't even run. I started to giggle. Well, why not? I was going to be killed by Ma and Pa Kettle. What a fine kettle of fish. I hummed Hi-ho the derry-O, the farmer in the dell, crazy to the end. But they just picked me up and carried me into their home and waves of pain made me shiver.

When I awoke I was in the softest bed. I could smell wood smoke and ash. Smoke without the stench of gasoline or metal. Out the window I saw the wife feeding my parachute into an open fire. I imagined it hurt her to burn all that silk, enough to make her daughter a tiered wedding gown and a fine bassinet for the first-born to boot. But it was death for them if the Germans found me on their farm, so they burned everything but my boots. And the wife, bless her, she kept my chunks of flak and put them beside the bed like touchstones. I don't know how long I was there. I have images of wavy pain and borscht, rough sheets but clean, and the meditative sound of a rocking chair. Eventually they packed me into a hay wagon and moved me west to new people, and this happened again and again, sometimes a short distance, sometimes far, like a slave on the Underground Railroad.

Who were these people who didn't even know my name, didn't speak my language, risking their lives for a nineteen-year-old boy, this string of hearts who willed me to *live*? Uncle Sam gave me a medal for breaking my ankle on a stone wall, but my injury seemed easy compared to the act of spiriting a single soldier all the way

to an English base on the Adriatic. I looked out at that argent sea and knew my war was over. The Limeys delivered me to Naples, back into the arms of Uncle Sam, who put a silver plate with seven screws into my ankle.

On the last day of summer I went into town. It was a starry, starry night and I found a tavern with accordion music spilling out in the street, candles on the tables. The town was full of soldiers and the noise of life, a bony dog barking on the step. I drank my beer and the barkeep filled me up again. She was as beautiful as hope, dark hair, smoke eyes. It was a busy night and she wiped her hands on the apron tied around the waist of her black dress. Soldiers were dancing with girls, inside, outside. I wanted to dance with the beautiful barkeep, smell her, feel her against my chest, rest my hand in the small of her back. I would have married her this very night, cathedral bells ringing down the alleyways. Intuitive girl, she saw my melancholy but mistook it for lust, slapped my arm with a smile, and splashed another drink my way. I tipped my pewter mug to the beautiful girl, to Jerry, to all that was lost, drank it down. I survived the war and that was that.

The Color of Fisticuffs and Bloodlines

*Never ask a mother if she would exchange
her life for the life of her child. The
answer may not always be yes.*

Japan, Winter 2010—Kimiko

Kimiko was born during an earthquake in Matsumoto, Japan, still elbows deep in her mother when the 7.4 struck. The doctor held on to Kimi, but the infant was slippery and, of course, still connected to her mother's body. The earthquake was a jumpy tumbler. There was an avalanche of white ceiling tiles, scalpels on the loose. The doctor struggled against the earthquake to bring Kimi into this world, a fight of samurai against Godzilla. Everybody was screaming. The doctor fell to the floor and Kimi went with him, placenta ripped from her mother's body. Kimi landed on the doctor, her tiny head protected by the doctor's chest. For an instant, his wild heartbeat pounded in her ear, the sound of a rolling ocean in a seashell. Then Kimi was slapped in the face with the placenta. The earth settled down with a final shogun-shrug, and suddenly everything was silent. That was Kimi's cue to cry.

The quake was felt throughout the Japanese Alps. In Kamikochi the trout jumped out of the Azusa River; half miscalculated the return. North in Shibu, snow monkeys soaking in the hot springs were insulted by the water aggressively slapping their furry, icicled faces.

Down in Matsumoto's old city, the Black Crow castle flew away and came back again while no one was looking. Just for a moment, while the earth was letting go, it flew.

Lake Tahoe, Nevada 2018—Fiona

Rand proposed to me right after I landed the best dismount of my career. I did a 180 front salto tuck and stuck it. As providence would have it, I was backlit by a beam of sunlight coming from a high window, standing in a halo of white chalk dust. The crowd went wild. In my head. In reality we were in the high school gym with about twenty spectators, and I didn't even place. Emily Garrett chewed gum while receiving her winner's ribbon, green-and-white stripes. She was going on to State. I think she won because she wore her leotard one size too small and favored leg splits from the high bar. And she was white. Black girls win track—because the results are black-and-white.

"Fiona, you don't need to watch this, let's go." Rand and I left the gym, and I was still sweaty and almost naked, barefoot, chalk dust ghosting me. I jumped up on his back and he took off for the forest that everyone knows should never be allowed to grow around a high school. It was spring, the dangerous pinesap time. He jogged the winter-softened pathways. "Listen Ducky, let's get married and kick this place. Two weeks to graduation," said Rand, spinning me off his back. I fell to one knee. He took that for a yes. I was never off balance. "I love that your feet are like bars of Lava soap." He pushed me back into the damp forest bed, one hand on my foot, the other traveling north. "I'm going to snort the chalk right off your thighs," he said, and I didn't know if that

was romantic. A beetle with blue-black wings walked over the mountain of me and flew away. Rand shimmied my legs apart with his hips and kissed me and I could taste grape jelly and peanuts, which isn't bad. But it isn't grown-up. A marriage proposal should taste of flint and wine. But that wasn't what stopped me, wasn't what caused me to flip him over. Let's face it, I have the thighs of a chastity belt. What I really didn't want was for Rand to see the bruises on my hips, every time I slammed into the uneven bars, blooms of wisteria and violet. The gum-purple of me. It seemed more personal, more private than my privates. I don't have words for such places, for such feelings.

"Nope," I said bouncing up, "not getting married. Rand, you're an idiot." Honestly, he looked relieved. The things boys will say to get laid.

"Was it the Lava soap line?"

"You really know how to get the pants off a girl."

"Well, technically, you're not wearing pants, so it wasn't that hard."

The forest breathed us out, the compost smell of us, and we left that place forever.

"But you know I meant it, Fiona," Rand said, reaching for my hand. I stopped for a moment and enclosed his hold, made Oreo hands.

George and Roxayn
Fiona was born when Roxayn was forty-four years old. The baby wasn't an afterthought or a surprise. She was a prizefight, a to-the-death struggle with Roxayn's body. Hormones and silver needles. Four pounds six ounces delivered on a December night when the clouds froze and fell to earth in a prickling of rime ice. Fiona came

out a lovely shade of lavender but oxygenated when the doctor removed the garrote Roxayn's body had so intimately placed around her neck in one last attempt to remain childless. Hearing Fiona's victory cry, Roxayn's rebellious body chose to bleed out and die rather than surrender.

Fiona wanted her mother as much as Roxayn had wanted her baby. Fiona wailed, called for her mother in the most instinctual way, but they passed in the night. Roxayn held her baby's hand and let it go. Fiona could have used her mother when she was in the woods with Rand, tried to ask her what it meant when she wanted to be touched and not touched at the same time. Maybe Roxayn was the beetle, leading by example. *Fly away, Fiona.*

Fiona's father is George and Fiona thinks he's the greatest. A sort of Father Goose for her, downy-white skin and hair so light it flies away in any puff of air. When people talk to him the push of their voice makes it look like he's trying to escape. But he isn't. Every night he's home. Wire half-glasses when he reads, Fiona tucked up in his lap. Good-night glass of milk.

George met Roxayn at the El Rancho Drive-in in the late 70s. Roxayn was pushing popcorn for summer money and he was buying popcorn and dumping it out back for the magpies so he could go buy more. George would hate to admit it, but he fell for Roxayn partly because of her color, fell for the conjured image of the yin-yang-ness of their twined and sleeping bodies. But Roxayn didn't need a doughboy. Her parents had money; Dr. Tallis, if you please, and her husband, Roman, TV sportscaster. Roman Tallis was on billboards—Reno's Dynamic 8. Granted, no one took him seriously—of course the black guy does sports. But Roxayn wasn't

running around with homies in hoodies and she certainly wasn't playing Guess Who's Coming to Dinner with white boys. The albino could buy all the popcorn he wanted. By his third purchase she had buttoned up the next-to-top button of her neon-orange polyester uniform. But George still got something he wanted: *Roxanne* announced the plastic tile name badge. ("Spellin' it with an A-Y-N will just confuse 'em," dismissed her boss, controller of the Bakelite labeling gun, master of the letter wheel.)

Internet porn was several garage inventions away. The best thing going in Reno was the sign for the Primadonna Club: Five girls, twenty feet of painted plaster each, and not just girls, but *showgirls*. And they were showing it. Practically tweerkin' it, fat thighs and sweetheart necklines. Feathers and fishnets. There was the American Giantess in the middle, flanked by her slightly smaller Spanish, Hawaiian, Chinese, and French sisters. Oh, a boy could dream. Despite their implied ethnicity, all were white, just like dress-up Barbie, the classic plastic tease. In San Francisco, in L.A., or even Sacramento, there were black people and Hispanic people mixing in like an infusion of probiotics. Everybody knows purebreds get hemophilia while mutts duke it out. But in Reno, George had never really even seen a black girl, not one pinned behind a counter, forced to put change in his hand, finger slightly tracing across his palm, lighting up his lifeline. Not one that almost glowed garnet, just below the surface.

Lila and Roman Tallis had moved to Reno from Richmond to get away from garbage strikes and shipyards, the big sound of steel, and the small sound of the corner homeless woman pushing the grocery cart with

the rusty wheel. Reno smelled clean, the Washoe Zephyr wind delivering the sharpness of spruce and sage. If there weren't any black kids in Reno, well, they would make some. Like cookies. Lila got a job teaching at the university school of medicine (token black professor) and Roman at KOLO-TV (token black broadcaster). Tokens pay the bills. They bought a house on Skyline, looking east to the manzanita-covered Pine Nut Mountains, where the ghosts of Paiute women weave baskets in an ever-setting sun. *Watch out for Falling Rock*, signposts warned, knowing what ghosts can do. Oakland doesn't have that kind of sign.

It seemed to the Tallises a good time to be black. The Jeffersons had their own TV show. People wanted to invite them over, made a point of using the china, decanted wine, never serving fried chicken. The awkwardness passed; they made real friends. But what were they thinking? Whom did they expect their kids to date, to marry? They had to ask themselves if *they* were the prejudiced ones, wanting to send their kids to a West Coast college, Berkeley, UCLA. Places the N-double A-CP assuredly stocks with black people, like a trout pond. They never directly said to Rex and Roxayn, *marry black, stick to your own*, but the kids knew. Lila and Roman embarrassed themselves. They had pushed so hard on the door of racism that they had no choice but to go through it themselves and accept that it swings both ways, like saloon doors.

When the El Rancho closed for the season, George didn't know if he would ever see Roxayn again. But he couldn't get her out of his mind. It didn't help that KGLR was blasting The Police—*Roxanne. You don't have to put out the red light*. He didn't think that of her, but once,

flirting with a fantasy and a DUI, he drove down Fourth Street looking for her, in case he could save her from her song. He drove past Louis' Basque Corner, past the Coney Island Bar, more or less looking for someone to punch in her defense. Young men never know what to do with themselves. It was a relief when college classes started, really for communities everywhere.

George loved the University of Nevada. He was always a sucker for September, the muffled sound of erasers behind the puff of chalk, the creak of an opening book. He took to studying outside, resting against one of the twenty-four Dutch elms lining the quad. The last of summer seemed to sequester in the tree house of leaves. Then one morning the air snapped and all the leaves turned gold, a ransom paid; the price of summer. The branches shook the leaves off as if they hurt and the gold accumulated on the ground. On the first of November a hobo-wind shuffled through the quad, spinning little whirlwinds that dervished the gold away.

All through the fall George's eyes tracked every black girl (very few), and one early embracer of Goth whom he kept confusing for black, that passed. No Roxayn. But he had at least some hope that she was there, because standing in line at the El Rancho, he had heard Roxayn say she was majoring in nursing, or mining, he couldn't quite pick it up.

Roxayn *was* there. A freshman to his junior. She liked to study in the depths of the library, bookshelf sentries on either side, discouraging nonsense with their straight spines. A tiny desk carved so many times it looked like it had Dutch elm disease. Dust motes, rather large in size, that made Roxayn wonder if they were disintegrated pages, if she was breathing in letters, words. She took a

deep breath and hoped for a haiku. Once a little mouse stopped by for a whisker of a chitchat.

Other kids stayed up late in cinderblock dorms watching *Saturday Night Live* on garage sale black-and-white TVs, went dancing at Del Mar Station. Roxayn was cloistering, wrapping herself in a social shroud of text. She knew it. She was worried about grades—her mom was a doctor, for God's sake, she couldn't bring home Cs. Maybe she should join the Black Student Union, but it seemed so expected. Why should she join a club based on her skin color? Maybe she should have gone to school in the Bay Area, where her tidy Afro wouldn't stick out like stick-out hair.

The alchemy of autumn gave way to the clear intentions of winter: *Cover the whole mess up with snow and no one will ever know what happened here. Start again next year; a Mulligan.* It was on such a night of obliteration that George happened to be looking for a philosophy book in the lowest level of the library. And there she was. There was no mistaking her. Her nail beds, the veins on her arms, they were amethyst in the dim spotlight of the desk lamp. She looked like art. George quickly darted into the book aisle next to her. He was so excited it exhausted him. Why should he even care about this drive-in girl? He sat down on the floor and maneuvered a few books to one side to get a look at her. Roxayn's peripheral vision caught the quiet shuffle.

The Noble H. Getchell Memorial Masturbator! she thought. The peril of the deep library. She got up with the intent of slamming the books back together on any digit that appeared in the gap. But nothing appeared until George came round the corner. "The Albino!" Roxayn said in her outside voice and immediately regretted it. He

wasn't technically an albino, just quite white and blond, plus that was racist to albinos. No, discriminatory. Her brain was a little jumpy. She did feel somewhat trapped and George could tell. He was walking the creeper line. *Truth or less than truth?*

The truth was he'd been hanging around the Black Student Union after he was denied entrance on the grounds of his race. His memory did a quick reboot:

"That's racist," George complained to the kid at the sign-in desk, a black student in an enviable paisley shirt George could never pull off.

"Man, you're not black. It's the Black Student Union. You got the Jot Travis. Go there."

"My grandfather was black." Take the long shot.

"Right. So you some lily-white pickaninny?"

"Don't use that word, that's not nice."

"Man, whaddya doin' here?"

George decided to confess. "There's this girl—"

"Ooooh," interrupted the desk monitor. "You after some Sister. There's only like twenty of us in this whole shit town and you gotta go after one of ours. Get the fuck out."

George dismissed the conversation with the desk monitor from his mind and decided not to go full confession. He could tell that Roxayn recognized him. "Hey, Roxayn, may I interest you in going for some popcorn?"

And she smiled! Is there anything more singularly beautiful on the face of the earth than a spontaneous smile, a shoulder that releases the cold?

The little mouse, the one with the silver whiskers, watched the whole thing from a quiet corner. He was eating a page from a James A. Michener paperback that the real *Noble H. Getchell Memorial Masturbator* had

dropped from his backpack. *Hawaii*. The mouse could eat the first hundred pages and make it a better book ...

George and Roxayn married after Roxayn graduated (mining!). George had a few more years to finish his PhD in education, but they were on their way. Both sets of parents were inwardly adjusting preconceptions of skin tones of future grandchildren, and outwardly absolutely inclusive. Pretty soon that switched. They became inwardly inclusive, Sunday family dinners, a joint trip to S.F., and outwardly discussing how beautiful (inside and out) their grandchildren were bound to be.

But no babies came. Ten years. George quit riding his bicycle, fast, down the ranchlands of Hash Lane. He went commando, and kind of liked it. He romanced Roxayn with pomegranates and Ethel M liqueur-filled cordials, little sips of whiskey since she self-banned alcohol. Roxayn romanced George by uncrossing her legs. They moved to Lake Tahoe, just thirty minutes away, but two thousand feet higher. If they couldn't have children they would surround themselves with forest animals, coyote concerts and the backdraft of eagles, snow that smelled like pinecones. They lived off Pioneer Trail down a long, hard-packed driveway they dubbed Bunny Ears Lane. In the winter they could hang a pot, cook campfire beans inside the stone fireplace, and watch the ice fern the windows.

Almost twenty years and they decided to give it one more shot. A lot of shots actually. IVF drugs had improved statistics (now their baby was discussed in terms of statistical probabilities). The drugs bloated Roxayn into a hot-water bottle, all sloshy and running to cold. Her skin lost its beautiful purple sheen and took on shades of ash, as if the Pope had burned all his lovely vel-

vet gowns and she was what remained. But it worked! Eight months of hormones and a fetus showed its little heartbeat on the monitor, fast and blurry as a hummingbird wing. Enter Fiona the Destroyer!

Well, we already know how this part of Roxayn's story ends.

Would Roxayn have been happy to give up her life in exchange for the life of her daughter? Never ask a mother that. Never ask. Not every mother would say yes.

Fiona

When I was a newborn I looked like an eggplant, purple-dark in George's white hands. To leave Barton Memorial without Roxayn, to truly burn her body to ash in exchange for this Howling, what a monstrous exchange. Stick your hand down the drain and turn on the garbage disposal – that kind of feeling. Why did they ever even want children?

Everyone who didn't know us and saw us together assumed my dad had rescued an orphaned African child, a UNICEF baby. This made him an automatic *good guy*. Women saw him stalled in the baby aisle and helped him pick out formula and offered diaper suggestions, cooed at me. And I answered in the secret language born before letters that we all lose. In the eternal words of P. D. Eastman, I asked, "*Are you my mother?*" I never stopped asking. Every time I blew out the candles I wished for her. And a pony.

Of course George tamped down his grief and raised up his daughter. He *is* a good man. He covered an entire wall of my room in sheets of North African cork. From disorganized cardboard boxes full of photos of his life with Roxayn he assembled a type of historic time-

line over the cork, oldest photos lowest. On light gray paper he wrote dates and places and broken poetry in tiny script and worked them in like a stone path for me to follow. He installed a library-style ladder so that as I grew I could climb up to the top, only five and half feet. Above that he had a mural painted—clear sky with the top leaves of a Red Dragon maple laced across. Here we could both visit Roxayn, pick a version of her, pick a fight, talk it out.

My mother was my room. "*Are you my mother?*" I sometimes asked the wall.

I was surprised when I returned home on the day I turned down my first marriage proposal to find my dad sitting at our kitchen table. I still had pine needles porcupining out of the back of my hair.

"Why are you home early, Dad?" I asked, carefully sitting across from him, hoping the needles wouldn't fall out and start embroidering some sort of naughty-daughter scarlet letter.

"How'd you do at finals?" he asked, ignoring my question.

Emily Garrett won."

He shook his head up and down, "White girl always wins." He didn't believe that.

"She might have been better than me," I finally admitted, out loud.

"You think I'm going along with that?" he asked. I smiled. I knew he wouldn't; I was the Simone Biles of his eye. "So ... two weeks to graduation ..." he continued. "All signed up for UNR, dorms. Big life."

"Yep. Where you goin' with this, Dad? You're all fidgety."

He pushed his feet out, leaned back in the chair. "I'm

retiring, Fiona. Hanging up the elbow-patch hound-stooth."

My dad was sixty-five years old, a tenured philosophy professor at Sierra Nevada College—students love his *Fear & Loathing* class. It's a forest campus, wood buildings with slanted green metal roofs, built to send snow avalanching. If I thought of my dad, I pictured him there, in a kind of academic diorama for me to move the image of "dad" around in. If not there, where would he be? Children want their parents to remain essentially the same, so the child can go away and know exactly where to find them. A time capsule in a foundation cornerstone.

George

George believes children cannot know the secret lives of parents. They can pick up traces, sediments and smells. Fly-fish their way through their parents' movements and hope to catch something big enough to eat. But parents, at least the good ones, learn how to hide in the deep. Fiona never knew that her father had a lengthy relationship with the college librarian. He loved to make love to Jessica with her wire-framed glasses askewing her nose, the bounce of her. They broke up because he couldn't bring himself to introduce her to Fiona as anything but *Ms. Winston*. How could he bring another woman into Fiona's life? It felt like he was betraying not so much Roxayn, but Fiona's mother. Of course this was a mistake. Fiona wanted a replacement mom; Roxayn was always two-dimensional to her. George never understood that.

George was happy with his life as a father and a teacher, he had activities. He was still on a softball team; their pitcher smoked Lucky Strikes on the mound and hotdogs

were served to the runners at first base. George smoked a little weed on solitary hikes, looking over Lake Tahoe, the water sometimes densely silver, sometimes so clear it ceased to even exist. He loved his dark daughter, the way her fingers turned purple in the cold, mud-warm in summer. Back when she still reached for his hand, needing just to be sure of him, and then running ahead again. She would always be ahead of him.

Now Fiona was going to college. She had pine needles sticking out of the back of her hair. She looked more like Roxayn, Roxayn at that age, every day. He had spent the winter making his plan.

Pulling his attention back to the kitchen table, George said, "I've decided to spend the summer in Japan." He paused to give Fiona time to picture pagodas and kimonos. Hello Kitty! Things he knew she liked. Then offered, "Come with . . . ?"

And just like that Fiona's life walked over the crooked bridge.

Roxayn

If we could save our days, could they be like thread? Spools of silky-fine summer days. Rough days of lumpy hemp macramé, chunky with driftwood and shockingly bright feathers. Days of anger, reeling spirals of red. Lanky nights of sex running in inky blue skeins. Workdays of wool. Childhoods spun from apron strings. Bobbins, coils, whorls of floss, loomed together; if each day were a thread.

Roxayn felt, or at least sensed, her body being lifted onto a gurney; the heartless sheet of metal was not as cold as she. She felt aware of the opening of the morgue roll-in freezer, the cloud that escaped its incubation, and

the ice-edged air did not chill her. She sensed her body being awkwardly dressed in her decades-old wedding sari; a perfect shroud for wrapping around her pregnancy-and-death-bloated belly. She could see the woman from Bangalore who wove the silk, red and orange, could see the aura of her fingers in the pattern. She could sense the loss of light and vibration of closure. And finally, everything around her turned to sari-shades, intensely saturated with heat, and it did not warm her. Warm air rises, up and away. Ghosts make themselves, white as ice.

Well, it's an afterlife. Once Roxayn got over the awful shock of dying and body disposal, she settled into her new freedoms and restrictions. She knew that at any moment she could let herself go, unravel the foggy threads that held her together. Dissipate. But it's hard for a new mother and a young woman in love with her husband, with herself, to let go. Love is the strongest floss. So she lingered. Tried to show George and Fiona she loved them. Remove obstacles for them, like survivor's guilt, that hard-to-remove heart stain. She was sometimes somewhat successful. She traveled. Saw all the major sites. One Thousand Places to See After You Die. She learned that Mount Everest is not the tallest mountain at all times. That water talks but is inane like a drunken aunt at a wedding, that bricks have a fascination with the rearrangement possibilities of earthquakes. Humans don't need to believe it for it to be so.

Roxayn waited for a body. She knew she would mostly lose her *Roxaynness* when she did this. But it was the only way she had a chance to get back to George, to Fiona—to herself—as anything more than a misunderstood moonbeam.

Kimiko

And now we are back to the beginning. The baby born during an earthquake in 2010, Matsumoto, Japan. No one died, not the baby or the mother. But the mother was only fifteen and although she would have liked to keep the little baby (Hello, Kitty!) her parents convinced her that adoption was the best for all concerned. Considering the pain she was in from having her earthquake-assisted delivery, she allowed the baby to go. In that parentless instant, when the child was not being called upon by anyone's love or expectations, Roxayn slipped in. This kind of thing goes on all the time. You don't know where your babies come from.

The baby was given the name *Kimiko—valuable child*—in hopes that she would be.

Kimi was transferred to a children's home in the city of Kanazawa, on the Sea of Japan. It was a dormitory-style house with a blue-tiled roof and a very important kitchen garden. The children rolled out their futons at night and slept with windows open, because orphans are never stolen. Other babies and children were adopted, new ones came, but it would not be easy to find parents for Kimi. She was a pretty child, slender as the word *lily*, tissue-paper skin, all her veins near the surface. Eyes with a shadow of lavender. But by the time she was four she had gained the nickname *Akimbo*. Everything about her moved in unexpected directions. The doctor said the Tourette's was caused by genetics, but Kimi knew it was aftershocks. She thought of it as her birth-quake, coming through in blinks and boinks. Tics and grimaces. It was disconcerting, and exacerbated when the children were called to stand in the *please-pick-me* line up for prospective parents. She looked like she had fleas.

Emiko was the head mother at the children's home. Emiko would not let the children make fun of Kimi in Emiko's earshot (although the Akimbo nickname stuck), but she couldn't make them like the tic-ing girl. Sometimes the child sounded like a bamboo grove knocking in a wind storm. To help make up for Kimi's alienation, Emiko brought Kimi into the kitchen and taught her how to make soba soup for twenty and then a proper matcha tea for just the two of them. Emiko had to make it look like work, or the kids would like Akimbo even less. She messed up Kimi's hair. In the kitchen, Kimi could twitch, drop an egg. Giggle.

At the end of March, the cherry blossoms emerged in pink to remind the world of the virtues of tenderness and poetry. When a puff of wind tugged a blossom lose, petals floated away like a tiny, gift-wrapped wish. It was around this time that a delivery of used Pokémon cards, dog-eared and abandoned, arrived at the children's home like a new batch of orphans. It was to great excitement that Emiko passed the cards out. She simply counted out an equal number for each child, unconcerned with the individual card's worth in the game. The *great swap* ensued. Here the skills of salesmanship and friendship came into play, neither of which favored Kimi. In each trade, Kimi gave a bit more than she received. But Kimi knew the rules of Pokémon, the value of each card. In her pocket she kept a faded but still powerful Shadow Lugia, the rearing, flying purple dragon. Kimi did not show this card, would not trade it. She hoped Shadow Lugia would help her sumo-wrestle her Tourette's, or turn her into a long-legged crane, so she could fly away on white, graceful wings.

Most Saturdays the children would go to Kenroku-en

Garden (on a year-round free pass given by the govern-
ment) and it was here that Kimi's quaking aspen of a
body would be most quiet. At eight years old she had
lived in the orphanage longer than any other child and
was mature enough to take care of the new babies. But
Emiko could see Kimi's limbs, her face, relax—or order
themselves in a different way when they passed into the
green. Mostly she let the girl wander; the child knew her
way around a koi pond.

Kenroku-en is an old and famous garden—one of
three designated *most beautiful* in all of Japan, a country
that would pitchfork those rose-arbor-adoring English
in pursuit of the gardening Pulitzer, if such a thing exist-
ed. *And why doesn't it?* they often ask.

Kimi didn't know she was rambling a pinnacle,
wouldn't have cared. On this most spectacular day in
late May she hopscotched the flat stones of Flying Geese
Bridge and headed to the arched Flower Gazing Bridge.
She had plastic Hello Kitty barrettes holding back her hair
and a Hello Kitty Pez dispenser, fully loaded, in her Hello
Kitty vinyl purse. Shadow Lugia squarely in her pocket.

Coming from another direction, crossing the crook-
ed bridge (over which a ghost can never pass), was an
overtly white man and a black woman in a rented ki-
mono. She certainly wasn't the only visitor in a rented
kimono, but she might have been the only black one.
Or purple one. Her skin was heartwood in the garden.

Kimi walked off of the arched bridge to get closer
to the muddy stream. The stands of iris were in bloom!
Banking both sides, the water-rooted flowers were a
ruffle of color. Kimi knew it was off limits to leave the
path, go into the water. She was Japanese—she followed
rules. But she was also a marionette to Tourette's, moved

by strings she could not see, seldom able to control her jerky twerks and impulses. She waded right into the iris bank, mud sucking her black shoes under like water beetles, her head really just above the flower-line. She sat down. Her head just below the flower-line. Her eyes submerged, sank, into the color of the petals. Petals the shade of fisticuffs and bloodlines. Who doesn't want to sink into the singular space, the infinite dash between blue-violet?

Fiona saw the little girl go into the stream, disappear behind the tall fan of sword-shaped leaves. The little girl did not come back up! She ran to the girl, losing her sandals, hitching up her kimono, stumbling into the water. The mud felt like a living creature beneath her reaching toes. Periwinkle silk waved around her knees; the kimono was ruined. Fiona didn't care. She pulled the little girl from the bank of flowers, lifted her into her arms, and for the first time since an ice-edged night eighteen years ago, their eyes met. A tsunami of the heart flooded them both, drowned them. They could barely hold on. Kimi's almond-shaped eyes blinked rapidly, an electrical storm of blinks. Fiona subconsciously recognized a *Roxaynness* in the violet-flecks, in the iris. From all the photos on her wall. Kimi recognized her own flesh, was somehow certain that this murky-purple woman was hers.

Kimi wrapped her legs around Fiona's waist, took Fiona's face in both of her muddy hands, and asked, "*Anata wa watashi no okāsandesu ka?*" [Are you my mother?]

Fiona had no idea what the little girl with the straight-across bangs was asking, but Fiona answered, "Hai." And so she was.

About the Author

The Franklin Avenue Rookery for Wayward Babies is Laura Newman's second collection of short stories. One story in this new collection, "Swisher Sweets," was a finalist for LitMag's Virginia Woolf Award for Short Fiction. Laura founded the "Heroin Committee," and she continues to work through JTNN.org to produce and run public service announcements to educate parents and the community about substance abuse issues. She is an Addy Award and American Marketing Association winner for the production of these PSAs. She lives in Reno, Nevada.

Acknowledgments

To my husband, Dave Newman, who is like the Rock of Gibraltar—covered in monkeys. Dave, you are my first reader and editor. You reject every rejection and amplify every success. My eternal optimist; I could not have done better.

To my daughter, Katie Boren. You are more than I could have ever deserved or earned. You are as necessary as air to me. To my son, Austin Boren. Our conversations go all over the world, and when I read you my stories, you really listen. And to your father, Kay, who is fishing the Milky Way.

To my father and mother, Louis and Ellen Vlasek. The two of you are my guideposts and trailblazers. You are both extraordinary and I take you with me everywhere.

To Debbi Engebritson and Rebecca Lack. What a golden kindness to gift your outstanding editing skills and personal time on both of my books. You chiseled and polished. To Jackie Shelton Hall, who said I must have a website and then created it and maintains it still. To Cat Stahl for my cover photo. You made me look not the way I do, but the way I feel. All four of you volunteered your massive skills without my asking! You are Berserkers one and all, and I bow to you.

To my agent, Kathy Green of Kathryn Green Literary Agency. Oh, you are everything. Thank you so much for taking a

chance on me. I am just another writer sitting at her kitchen table with a laptop without you.

At Delphinium Books, thank you to Editor Jennifer Ankner-Edelstein, the first person at Delphinium to read and see merit in my manuscript. Thank you to copy editor Nancy Green, who kept me from calling mountains (massifs) dogs (mastiffs) and from disrespecting the flamingos. Your attention to format and detail is exquisite. And to Colin Dockrill for the work of art that is the cover and for the pink feather on the back.

Thank you especially to my editor, Joseph Olshan. Joe, this is a stronger book because of your careful, thoughtful work, and you did every step with kindness. I was so nervous, and from our first conversation, I knew I was safe. You are exceptional as an editor, author, and person. You took me from crayons to perfume.

To Lori Milken, publisher of Delphinium Books. You amplify writers' voices and hand us our dreams, in hardcover no less! I cannot ever thank you enough.

Lastly, to my newest favorite, Jaxon John Trautmann Aguilera. Oh, the places you will go! I'm tagging along for as long as I can.